DEATH
on a
SILVER TRAY

DEATH
on a
SILVER TRAY

ROSEMARY STEVENS

BERKLEY PRIME CRIME, NEW YORK

DEATH ON A SILVER TRAY

A Berkley Prime Crime Book
Published by the Berkley Publishing Group
A Division of Penguin Putnam Inc.
375 Hudson Street, New York, New York 10014

The Penguin Putnam World Wide Web site address is
http://www.penguinputnam.com

First Edition: May 2000

Library of Congress Cataloging-in-Publication Data

Stevens, Rosemary.
Death on a Silver Tray : a Beau Brummell mystery / by Rosemary
Stevens.
p.   cm.
ISBN 0-425-17468-9
1. Brummell, Beau, 1778–1840 Fiction.   I. Title.
PS3569.T4524D43   20001
813'.54—dc21   99-43090
CIP

Printed in the United States of America

10   9   8   7   6   5   4   3   2   1

AUTHOR'S NOTE

Besides Beau Brummell, other characters in this book were also real people living in 1805. They include: the Prince of Wales, the Duke of Clarence, the Duke of York, (and his mistress, Mrs. Clark), the Duchess of York, Viscount Petersham, Lady Salisbury, Robinson, John Lavender, Scrope Davies, Edmund Kean, Poodle Byng, Lumley Skeffington, Lord Yarmouth, Old Dawe, Juan Floris, W. Griffin, Weston, Meyer, and Guthrie.

Of course, their dialogue and actions in the story are purely fictitious.

ACKNOWLEDGMENTS

For their unfailing support and encouragement, I wish to thank Barbara Metzger, Cynthia Holt, and Carolyn Greene.

Special thanks for her research assistance goes to my friend Melissa Lynn Jones. Melissa is perhaps the foremost authority in America on Regency language and social history. I am also indebted to Paul Cox of the National Portrait Gallery in London for his kindness and generosity in regards to the likenesses of George Bryan Brummell held by the Gallery. I do want to say, however, that any errors contained in the story are solely my own.

As always, I want to thank J. T., Rachel, and Tommy Stevens. You have my love.

*This book is dedicated with love
to my husband, J. T.*

1

The boredom that so frequently troubles me was, for the moment, joyously at bay. With an expression of good humor firmly in place, I hurried out of the small art gallery in Pall Mall and turned in the direction of White's Club.

I had a mission and meant to accomplish it.

"Mr. Brummell! Oh, Mr. Brummell!" A young woman seated in an open carriage frantically waved her lace handkerchief with one gloved hand, trying to capture my attention. Above the noise in the street, she called to her driver. "Stop, coachman, do stop! I wish to speak with Beau Brummell."

Her servant obeyed the command, guiding the horses across the cobblestones until the carriage came to a halt by the curb.

So great was my desire to reach White's that for the barest instant I considered ignoring the woman, whom I recognized as Lady Kincade. I immediately discarded the idea.

It would never do for me to shun her. If I did, and the slight was observed by a member of Society, or the Polite World as it is sometimes called, a calamity Lady Kincade did not deserve might ensue. No one would send her cards of invitation to their dinners or parties, thinking I had found her less than acceptable.

Absurd, you say? Well, privately I agree with you. But why should I not revel in the power the English aristocracy of 1805 has given me? I am only human, you know.

Besides, Lady Kincade is a pretty butterfly of a girl, hardly out of the schoolroom and newly married. She wants to cut a dash among the *Beau Monde* and make her husband proud.

Of course, she should never have boldly hailed me in the street that way, but, somehow the sight of her cherry and white striped gown, matching cherry-colored bonnet, and the face of an angel, made one forget such things.

I stepped to the door of her carriage, swept off my tall hat and bowed. "Good afternoon, Lady Kincade. What a brave girl you are, facing a chilly late September day in an open vehicle."

She giggled. "La, Mr. Brummell, you know we ladies feel it is not fashionable to be seen in a heavy wrap. And I will suffer any inconvenience to be stylish."

That was a fact. Her pale flesh had a bluish cast and bumps from the cold. I repressed a desire to hand her my greatcoat.

"My husband and I are on the point of leaving the city for Brighton, even though there are still people in Town."

By this Lady Kincade did not mean that London only had a few souls haunting its streets. Quite the contrary was true. Scores of men and women populated London. Lady Kincade referred to those genteel people in the highest circles who tended to drift off to their country estates after the social season was over.

Her lips formed a pout at the thought of missing any London entertainments, but then her face cleared. "Kincade has heard rumors that the Prince is going to the seaside town and we want to be ahead of the crowd." She looked at me expectantly.

"Wise of you, I am sure," I said casually.

She clapped her hands in a youthful display of enthusiasm. "Then the Prince must intend on going to Brighton. You are his closest friend and would know his plans," she said with a delighted smile. She reached over and picked up a package from the seat beside her. "I beg that you will indulge me with another favor and examine this cloth I just purchased."

I dutifully spent the next few minutes pondering whether the marigold silk or the honey-yellow crepe would be better with Lady Kincade's complexion. Inspecting the costly materials, I became caught up in their beauty.

At length she said, "No wonder you are the arbiter of fashion and called 'the Beau.' You possess the most exquisite taste, Mr. Brummell. I hope I shall see you before long in Brighton."

"Surely Fate will not deny me the pleasure, my lady," I told her and, with a last bow, I strolled away.

Yes, she did flatter me to no end, I suppose. Manfully, I contrived to suffer through it. Nevertheless, I turned onto

St. James's Street where I was less likely to be waylaid by any female. Ladies simply do not parade up and down the street where gentlemen's clubs are prevalent. Should a lady walk or drive her carriage past these male sanctuaries, she would be inviting comment on her person. Very fast behavior indeed.

Fading sunlight filtered through the fog and soot that perpetually plagues London. I gave a mental nod of thanks to my indispensable valet, Robinson. He had had the foresight to lay out my black velvet greatcoat when I told him I intended to visit Talbot's Art Gallery. My bones detest cold weather.

On the other hand, I cursed the sedan-chair maker who had assured me my new vehicle would be ready two weeks ago. I have no patience with those who make promises they cannot or will not keep. When all is told, a man is only as good as his word.

I vowed then and there that if the merchant failed to produce the chair shortly, word would rapidly spread through London that Beau Brummell had declared W. Griffin, Sedan-chair Maker to His Majesty King George III, *unfashionable*.

I am not stretching the truth when I say a merchant would sooner spit on a duke than have such an adjective applied to his place of business by me. *En garde*, Mr. Griffin!

Arriving at my destination, I slowed my pace and ambled into that exclusive terrain of four hundred and fifty privileged gentlemen, White's Club.

We gather here not just for convivial conversation, but

also to discuss topics of a broader scale: politics, literature, science, drama.

White's is, of course, still a good place to read one of the myriad of newspapers kept there or to place a wager in White's famous Betting Book as to, say, which opera dancer might bestow her favors on which peer of the realm first. Important matters, you understand.

I stood for a moment, no longer, or I risked being hailed by another acquaintance, on the threshold of the club's morning room. I looked among the potted palms, the dark, heavy furniture, and the green, baize-covered tables where fortunes have been won and lost, searching for my friend, Petersham. He was not among the card players, where he could usually be found.

I did not trouble myself to step back to the billiard room. Only on rare occasions can the viscount be roused to such a vigorous activity as billiards.

I lifted my Venetian gold pocketwatch by its chain and checked the time. Petersham never leaves his house before six in the evening. It was fifteen minutes past six.

"Delbert, has Lord Petersham arrived yet?"

The footman sprang from his place and bowed his white-wigged head. "He has, Mr. Brummell. His lordship is abovestairs in the coffee room. And, sir, 'He is a soldier fit to stand by Caesar.'"

I paused a moment. "*Othello*. Thank you, Delbert." Trust White's to have a footman who quotes Shakespeare. Though he continues to try, Delbert has not yet caught me out.

I handed Delbert my hat, my walking stick with the

gold lion's head, my kidskin gloves, and my greatcoat, then ascended the stairs.

Here I found the languid viscount in a leather armchair next to a comfortable fire reading a copy of *The Gentlemen's Magazine*. I eased myself with practiced grace into a matching chair. I am blessed with reasonable height and a frame still lean, despite the zeal with which I appreciate fine cooking.

Shaking my head with mock dismay, I asked, "When are you going to shave, Petersham? Or are you hoping to flap those things and fly?"

Viscount Petersham tossed the magazine aside and patted his side-whiskers complacently. "Bothers you, don't it, that I'm not one who will follow your fashion dictates." He favored me with one of his famous winning smiles. I may have a highly sought-after smile myself, but it is really nothing out of the common way. Petersham's whole face brightens when he grins, delighting the recipient.

"A gentleman should be clean-shaven. Are you hiding something under that forest of hair?" I asked in a teasing tone. Then, because I am, sadly, a perfectionist, and one with the added burden of having a sharp eye for detail, I could not resist adding, "Oh, and by the way, the left side has been trimmed shorter than the right."

I knew he would not take this observation badly. He and I first met back in the late 1790s when we both served under the Prince of Wales in the Tenth Light Dragoons. Some of the officers had made sport of Petersham because, although he is a tall and handsome fellow, he is not known for his physical strength and in fact suffers from asthma. I cannot stand a bully and often found myself coming to

Petersham's defense. Our resulting friendship has grown over the years.

"Something to hide? I?" the viscount replied with false severity. He stroked his whiskers as if checking for the uneven length I had mentioned. "Why, I am the most amiable and blameless of men. My foremost passion in life is snuff boxes."

I signaled a footman to bring a bottle of claret. Petersham had given me exactly the opening I needed. "Speaking of snuff boxes, I saw a particularly charming one this afternoon."

Petersham dropped his hands from his whiskers, instantly alert to the news. This is a lad who has a different snuff box for every day of the year. True gentlemen disdain smoking tobacco, but the taking of snuff is a fashionable habit, one, if I might add without seeming immodest, that I have helped raise to an art form.

At the moment, I did not miss Petersham's air of excitement. Indeed, I had counted on it. "A precious little gold and enamel box with an uncommon scene portrayed on the lid," I elaborated. "It looked to be Venus as a mermaid reposing on a shell done in mother of pearl. Matched black pearls adorned the four corners of the box."

The viscount actually exerted himself to lean forward in his chair. "Whose was it?"

I took a sip of claret before I answered, savoring the flavor. There is no better liquid refreshment. Unless, of course, it is aged brandy, a good Madeira, or canary wine. My motto is, "When your spirits are low, get another bottle."

But, back to the matter at hand. I replied to the viscount's question. "Who the box belongs to is a puzzle, Petersham. You see, I was at Talbot's Art Gallery when I noticed it. Mr. Talbot has acquired a private collection and the snuff box is among its contents. He is about to put it up for auction." I saw a flash of recognition cross the viscount's face.

"Must be Sidwell's. I heard he was running short after high play at the gaming tables. It don't surprise me that he's resorted to selling off valuables."

Nodding as if in possession of this information all along, I took another sip—very well, perhaps it was more of a gulp—of wine.

Petersham stared off into the distance. "I know that Sidwell, like you, is mad for paintings. But I never thought the old cove would have such a prime snuff box. Say!" he cried suddenly, turning back to me with a look of horror dawning on his face, "You wouldn't be thinking of bidding on it, would you?"

"Rest assured, my friend, that while you know I collect the occasional snuff box, I would never bid against you." Then, as if the matter held little interest for me, I said, "Though, now that you mention it, there is a painting I am half inclined to bid on."

Petersham took the bait. "Which one?"

"A lovely Perronneau, which would enhance my modest collection. It is of a girl and her kitten. I have a fondness for animals, you know, and own a few of Stubbs's paintings of dogs, foxes, and horses. I feel I should like the variety of having a painting depicting a cat."

Petersham supported the idea without delay.

We looked up from our conversation as a particular

confidante of Petersham's approached us. The man, whom I had seen about, and of whom I had a vague recollection, was Lord Munro. He is of average height and possesses very pale, almost white-blond hair which he wears in a wispy style. He lingered a few feet away from where we were seated, his gaze on the viscount. Just precisely what their relationship is, I have no idea. Sometimes, it is better not to inquire about these things.

Petersham excused himself and rose. He spoke to his friend in a low voice, his lips close to the other's ear. Lord Munro placed a possessive hand on Petersham's sleeve, then he nodded and moved away.

"Sorry for the interruption, Brummell," Petersham said, returning to his seat. "Munro is feeling neglected and wanted to make plans to see the fireworks tomorrow evening at Vauxhall Gardens. We haven't been to Vauxhall for a while."

Petersham and I resumed our chat and discovered we were both to attend the same musical party later in the evening. After we parted, I felt exhilarated at having accomplished the first part of my mission. I had no doubt the viscount would make my desire to own the Perronneau painting known in aristocratic circles. That would increase the odds that I would be the sole bidder. No one in the exclusive Mayfair area of London in which I run tame would think the painting important enough to bid against me.

Devious, you say? Well, I admit I can be sly in getting what I want. And, lest you think me a cad, I confess I did feel a twinge of guilt over my methods. But really, what harm had I done? Petersham benefited by our conversation as much as I did. He gained the knowledge of the existence of a snuff box sure to send him into transports of joy.

See, there, one can justify one's selfish ways if one but tries.

I must tell you, though, that even years after attaining my position in the *Beau Monde*, it still amazes me that I have risen to such heights. That a Society which eschews association with anyone whose family cannot trace illustrious roots back to the time of William the Conqueror would bow to the opinions of a twenty-seven-year-old man with no aristocratic lineage—and worse, no immense fortune—astonishes me.

But then, who am I to question their judgment? I keep my doubts well-hidden, preferring to present a fearless, completely independent demeanor to the public lest they topple me from my invisible throne.

After all, this is what my father had wanted for me. When he sent me off to Eton all those years ago, his sole hope was that the aristocratic connections made there would enable me to become somebody. If he were alive today, perhaps he would be pleased with the end result. Perhaps. It had never been easy to please Father. And since he and Mother had died within a year of one another when I was fifteen, my opportunity to gain their approval was gone.

Even so, I often envision what my parents, especially Father, might think of my present position in the Polite World. Possibly he would appreciate the fact that despite my guiding influence over fashion, there is nothing to call attention to myself in the way I dress. Unless one counts elegant perfection. But, truly, once I finish the long daily ritual of bathing and dressing, dubbed The Dressing Hour by myself and my valet, I give no further thought to my appearance.

Until, that is, it is time to change clothes again.

My doctrine is simple. I have a violent dislike of extremes and of vulgarity. I believe in good tailoring and demand excellent cuts to my clothing. I wear little jewelry other than my father's watch, which hangs from a chain attached to my waistcoat, and my quizzing glass. The latter is a circular magnifying lens of moderate proportions that I wear suspended from a long, slim black cord around my neck.

Up until recently, gentlemen's clothes have been characterized by fussy, frilly, and elaborate stuff. When my friendship with the Prince of Wales helped open Society's doors to me, I soon replaced what was regarded as fashionable for gentlemen with a smooth, sleek, uncluttered look.

A heady triumph.

Another thing I take pride in accomplishing is maneuvering the ways of Society toward cleanliness. I shudder every time I think of, or am forcibly reminded of, the custom of covering oneself with perfume to conceal unpleasant odors. Cleanliness, after all, can only promote good health. Dirt must lead to diseases. I cannot understand why everyone does not accept the idea.

At any rate, I was in a good mood when I entered my house in Bruton Street.

The ground floor contains a modest hall, which leads to a nice-sized bookroom. Here, the best editions of chiefly French, Italian, and English literature line the shelves. It is a warm chamber where I can spend hours indulging in two of my favorite pastimes: reading and letter-writing.

Down a narrow corridor to one side are the stairs leading to the kitchen. Robinson's sitting room and bedchamber are on the other side. The upstairs boasts a large drawing room, larger in fact than in some town houses, I am pleased to report; also a dining room and my bedchamber. It is the perfect arrangement for a gentleman about town.

Robinson met me on the stairs. He promptly reversed his direction to follow mine. "Good evening, sir."

"Hello, Robinson. Getting devilishly chilly outside."

"Yes, sir. Fires are burning in all the rooms. I know how you dislike the cold."

"Very good." As I said, he is an excellent manservant. He knows it, too, the devil.

"André has instructions that you will be dining at home this evening. He is preparing his recipe for chicken in mushroom and wine sauce."

I breathed a sigh of anticipation. What is better than good food, well prepared and well presented, accompanied by an appropriate wine? Very few things indeed. André, while he costs the earth, knows his craft. His skill in preparing lobster patties, another of his many specialties and my particular favorite, is most appreciated. I make sure he is rewarded and remains content in his position. Needless to say, invitations to the small, but exquisite, dinners I occasionally hold are coveted and not just for the company of yours truly.

We entered my chamber. A tented bed with ivory silk hangings dominates the room. In here, I have every appointment a gentleman of fashion might desire, and a few more. Very well, more than a few. For sequestered from prying eyes are my most prized possessions, including my best Sèvres porcelain pieces.

I walked over to a crescent-shaped side table and ran a caressing finger across the surface of a recent Sèvres acquisition. It is a tortoise-shell plate with a parrot painted in the center. I am cheered simply by gazing upon the delicate, fragile piece which is representative of the best art man can accomplish.

While, for the most part, I am happy with the life I have achieved, there are times when I feel my cherished art pieces are my only real friends. Society expects much of me. I am to be witty, have the best of manners, be expertly dressed, and remain ultimately cool at all times. In front of my Sèvres porcelain, I may wear my older silk dressing gown and slouch.

But I grow maudlin. I do have true friends—Viscount Petersham, whom you have met, Lumley "Skiffy" Skeffington, Scrope Davies, "Poodle" Byng, Her Royal Highness the Duchess of York, whom I am privileged to call "Freddie," and, great heavens, the Prince of Wales himself.

Realizing I had remained silent for several moments, I turned around and saw Robinson observing me curiously. I straightened my shoulders. "Was there anything in the post to interest me?"

Robinson flipped through a dozen folded vellum squares before selecting one and handing it to me. "The Duchess of York's weekly missive, a trifle late, sir."

"Oh good. I shall read it now before I dress for dinner. The naughty girl has taken her time writing, and after I sent her two long letters. Ungrateful little wretch," I declared with no small measure of warmth.

Frederica, daughter of a Prussian king and married to King George III's second son, the Duke of York, is one of my most cherished acquaintances. She is also my closest female friend.

Dearest George,

What must you think of such a slow correspondent? I can only imagine you are justifiably cross with me for not answering your last letters. But I console myself with the reminder that you are much too kind to ever remain out of charity with me for long.

I trust the reason for my delay in writing may also hasten your forgiveness. My dear Minney has had her pups. Five of the most darling little creatures, George, all soft black fur and big brown eyes. At last we can determine who the scamp was that got her in a family way, and thereafter paid no particular attention to her. It is my precocious boy, Legacy, who is the indifferent Papa. But, never fear, we shall bring the rascal about. Rather than giving him the run of the estate, I have sequestered Legacy with his new family and have high hopes for their future. Old Dawe tells me that yesterday, when he took Minney her food, Legacy actually let her have a good portion of it after devouring the lion's share himself.

This, by the way, brings the count of dogs at Oatlands up to one hundred and seven. I expect to be

*quite occupied here for the rest of the week, but I
shall not fail to write again within the next few days.*

*Yours, ever, and truly,
Freddie*

Still chuckling over the antics of Freddie's treasured
pets, and contemplating what gift I could take them on my
next visit—a leather ball? a length of rope knotted at both
ends?—I stripped off my clothes and eased myself into the
copper tub Robinson had filled with hot water. Ah, now
that felt good.

How could members of Society disdain immersing
themselves in water? Some actually believed one could
become ill by doing so. How ridiculous.

I wished I could indulge in a good long soak, perhaps
read the rest of my correspondence, but I needed to get on
with the preparations for the evening. Exiting the tub, I
dried myself with a soft cotton cloth, donned my Floren-
tine dressing gown, and sat at my dressing table.

Robinson ceased building up the fire and came to attention.

"I shall be attending the Perrys' musical party directly
after I dine, Robinson."

With these words, The Dressing Hour officially began.

Robinson whisked himself over to one large wardrobe
and pulled open its mahogany doors. Inside, snug in their
appointed places, nestle my selection of evening clothing.
With few exceptions the pieces are dominated by my preferred costume of dark blue coat, white waistcoat, and
black breeches.

Robinson extracted one of the superbly tailored coats, a deep slate blue, and laid it reverently on the bed. He selected a fine white lawn shirt, a pair of black, silk-lined Cassimere breeches, and a luxurious white brocade waist-coat.

"Are those the new breeches Meyer made for me?" I asked.

"Yes, sir," Robinson answered, bringing the garment for me to inspect.

I ran my hand expertly over the soft material, studying every seam and button. To scrutinize the lining better, I turned the breeches inside out. Tailors vie for my custom because if they please me, they gain the business of scores of stylish gentlemen, thus enabling them to line their own pockets with money.

The lining appeared satisfactory, yet something bothered me about the breeches. I turned them right side out. A frown creased my brow as my gaze fell on the two buttons spaced a few inches apart on the waistband.

I drew in a sharp breath.

"What is it, sir?" Robinson asked, alarmed.

"These . . . buttons . . . do . . . not . . . exactly . . . match," I said in a voice faint from shock.

It is difficult to say which of us was the more unnerved. Robinson seized the offending garment from my fingers and examined it himself. "Reprehensible! We shall speak most severely to Mr. Meyer." He swiftly folded the breeches and consigned them to the bottom of the ward-robe to be dealt with later. "Now let us put the disturbing incident behind us and continue," he suggested in a bracing tone.

Robinson chose another pair of breeches and laid them out for my approval. I went over them with painstaking precision and could find nothing amiss.

You feel I am overly critical? Not at all. Dressing is an *art*. You would not want an artist to paint your portrait showing you with a blemish on your face, would you? I rather thought not. Why should clothing not be equally flawless?

At the washstand, Robinson filled a Chinese bowl with warm water and assembled the shaving supplies. He said, "I heard from Lord Culver's man that his master has resorted to wearing false calves."

This intelligence was undoubtedly shared in order to distract me from the Disaster of the Breeches, but it did not.

"Sir, you must unclench your jaw, else I will accidentally cut you with the razor."

I contemplated the sharp blade and thought of Meyer's throat. What if I had gone out in public dressed in breeches with mismatched buttons? My reputation would be in tatters. I could almost see Father's look of disapproval.

With only a light whiff of Floris's citrus scent clinging to my freshly shaved face, I began the nerve-racking chore of dressing. Robinson and I have a mutual goal: perfection. Nothing less will do.

Tonight, this resulted in Robinson's removing one starched length of white linen after another from the wardrobe. Every one of our attempts at tying the perfect cravat failed. It cannot be said at whose door the fault for this could be laid. Robinson did his part in winding the starched cloth around my neck, and I carefully lowered my head to arrange the folds. Robinson tied the ends into an intricate knot with the skill of an artist. But the least error on either of our parts could ruin the whole composition, and a new cravat must be produced.

Standing in the center of a sea of discarded linen, I felt my temper rise. When yet another attempt resulted in an unsatisfactory outcome, I said, "Oh, devil take it, Robinson, get another neckcloth."

The valet moved to the wardrobe and suddenly stood stock-still.

Looking up to see what had rendered him immobile, I saw there was only one remaining length of cloth in the wardrobe.

Our eyes met.

"Is the laundress coming this evening with clean linens?" I asked between my teeth.

Robinson swallowed. "I am afraid not until the morning, sir."

I sighed. "Well, I suppose we had best get this one right."

Several tense moments followed but, happily, with Herculean efforts we at last achieved success. I found myself relaxing enough to remark, "We may soon have another treasure to add to our walls. A painting."

Robinson's deft hands helped me into a faultless pair of breeches, my waistcoat, whose buttons matched to a shade, and the slate blue coat. The latter was no easy task since, once donned, the coat had to fit without a single wrinkle.

"How wonderful, sir. May I inquire as to the nature of the painting?"

"A lovely Perronneau, Robinson. It is painted in shades of pale blue with touches of ivory and grey. The cat looks especially lifelike."

"A cat, sir?" Robinson pursed his lips in a gesture well known to me. It indicates my fastidious valet's disapproval. Robinson's golden blond hair, expertly combed in the short Brutus cut, seemed to stand on end at the very mention of a feline.

"Come now, man, we have birds on our porcelain and paintings of dogs and horses," I said, slipping into thin, black shoes. "A cat would be a welcome addition. Besides, I should be able to obtain the painting for an excellent price. It is owned by Lord Sidwell, and I believe he is in need of funds."

I let the words drop in an offhand manner and waited. Robinson did not fail me.

"I beg your pardon, sir," he said, his clear blue eyes glowing with excitement. "You know how I abhor repeating gossip, but . . ."

I barely managed to restrain an outright snort at such utter nonsense. Robinson prides himself on his league of chattering valets, butlers, underbutlers, footmen, and maids who can always be depended upon to talk about their lords and ladies. Heaven knows Robinson's knowledge of the latest news rivals the *Morning Post*, and his propensity to share it is equally fervent.

"Do go on," I encouraged him shamelessly.

"Well, sir, it seems Lord Sidwell is preparing to, er, retire to his country estate. It is said he needs to take himself away from the temptations of London, especially from the gaming tables." Robinson lowered his voice. "There is talk that he might even be forced to sell his town house."

Now that was distressing news. I paused in the act of arranging my hair with one of Floris's smooth-pointed combs. Robinson took the comb and finished my hair. Then he pulled out a bottle of Eau de Melisse des Carmes lotion and began rapidly massaging it into my fingers.

I wanted the painting, make no mistake, but I felt a twinge of pity for the old man who was forced to part with it. Gambling fever ran rampant through London, and sometimes I feared going too far myself. Tradesmen could be put off, but a debt of honor, such as a gaming debt, must be paid at once.

Finished with the hand cream, Robinson put the top back on the bottle and stood waiting for my pronouncement.

I gazed into the tall mahogany-framed dressing glass. A convenient article, it rested on castors and could be moved about the room at will. The dressing glass had two brass arms, each containing a lit candle. In this light, I studied the full length of my appearance critically, not missing a single detail. I made one final adjustment to the folds of my cravat.

Robinson pulled a square of linen from his pocket and wiped his brow. By now you may have realized that The Dressing *Hour* is a bit of an understatement.

Content, I turned to leave the room, vigorously pushing aside thoughts of ruin at the gaming tables. I need not worry. Such an ignominious end would never befall me.

For if one got too deeply in debt there were only two

alternatives. Flee the country. Or place a pistol to one's temple and pull the trigger.

And death, social or actual, held no appeal for me.

Little did I realize how much a part of my life it would soon become.

2

Fans fluttered and jewels flashed in the candlelight of the crowded drawing room of Lord and Lady Perry's Grosvenor Square town house.

The large square chamber was done in the neoclassical Adam style, with the carpet woven into pleasing geometrical medallions, a design echoed in the painted ceiling. Delicate shades of cream and olive with rose-colored accents were repeated throughout the room, complementing each other. Rows of gilt chairs sat facing the ornate fireplace, next to which the tenor would perform for the distinguished guests. I noticed a magnificent harp stood positioned in front of the chairs and gathered we would be treated to its soothing sounds.

Among the crowd of people one man stood out. I gazed at him curiously then went to greet my hosts.

"Brummell! Glad you could attend," Lord Perry welcomed me. Perry is a well-favored man about thirty years of age with a strong profile. An earl in command of three income-producing estates, he had been a much desired bachelor until only a year ago. At that time, defying the predictions of matchmaking mamas who thought their daughters' dowries would attract the earl, the former Miss Bernadette Martin, a demure lady, both of countenance and of pocketbook, captured his heart and became his wife.

Lady Perry, a petite brunette, was fashionably attired. She wore a dainty, pale pink gown designed in the new classically inspired mode. The styles taken from ancient Rome and Greece make for gowns constructed of the lightest materials, cut low on the bosom, and draped in a clinging manner like a goddess in Greek mythology.

She smiled at me. "Mr. Brummell, how kind of you to come. Now the success of my musical party is guaranteed."

She had a teasing gleam in her velvet brown eyes I could not resist. "My lady, your triumph has nothing to do with me and everything to do with your beauty and charm. Why, you are a woman of great achievements. Only think, you have managed the near-impossible feat of prying Perry away from his music sheets and pianoforte."

"Now, if only I could persuade the beast to play for us this evening." Lady Perry gave her chagrined husband's arm a playful rap with her fan. A silent message of affection seemed to pass between them before she directed her attention back to me.

"Mr. Brummell, please do stay for a bit after the music. I am serving a light supper and asked Cook to prepare lobster patties especially when I heard they are your favorite."

"Perry," I exclaimed, a hand over my heart, "I am in love with your wife. You had better beware."

"Ah, but Brummell," Perry said, "*she* is not in love with *you*."

We all chuckled. Then, seeing another guest enter the drawing room, Lady Perry excused herself. Perry and I watched her retreating form.

"You are indeed fortunate to have such a charming partner for life," I said softly. "But then I have long admired your intelligence."

"Thank you. Bernadette is indeed a treasure." Perry tore his gaze from his wife and turned to me. "Look here, though, I am sorry to tell you Sidwell sent his regrets and is not coming. I collect you would like to question him about that painting by Perronneau you are so intent on owning."

I turned a quizzical eye toward Lord Perry. "Whatever can you mean?"

He waved a hand indicating the room. "It is the talk of the evening that you are adamant about buying the Perronneau that Sidwell commissioned Talbot to sell. I daresay until tonight not a soul knew about the painting, or the auction itself for that matter, as it is rumored to be rather small," Perry said. "I cannot think who brought it up, but we have all been heartily warned off under the threat of the most dire consequences should we bid against you."

Devil take it! I barely stopped myself from groaning aloud. Petersham had gone too far. I had merely wanted him to pass a quiet word that I desired the painting, not become the town crier!

Out of the corner of my eye I saw a somewhat shame-faced Lord Petersham accepting a glass of wine from a footman. He ducked his head and meandered away in the opposite direction when he saw me. I vowed to switch around his alphabetically arranged jars of snuff the next time I visited his quarters.

In a cool tone, I replied to Perry, "Yes, I intend on demanding pistols at dawn for anyone who dares cross me."

Lord Perry smiled. The conversation turned to his favorite topic, music, and after several minutes we were joined by a short man wearing spectacles. His sandy hair had been pomaded and combed into a simple style, and his neckcloth was tied in an equally simple manner.

"Mr. Dawlish," Perry said with satisfaction. "I know you are not much inclined to join social gatherings, but I thought the lure of a musical evening would be too much for you to resist."

"Your lordship," Mr. Dawlish said, making a stiff bow, "I am honored by the invitation. The Bible tells us David would take his harp and play, and Saul would obtain relief from the evil spirits that plagued him. I could not miss an opportunity to hear music from such an instrument."

"And I am delighted you are here. I hope to persuade you to share your expertise on the harp's origins. My quest for musical knowledge never ceases," Perry told him. "Allow me to introduce Mr. George Brummell."

I accepted Perry's introduction to the Reverend Mr. Cecil Dawlish, the rector of a parish in London, listening with one ear as Perry explained how Mr. Dawlish and he had met at a concert and had subsequently enjoyed numerous spirited conversations about composers and instruments.

I was preoccupied with Mr. Dawlish's appearance. He was dressed in a black coat and breeches, as clerics are wont to do. In truth, I feel a gentleman clad in a black coat, in addition to the correct style of black breeches, gives the appearance of a magpie. Colors in a coat, so long as they are in good taste, are much to be preferred.

These thoughts of what is fashionable in a coat and what is not, reminded me that I was curious to know the identity of the mysterious guest I had observed upon my arrival.

Before Perry and Mr. Dawlish could cross the room to inspect the harp, I said, "One moment, Perry. Who is that man standing alone by the window?"

I referred to a diminutive, golden-skinned man dressed in unusual, to say the least, garb. His single-breasted silk coat, the color of pineapples—not a color I can approve in a gentleman's coat—buttoned all the way down the front, and possessed only a small collar, which folded upward. A double row of gold embroidery lined the front of the coat, and his trousers sported the same embroidery down each leg. The garment was tied at the waist by a bright red sash.

Lord Perry turned his gaze in the man's direction. "That is Mr. Kiang, an emissary from the King of Siam. He has been in England almost a year and is reputed to be from one of the best families in Siam. We have not seen him in London for a while as he has been in Bath and Brighton.

You must have been in the country at Belvoir or perhaps at Oatlands the last time he was in Town."

I raised one eyebrow. "I must give the name of his tailor to Grimaldi."

Lord Perry appeared puzzled for a moment. "Grimaldi? You mean the famous clown?"

I drew in a deep breath. "Just so."

Comprehension dawned, and Lord Perry laughed. The rector merely looked perplexed. I moved away and procured a glass of wine.

Abruptly a hush fell over the room, and all eyes turned toward the double doors to the drawing room. Ladies sank into the deepest of curtsies. Gentlemen bowed low.

George Augustus Frederick, Prince of Wales and Heir Apparent to the throne of England, made his entrance. The tall, rather bulky man, known as the First Gentleman of Europe—a title I admit I covet—conversed easily with those present as he made his way through the crowd. He craved the admiration and affection of all, and in my opinion, his engaging manners made it simple for the public to overlook his extravagance and self-indulgent nature.

A gruff voice at my elbow distracted me.

"Prinny still sulking since his latest attempt at taking over the government failed? He has only to bide his time. The King is mad as a March hare. Our Prince will get his regency yet."

"Lady Salisbury, I am delighted to see you," I told her and meant it. She is a tiny but sturdy woman, with heavy black arched eyebrows accentuating her strong-willed face. I bowed over her hand. "I thought you would have removed to the country in preparation for the hunting season.

How is it that the Diana of Hatfield is in Town?"

"Hmpf! How indeed. James had some tiresome business to attend. Otherwise, we would both be home at Hatfield. This morning I was in Green Park, and the nip in the air made me long for the thrill of the chase."

I nodded in understanding, though I cannot personally tolerate the hunt. Only consider the inevitable mud which would be splashed on my topboots. Not to mention the early morning hour which leaves me with little time for a proper bath or the intricacies of The Dressing Hour. No, hunting is not an activity that can appeal to me. I believe I like it even less than the fox does.

Nevertheless, I adore the company of the plain-speaking Marchioness of Salisbury. Long ago, she had been Prinny's mistress, and now she rules the highest of fashionable assembly rooms, Almack's.

"Don't think your clever tongue can divert me from the subject at hand, Brummell," she scolded, a steely look in her eyes. "Prinny fumed through the spring and summer. Has it been long enough for him to recover, or is he still brooding over forming a regency and ruling the country?"

I considered the question and found myself reluctant to answer it, not wishing to speak ill of the Prince. "While I believe the Prince to be somewhat impatient in the matter—"

"Hah!" barked the marchioness.

"Yes, er, as you say, my lady, the King is not well, and I think our Prince will get his way before long."

"Perhaps he won't, after all. In January, the King read the Address at the opening of Parliament as clear as that crystal goblet you're holding and—" She stopped abruptly, then gasped. "Oh, Lord. Here comes Prinny."

Outrageously, Lady Salisbury slipped away before the Prince of Wales could reach us. It was left to me to soothe the frown creasing the royal brow. "Sir, may I compliment you on your coat?" This was a tactic sure to bring him pleasure.

"You like this one, eh, Brummell? I recall two weeks ago I almost left the opera when you raised that damned eyebrow of yours at my new leek-green coat."

"The color will not be fashionable, sir. The coat you are wearing now is a great improvement. The seams are particularly well-tailored." They would have to be, to hold the Prince's ever increasing weight.

"You know I rely upon your judgment. Hey now, it's going about that some auction's caught your eye. Anything there I'd be interested in?"

Many people liken the Prince to a sulky child. Behind his back, of course. Indeed, the look he leveled on me at the moment brought to mind a youngster kept out of a favorite game and none too happy about it.

I felt myself tense, though I trust I kept my expression impassive. Using only my left hand, I pulled a black and turquoise snuff box out of my pocket and flicked it open. I took a pinch with my right hand and delicately inhaled. My hands are beautifully pampered, I must tell you. In addition to massaging them daily with Eau de Melisse des Carmes cream, Robinson carefully trims my fingernails and buffs them to a healthy shine.

The Prince watched my every move, reached in his pocket for his own snuff box, and mimicked my actions.

Meanwhile, I contemplated my predicament. The Prince

was known to have a penchant for collecting. In fact, he was a well known and generous patron of the arts.

If I waxed enthusiastic about the Perronneau, the Prince might conceive of a notion to possess it. On the other hand, seeing how everyone in the room apparently knew of my interest in the painting, it would not serve to deny it.

"Poor Sidwell is having to sell up to recover gaming losses. I thought I should help by purchasing a small Perronneau," I said at length.

"Pretty thing, is it?" The royal eyes narrowed.

"Yes, sir, especially if you care for cats."

"I'm partial to all animals, as you are, Brummell. I might have to attend the exhibition tomorrow afternoon."

"Are you sure, sir?" I inquired gently. "If I thought you would like it, I would have planned to purchase the painting for you."

The Prince preened a bit at this evidence of subordination. "That's good of you."

I assumed a look of sorrow. "I would have, you see, had it not been for the fact I knew the cat would remind you of that unfortunate wager you made with Charles Fox a few years back. You lost thirteen to one as I recall."

The Prince's face clouded. "Yes. I remember it well. Fox boasted he could determine on which side of Bond Street the most cats would be seen. I accepted a bet on the subject, and damned if Fox didn't win merely by picking the sunny side of the street."

I nodded sympathetically.

"No, I would not care for the painting at all myself," the Prince said petulantly. "And if you say there's nothing else of interest, I might as well amuse myself with my guests at Carlton House for the rest of the week. After that, I'm leaving Town for an extended time. I've decided to go to my Pavilion in Brighton. Call on me before I go, Brummell."

"I shall consider myself honored to do so, sir," I assured him, and the Prince wandered away.

As I said, I can be determined and a trifle devious when it comes to getting what I want.

I looked about for a footman so I might obtain a fresh glass of wine. Lord Perry keeps a devilishly fine cellar. Also, I wished to satisfy my curiosity about Mr. Kiang, the emissary from Siam. I noted the arrival of the tenor and judged I did not have long before the entertainment began.

Scanning the elegant gathering, I saw the Siamese man toward the back of the room. I moved in his direction, just managing to exchange my empty glass for a full one before I reached him.

"An excellent wine, would you not say?" I asked by way of opening the conversation.

The emissary turned his slanted eyes in my direction. He gave a brief bow. "You are correct. I have purchased much wine and brandy in England to take home to my King."

My knowledge of Siam was limited, but I was aware of its recent bloody history. "A distinguished ruler, your King Rama. He has succeeded in finally defeating the Burmese and uniting your country."

A little knowledge goes a long way. Mr. Kiang appeared impressed by my comments and willing to take a stranger into his confidence. We chatted for a few moments about Siam.

"You are wise," he said abruptly. "Perhaps you can help me. I am in England almost a year now obtaining many beautiful art pieces to take back to King Rama to adorn the new palace in our capital city of Bangkok."

I cannot like English art treasures going overseas, but I held my tongue. For once. I picked up my quizzing glass, held the magnifier to my eye, and studied the man's garish coat. My eyebrow must have soared to the upper reaches of my scalp, but he did not seem to notice.

Mr. Kiang went on speaking. "I want to bring back only the best for my King. I understand there is a Mr. Brummell in London who declares what is in good taste and what is not. Do you know him?"

I let my quizzing glass fall back to my chest. "Somewhat."

Mr. Kiang lowered his voice. "It is said this Mr. Brummell wishes a painting of a girl and her cat that will be auctioned the day after tomorrow."

"Hmm. What you heard could be merely a rumor."

"No, no. No rumor," Mr. Kiang declared. "I have heard it said here in this very room by these people of high rank."

"Who would never lie," I murmured.

"Excuse me?"

"Nothing. Do go on."

"A painting that a man of taste says he wants must be a painting for the King of Siam," he insisted.

I felt a twinge of alarm. My desire to own the Perronneau had grown by the hour—and by the number of rivals for its ownership. I took a sip of wine, then assumed a benevolent expression. "I do not like to be a party to rumors, but you seem like a good man, eager to serve your country."

Mr. Kiang agreed fervently.

I acted as though I had come to a decision. "Then I shall tell you. Just between you and me, I happen to know that Brummell is nothing but a foolish, idle dandy with no thought in his head other than his appearance. Pay no attention to anything he says."

Mr. Kiang seemed startled. "Shh!" he admonished with a finger to his lips. "This Mr. Brummell is said to be a friend of your Prince. You would not like for him to hear you speak so rudely of his friend."

"Calm yourself, sir," I said, glancing around to see the Prince of Wales flirting with a woman a good twenty years his senior, exactly the sort Prinny liked. "The Prince is occupied with conversation."

"Even so, I hear Mr. Brummell is a very powerful man. You would not want anyone to overhear what you say."

"Powerful, yes. But power does not equal taste, does it? No, of course not. Take my advice and contact Christie's auction house. They would be a much better source for you than a small gallery like Talbot's."

Feeling smug, I sauntered away from a frowning Mr. Kiang. I was sure I had put a spoke in the emissary's wheel. I prepared to enjoy the music and selected a seat next to a lady who blushed furiously.

Petersham, seated a few rows away, caught my attention and shrugged an apology. I graciously smiled my acceptance.

No, I had absolutely nothing to fear. Tomorrow afternoon, I would attend the exhibition to dampen any other burgeoning interests. By the following evening, the Perronneau would grace one of the walls of my home. The only question was which one?

A few minutes later, I lost myself in the tenor's rich voice.

I would not have been so sanguine had I any inkling of what would transpire at the exhibition and the events that would soon follow.

3

The next afternoon, I hired a coach to take me to Talbot's Art Gallery. However, I did not leave my rooms before writing a scathing message to Mr. Griffin, the sedan-chair maker. This was the last time I wished to travel about Town without the comfort of my own conveyance.

The exhibition began at three o'clock; thus I knew that Petersham, the slug-a-bed, would not be on the scene. Nonetheless, I did not anticipate how many members of Society would be there. Entering the gallery, I groaned when I saw the crowd gathering around the Perronneau painting.

Lord Perry stood contemplating a lute. I joined him. "Good afternoon, Perry."

"Oh, hello, Brummell. Would you look at the workmanship on this lute? South Indian if I am not mistaken."

I raised my quizzing glass and examined the instrument. "A lovely piece. Ivory inlay."

"Indeed. And mark the delicacy of the paintings of the deities on either side of the strings. You know, Brummell, they say you can tell a lot about a person by the art he collects. I never knew Sidwell had such a whimsical side. I thought the only music he appreciated was the music of the dice-box."

"You must bid on the lute, Perry. Someone with your passion for music should own it."

Lord Perry glanced around the room, then indicated Mr. Kiang with a slight nod of his head. "I wonder if the rest of us are wasting our time here. The emissary from Siam seems determined to make off with the lot."

I turned in the direction of Mr. Kiang and received a mocking salute.

I puzzled over this briefly, until a commotion coming from the front door captured the attention of the room.

Lord Perry said, "What the deuce? Here is the dowager Countess Wrayburn. I have not laid eyes on the old harridan in years. Probably since the Season of '03 when she proclaimed the future Duchess of Wiltenshire 'trollopy-looking.' "

"I remember," I said, recalling that the Countess never had a kind word for anyone. "Fortunately, she does not go about much anymore."

In the loud voice often adopted by the near-deaf, Lady Wrayburn shouted at her companion, a frightened, but rather pretty, young lady about twenty years of age. "You stupid child! I told you I didn't need this heavy cloak! I'm sweating like a farmer's wife! One of my shawls would have served! Here," she yelled, reaching claw-like hands up and pulling off the offending garment. She heaved it at the younger woman. "You lug it about for the next hour, you ninnyhammer!"

"I am sorry, my lady," the companion replied quietly. She then held up her hands as if to ward off a blow. The cloak fell to the floor.

"Damn you, girl, pick that up!" the dowager screeched.

The command was instantly obeyed.

Lady Wrayburn and her trembling companion moved into the room to study a drawing. Now that the ugly scene appeared to be over, the gaping onlookers turned their attention back to the art pieces on display.

"A thoroughly unpleasant woman," Perry remarked in an undertone.

"Her comment comparing herself to a farmer's wife is not that far off the mark," I ventured. "Though I would be willing to wager many farmers' wives have better manners."

"You would wager on most anything, though, would you not, Brummell?" Lord Perry asked with a mocking smile.

Before I could deliver a rebuke to this cocky observation, the front door swung open, and to my astonishment, Viscount Petersham, looking exceptionally pale and with dark circles beneath his eyes, entered the room. "Good God, Petersham, is that you? I cannot remember when I have seen you out so early."

"And there's a valid reason for it," the viscount moaned. "I'm not myself until the evening. It'll be a deuced miracle if I don't bring on one of my asthma attacks. But I had to come see that snuff box you described, despite the ungodly hour."

That was understandable.

Lord Perry exchanged greetings with him, then moved away to view a stunning painting by Raphael.

Petersham, who had glanced around and determined who was in attendance, spoke to me in a low voice. "I thought by now one of Lady Wrayburn's enemies would have choked her to death with her own ghastly tongue. What's she doing here kicking up a dust?"

"Defying death and making life hell for those around her," I replied. "Come on, I know you want to see the snuff box."

We moved past a display of Chinese drawings to where the snuff box sat on a tall pedestal enclosed with glass. A card next to it indicated it had been made only a year before by Mssrs. Rundell and Bridges, jewelers.

Lord Petersham gasped in ecstasy. "It is exactly as you described, Brummell. Venus as a mermaid. It would make some men want to join the Royal Navy."

From across the room, the shrill voice of the dowager countess intruded. "What's everyone making a fuss over that Perronneau for? It belongs in the dustbin! Cats! I can't abide them! I want that painting by Raphael!"

Her remark about cats came as no surprise to me. Does it not stand to reason someone like Lady Wrayburn would not appreciate the gentle beauty and fine intelligence of felines?

About to turn my attention back to the snuff box, I noticed Mr. Kiang approach. When he was a few feet away, he stood in a posture that indicated he was waiting to speak to me.

"Excuse me a moment, Petersham," I said, though I doubted the spellbound viscount, who had not taken his eyes from the snuff box, heard me.

"Good afternoon, Mr. Kiang," I said. My gaze immediately focused on the buttons of the Siamese man's coat. They were fastened incorrectly.

What was going on? I thought irritably.

First the buttons on my new breeches were not matched properly. Now the buttons on this man's coat refused to align themselves in an orderly fashion. Had the world of buttons gone mad?

I struggled to ignore the imperfection. Mr. Kiang's next words helped.

"So we know each other's name, *Mr. Brummell*. You are a very clever man. But not clever enough in this instance."

"How is that?" I inquired politely.

"After our conversation, I felt remiss in not knowing the identity of the gentleman who had advised me not to pay attention to what *Mr. Brummell* said." He fixed me with an unyielding glare.

"I did warn you."

The Siamese man's eyes narrowed. Then his face cleared. "I admit I was angry at first. Then I found I admired your tactics. You are a man who knows what he wants and goes after it."

I made a slight bow.

Mr. Kiang continued. "Because you desire the painting so greatly, I have decided it is truly special."

I felt like kicking myself.

Mr. Kiang took a step forward. "Nothing can stop me from acquiring that painting for my King Rama. Nothing and no one."

"We shall see." My voice was controlled, but I fought a mounting irritation. I returned to Petersham's side, fighting to maintain my well-known reserve.

Petersham tore his gaze away from the snuff box. "Who was that fellow with the dreadful coat?"

I quickly described what I knew of Mr. Kiang.

"Egad. I hope he doesn't want this snuff box."

"Never fear," I said coming to an impulsive decision. "I shall take matters into my own hands. I have it on good authority that Sidwell is rusticating at his country house. I shall hire a coach and drive out there tomorrow. I will buy the painting and the snuff box from him outright. Then I shall return to Town before the auction to claim our prizes. Perhaps I will let Mr. Kiang see what a gracious winner I am."

"I say! There's a plan," Petersham approved with a happy grin. "I'd go with you, I assure you, but since you're going during the day—"

"My lady's maid has got herself with child! What? I'll kill the harlot!" The now familiar piercing voice of Lady Wrayburn exploded into the room and arrested everyone's attention.

A shocked silence fell.

The dowager countess and her companion stood before a small sculpture by Donatello, called "Madonna and Child."

The companion, I perceived, was in tears, though trying

valiantly to hide the fact. "Please, my lady. I did not mean to say anything. Lizzie has known for several weeks now, and we . . . we were frightened to tell you. Just now, when I saw this sculpture, I spoke without thinking."

"Without *thinking*? You are not able to think, Miss Ashton! Thinking requires a brain, an organ of which you are not in possession!" Lady Wrayburn struck her cane on the floor for emphasis. "How dare she? And how dare *you* keep this from me? I shall have you both turned off without references!"

Miss Ashton seemed to shrink at the threat.

The dowager countess appeared on the brink of apoplexy. "And after I took both of you in! She was without skills, so I had to train her! And you had no place to go after that wastrel you called 'father' died!"

"Please, my lady," Miss Ashton begged, obviously humiliated, but maintaining her dignity. "Calm yourself. Let us go home and speak of this. I know you will make a compassionate decision once you have had time to reflect—"

"Reflect!" Lady Wrayburn shrieked. "The only thing I shall be reflecting on is what a fool I was to trust either of you! And who will do my hair now that Lizzie is in disgrace?"

What a vulgar scene. Drawn by the way Miss Ashton fought to maintain her composure while clearly frightened of her employer, I could not stop myself from intervening and moved to stand in front of the countess. "Lady Wrayburn, may I help you to your coach? You seem to be unwell." Indeed, a severe case of cruelty afflicted her.

"What? Is that you, Brummell? Still leading the Polite

World about with your beef-witted ideas on bathing and clean linen? I don't need any assistance from you. I'm perfectly capable myself. Have to be. I'm surrounded by fools and betrayers!" In a fit of fury, she seized the Madonna and Child sculpture and banged it down on its pedestal.

Mr. Talbot rushed to protect the valuable piece of art.

The dowager countess stamped out of the gallery, cursing her companion and her lady's maid the entire way.

I stood by watching in frustration. Miss Ashton cast me a swift look of gratitude before following her employer out the door.

"How gothic," Lord Petersham drawled. "I need a drink. Maybe even a bottle or two. What say you, Brummell? Will you join me at White's?"

"Yes," I replied absently.

I do not know why I was so affected by what had happened. Servants are commonly mistreated in London, but Miss Ashton had seemed a gently bred girl. And her azure-colored eyes were divine.

Lord Perry announced his intention of going home and telling Lady Perry about the lute, so it was left to Petersham and me to join our friends at White's. In the coach on the way over, Petersham kept up a stream of conversation about Lord Sidwell and his collection. I listened and answered appropriately, but my mind was on the scene we had just been treated to.

I could well imagine the sort of life Miss Ashton had to endure at Lady Wrayburn's hand, considering that the older woman thought nothing of berating the girl in a public place. Even if Lady Wrayburn decided to keep the young miss, her future did not bode well. In time, Miss Ashton's air of distinction might be crushed. In its place would be a dull, spiritless view of life. I hated to think of beauty being spoiled that way.

What was worse, though, was the more likely result of Miss Ashton's being tossed out without a reference. What future would she have then? One on the streets, no doubt. With her looks, she was sure to find a man willing to set her up as his mistress. *If* she would to accept such a fate. The proud set of her shoulders told me she might prefer a final, but high-minded, stroll into the Serpentine River.

And what of the pregnant lady's maid? Her plight was even more desperate.

The entire episode left me indignant. I wished I could think of a way to help the two women, but a solution failed me. Were there not innumerable females reduced to poverty across England? I could not play knight in shining armor to them all.

Once at White's we were joined by young Scrope Davies, who should have been hard at his studies at Cambridge but rarely was to be found anywhere near that university. The party grew merry in time, with Scrope relating the details of a horse race he had won a large sum on, but I was restless.

I was not looking forward to tomorrow's two-hour ride out to Sidwell's estate either, but there was a posting house on the road, which could be counted on to supply me with an excellent meal. That would make my trip more tolerable.

Still, I tossed and turned later during the night and was unusually impatient the next morning when dressing. After struggling with my cravat for almost a quarter of an hour, I dispensed with Robinson's assistance, much to that man's mortification.

I heard the knocker sound downstairs and decided that whoever it was would have to be told I was not at home. I must be on my way to Sidwell's if I wished to return to London by the time of the auction.

Satisfied with my Venice-blue coat, buckskin breeches, and gleaming Hessian boots, I picked up my hat, selected a carved ebony cane from my collection, and closed the door to my bedchamber behind me.

I had almost reached the stairs when Robinson stopped me.

"Sir, one moment, please."

I held up a restraining hand. "I am not at home to anyone who has had the misfortune to call." I put my foot on the first step.

"Sir!"

"What is it?" I demanded impatiently, swinging around to face him. "The hired coach is waiting out front."

Robinson assumed an injured air. "I am sorry to delay you, but thought you might wish to know that Her Royal Highness the Duchess of York is in the drawing room."

I stood thunderstruck. "Good God, man, what is she doing in Town? She rarely leaves Oatlands." I felt my chest tighten in alarm.

I gave Robinson no chance to reply. I hastened past him and threw open the double doors to the drawing room. There was Frederica, the Royal Duchess herself, seated in a chair. My heart raced.

"Freddie! What in heaven's name are you doing here?

Not that I am anything less than delighted to see you." I paused only long enough to deposit my hat and stick on a nearby table, then rapidly crossed to her side and bowed.

She rose to clasp both of my outstretched hands. We stood like that for a moment looking at one another. She is a small, dignified lady of some thirty years. Her brown curly hair was held back from her face with a pale green silk bandeau which matched her gown. A few tendrils of hair framed her face, the rest fell to her shoulders. Her normally serene countenance was marred by worry.

"Oh, George," she said in her sweet, light voice. "I am much distressed."

"Please sit down," I said, indicating a chintz-covered sofa. I took the place next to her, apprehension filling me at this unprecedented visit. I often spend weekends at Freddie's country estate, Oatlands, but she has never come to my rooms. This is, after all, a bachelor's residence. And I had just had her letter telling me of the new puppies and her prediction that she would be a busy lady this week. "Tell me what is wrong, Freddie."

"Forgive my manners, George. I know I should be complimenting you on this enchanting room—"

"Never mind that now!" I blurted. "Are you ill? No, I can see you are the picture of beauty and health."

That brought a tremulous smile. "You are always the perfect gentleman."

"Do you need tea? A glass of sherry, perhaps?"

"No, thank you, dear. I shall tell you the news straightaway. Lady Wrayburn is dead!"

I am uncertain what I had expected, but it was not this. Confusion was my first emotion. "I am afraid I do not understand, Freddie. I saw the lady yesterday, and she had plenty of life in her, let me tell you. Was it her heart?"

Before the Royal Duchess could reply, I muttered, "Forget that. The woman had no heart. Recollect the time you rescued that old hound she ordered shot because his bad hip made him limp?"

"I remember it well, but listen to me, George. The countess was murdered!"

My eyebrows rose incredulously. "Murdered? By whom?"

"That is the problem. The police office at Bow Street thinks Miss Ashton, her companion, poisoned her. But I know, George, I simply *know* that cannot be true. You see," she ended on a soft wail, "I recommended Miss Ashton for her position with the countess, because I knew her father."

"Good God, Freddie," I managed to utter.

"People will talk about how I gave my approval to her character, and there could be a scandal. But more importantly, what will happen to Miss Ashton? I cannot stand by and do nothing. That is why you must help me . . . and Miss Ashton."

"Freddie, I am Beau *Brummell*, not Bow *Street*. What can I do?"

"There is only one thing to be done, George. Find out who really killed Lady Wrayburn." Her Royal Highness turned the full force of her compelling blue eyes on me.

Alas, I never have been able to deny her anything.

4

"*Freddie, how can* you be sure Miss Ashton did not murder Lady Wrayburn?"

"George!" the Royal Duchess cried, drawing her head back and looking at me askance. Sitting next to her, I could feel the outrage emanating from her.

Thankfully, at that moment Robinson entered the room bearing a tea tray. Excellent timing, I thought. Another minute and Freddie might have left in high dudgeon, never to see me or write to me again. A fate I could not endure.

As it was, several moments passed while Robinson carefully placed a plate of tiny cakes within Freddie's easy reach, and she poured the tea. The entire time he was in the room, Robinson smiled at her. He did not make as if to leave until he was certain her every comfort had been seen to. I nodded to him gratefully, and he so unbent from his pique at my earlier curt treatment of him that he spared a strained smile for me.

After Robinson left, I said, "Now, pray do not fly up into the boughs, my princess. My asking about Miss Ashton's possible guilt was a necessary question."

Freddie sat in composed silence, her cup and saucer untouched on her lap, a look of frozen hauteur on her face. Not even the use of my pet name for her induced her to thaw.

I placed my teacup on the table and flung out my hands in a helpless gesture. "Very well then. If you must know, when I saw the two of them yesterday at Talbot's Art Gallery, Lady Wrayburn treated those present to quite a scene. Miss Ashton apparently kept a secret from her mistress about one of the other servants. The lady's maid is—how shall I say this delicately?—in a family way."

"No," Freddie gasped, her teacup rattling as she set it down.

"Yes. Lady Wrayburn threatened to throw both women out of the house. Her tongue was sharp enough to slice a marble statue. But I suppose you would have me believe she died of a disorder of the digestive organs."

Freddie stood, and I immediately followed suit.

"George," she said, her tone admonitory. "I know what kind of woman the countess was. But I assure you Miss Rebecca Ashton could not possibly have murdered Lady Wrayburn. You see, Miss Ashton is the daughter of a viscount. She would *never* forget her breeding and manners to such an extent that she would be involved in something as vulgar as murder."

Freddie can be very much the *grande dame* when she chooses.

"Ah, a viscount's daughter. I did not know. Of course you are right then. Miss Ashton could not have been involved," I assured her, and we resumed our places on the sofa. Freddie apparently missed my tone of irony and appeared mollified by my sensibility to Miss Ashton's upbringing.

But privately I remembered the ugly scene at the gallery. Could anyone who witnessed the cruel way Lady Wrayburn had treated her companion, and the threats she had made to toss the girl out on the street, doubt that Miss Ashton, or anyone in her circumstances, could be driven to murder, aristocratic background or no? I hoped Freddie's assessment of Miss Ashton's character would prove correct.

"Now that we have established Miss Ashton's innocence," Freddie said, her voice once again its normal sweet, light tone, "I can tell you it was Lady Wrayburn's evening glass of milk which someone poisoned, subsequently causing her death."

Dash it! Worse and worse! I raised a hand to my brow. "Did Miss Ashton personally give her the milk?"

Freddie heaved a sigh. "I suppose she did, George. She was Lady Wrayburn's companion, and it was most likely her duty. Although it is possible the lady's maid brought it up to her. I have not spoken with Miss Ashton yet, you see, because I came here first to enlist your help."

The skeptical expression on Freddie's lovely face clearly implied she doubted her judgment in doing so. It caused me to feel a pang of guilt. "You had best tell me everything you know. To begin with, how did you find out about the murder?"

Freddie reached into the pale green silk reticule which hung by a satin cord from her wrist. She pulled out a folded sheet of parchment and handed it to me. "A messenger brought this to Oatlands."

The letter was written in a precise hand and dated in the small hours of the morning.

May it please Your Royal Highness, I write this letter on behalf of my friend, Miss Ashton. It grieves me to be the bearer of bad tidings, but Miss Ashton's employer, Lady Wrayburn, has been called home to her Maker this very night. Miss Ashton sent word to me, not only for spiritual comfort for herself, but also because I am the rector of Lady Wrayburn's parish.

Unfortunately, the doctor tells us the older lady was helped on her journey by some sort of poison added to her evening glass of milk. An investigator from the Bow Street police office arrived at Wrayburn House and questioned everyone in a most dreadful manner. Dear Miss Ashton is quite overset. Not only has she lost her employer, but she fears the investigator thinks her the most likely perpetrator of the crime. I am sure you will agree, Miss Ashton could never be guilty of such a sin against God.

I know you have stood Miss Ashton's friend in the

*past, and beg that you will come to her aid now in
her hour of need.*

*Most humbly your servant,
Cecil Dawlish*

My eyebrows rose in surprise. "Why, I know Mr. Dawlish, Freddie. We met the other evening at Lord Perry's
musical party. The rector has a weakness for music."

"Well, I am grateful Mr. Dawlish had the foresight to
write to me before the situation grows worse. As I said, I
knew Miss Ashton's father. Lord Kirgo came to many of
my weekend parties at Oatlands. Perhaps you remember
him."

"Yes, in fact I do. Bit of a fribble, was he not?" More
than a bit, I recalled. The man was rarely seen without a
bottle, flask, or glass of spirits in his hand.

Freddie looked past me and a slight frown marred her
ivory brow. "Charming, but yes, he was a rackety sort. He
died after an incident with Mr. Peepers."

"Who?"

"Mr. Peepers. One of my monkeys. You know how I
like to keep a little colony of them on the lawn outside
my bedchamber window. Their antics often relieve my
boredom. Such entertaining little fellows."

She looked to me for agreement and I nodded politely.
In truth, I avoided the creatures when possible. One of
them had ruined a pair of my pantaloons in a most rude,
uncivilized way. I must say that if the action was meant
to be a statement on the validity of the garment's style,
the monkey had more hair than wit. The pantaloons were
cut with the precision of a surgeon's knife, and their color,

Skeffington brown, was one I had just brought into fashion and named after my friend, Lumley Skeffington, who first brought the shade to my attention.

I turned my thoughts from my desecrated pantaloons back to Freddie's story.

"Mr. Peepers had climbed up the side wall and perched in Lord Kirgo's window. The monkey is fond of spying on people, don't you know. That is where his name comes from. At any rate, as best as we can put the events together, it was early morning and Lord Kirgo was lying in bed, suffering from a disordered spleen brought about from the previous evening's indulgences—"

"You mean he was drunk."

"Quite," Freddie agreed. "I imagine his head hurt terribly, poor man. At any rate, we can only gather that Mr. Peepers sat chattering away on the window sill annoying Lord Kirgo to no end. We believe that Lord Kirgo went to chase the monkey away, and in his lordship's unsteady condition, fell out the window to his death. Old Dawe, my footman, found him in the rhododendrons."

I raised a hand to cover a barely suppressed smile at the mental picture the tale evoked. Freddie glanced at me sharply, and I brought myself under control.

"Lord Kirgo left Miss Ashton with nothing but debts. She sold everything and had to resort to taking a paid position. I helped her gain employment with Lady Wrayburn. It was not what I would have liked for her, not at all. I would have preferred to sponsor her coming out in Society instead, but Miss Ashton is an independent sort and had no wish to marry. That was over a year ago."

"Perhaps her decision to remain unwed will change

now. Miss Ashton is hardly a fusby-faced old maid at her last prayers. And there are few options other than marriage for a gently bred girl," I pointed out.

"Unless she is sentenced to Newgate." Freddie gazed at me intensely. "George," she said, reaching over and placing her hand in mine. "My carriage is outside. You will come along with me now to see Miss Ashton, will you not? You are so very observant, dear. And an excellent judge of character. If anyone can find out what really happened last night, I am confident it is you."

Staring down into Freddie's pleading eyes, I could not help but take pride in her belief in me. I would have puffed out my chest, but I had on a rather tight-fitting waistcoat.

Freddie's gloved fingers tenderly squeezed my hand. The pressure filled me with warmth. All thoughts of my plans for the day and the Perronneau painting fled from my mind. Mr. Kiang would win that round after all. Loss of the painting was a small price to pay to retain Freddie's admiration.

I rose to my feet, still holding her hand, gently bringing her with me. "None of your monkeys are hiding out in the carriage waiting to ambush me, are they?"

Our arrival at Wrayburn House was not greeted with any great ceremony. The knocker had been muffled, straw had been spread in the street to lessen noise from passing carriages, and forbidding black crepe hatchments were draped over the front door.

The latter was opened by a gloomy butler, dressed in

black, whom Freddie addressed as Riddell. In somber tones, he informed us that while the family was unavailable, he would send for Miss Ashton.

Following Riddell's silent footsteps, I decided the funereal air which permeated the house went beyond the death of its mistress. Despite the obvious cleanliness of the furnishings, carpeting, and draperies, the rooms held a dreary, unused feeling, as if there was no life to be found within their walls. The dark furniture, and the equally dark draperies sucked light from the room and added to the depressive atmosphere.

"Poor Miss Ashton," Freddie whispered when Riddell left us alone in a small chamber which I supposed served as a second drawing room. "How dreadful to live in such grim surroundings when one is young. I wonder how her soul managed to survive."

Perhaps it did not, I mused as we seated ourselves on an uncomfortable brown settee.

But when Miss Ashton joined us a moment later, all thoughts of a young lady driven to the depths of despair by a domineering tyrant of an employer vanished from my head. Here was that mixture of composure and fear I had perceived at the art gallery the day before. Surely no soulless being could project such emotions. Or possess such divine eyes.

"Your Royal Highness!" Miss Ashton exclaimed upon entering the room and seeing Freddie. A look of happy relief spread across her features. "How wonderful to see you. Mr. Dawlish must be responsible for your coming to me." She dropped into a deep curtsy, then straightened and glanced at me.

"Yes, 'Becca, I did have a note from Mr. Dawlish and must remember to write and thank him for it," Freddie said. She gave the girl a quick hug, then turned to me. "George, this is Miss Rebecca Ashton. 'Becca, Mr. Brummell."

I had risen at Miss Ashton's entrance and made a slight bow at the introduction. She stood nonplussed for a moment, but quickly recovered.

A tall, slender girl with excellent posture, she wore a simple black mourning gown, made of that dull, loathsome material called bombazine, which heightened the translucence of her skin. Tiny curling tendrils escaped from a mass of dusky blonde hair on which a black cap with trailing ribbons had been placed.

"Mr. Brummell, of course I know who you are and am honored by your presence. I thank you for coming to my assistance yesterday at the art gallery."

"I am uncertain whether or not I rendered any aid under the circumstances," I said as we took our seats. Miss Ashton sat across from Freddie and me in a walnut armchair.

"Oh, but you did. You distracted Lady Wrayburn from her . . ." Miss Ashton appeared uneasy, searching for the right word to describe her late employer's behavior.

I rode to her rescue. "Tirade?"

A hint of color invaded her cheeks. "Well, yes, actually. But I fear I was to blame for provoking her ladyship."

" 'Becca," Freddie said gently, "George has told me what transpired. Are you and the lady's maid, was it? in need of a place to go?"

Miss Ashton twisted a handkerchief between her fingers. "No, I thank you, we are not. At least, not at present.

Lizzie and I have been told by Mr. Hensley, Lady Wray-burn's younger son, that we may stay on for a while, at least until the household settles down from . . . I mean to say, after the d-death—"

The young girl broke off, raising the handkerchief to damp eyes. I was reminded of the seriousness of the crime involved and vowed not to let those eyes, the color of a faraway sea, blind me to any truths about the young lady's possible role in the murder.

She tucked the handkerchief away and gracefully accepted the tea tray from a returning Riddell who actually unbent enough to smile at her. I was surprised his lips did not crack from the effort. She placed the heavy tray on a table between us, and poured a cup for Freddie, then me.

I had had enough of tea for the morning, but reached out for the offered cup and saucer. I noted Miss Ashton's slim fingers and tried to imagine them adding poison to a glass of milk which would bring on a permanent sleep.

It was not a pleasant image.

5

When I raised my eyes from the cup of tea we both still held, I found Miss Ashton watching me steadily. In that second, the expression on her face changed to one of defensive pride, as if she knew I was weighing the possibilities and was determined to rise above my suspicious scrutiny. She had courage.

And there was something more. Or more accurately, something lacking. Confidence. Though she put on a brave face, Miss Ashton's demeanor said that life had not been fair to her in the past, and she feared fate might hand her worse in the future.

For the time being, I decided I would give her the benefit of the doubt and abide by my initial impression that she was innocent of any wrongdoing.

"Miss Ashton," I said, after taking a sip of tea, "we have come here this morning for two reasons. First, to ascertain that you are in no danger of losing the roof over your head. You have reassured us on this point. Secondly, we wish to learn as much as possible about the events of last evening so that we may . . . er, protect you from any unpleasantness."

Miss Ashton squared her shoulders and fixed me with a forthright gaze. "What you mean is you want to know if I was the one who poisoned her."

" 'Becca!" Freddie exclaimed, setting her teacup on the table with a sharp click. "Neither of us thinks you had anything to do with this terrible matter. Anyone who does possesses not a grain of sense."

"Mr. Lavender, the investigator from Bow Street who was here last night, seemed an eminently sensible man, and I daresay he is convinced I am the most likely suspect."

Miss Ashton raised her chin during this pronouncement, but I noticed it trembled a bit toward the end of the speech.

"Stuff and nonsense!" Freddie cried.

"Not a bit of it," Miss Ashton said. "I-I wondered at first if I had not been responsible—"

"What?" Freddie demanded, taken aback.

I studied the young woman. "Perhaps you might begin with what happened when you returned to Wrayburn House after the exhibition, Miss Ashton," I encouraged gently, putting on my best sympathetic expression. The one that has been known to extract information out of the most tight-lipped member of Society.

Miss Ashton glanced at me, nodded, and took a deep breath. Releasing it, she began, "When we returned home, I tried my best to act as if nothing had happened at the art gallery. Lady Wrayburn complained that her feet hurt. I offered to fill a basin with warm water for her to soak them, but she refused. She feared she might catch a chill. So, I helped her undress and got her settled comfortably into bed, hoping and praying she had forgotten the news about Lizzie.

"She had not. Directly after I brought up her dinner and read to her until she finished her meal, she commanded me to send Lizzie to her.

"One really cannot argue with Lady Wrayburn," Miss Ashton explained, looking at me. I nodded in understanding, took a another sip of my unwanted tea and waited for her to continue.

She turned her face away as if mentally viewing the scene again. "I hurried up to the attics to fetch Lizzie. She has been laying down a lot lately because she has been feeling poorly. She is sick every morning and worn out completely by evening. It is a shame what women in general—I speak now of women not of the Nobility—have to endure during their lives. They are at the mercy of the kindness of others. It quite makes me angry."

Miss Ashton's hands had clenched in her lap, and her jaw hardened.

Freddie's expression was set, and I knew she was thinking that it was *not* only women in the lower orders who suffered. I wanted to reach over and touch her, reassure her that she had me to rely upon, but I knew such an action would be inappropriate and only embarrass her in front of her young friend so I restrained myself. A few silent curses at the Duke of York were all I indulged in before turning my full attention back to Miss Ashton's words.

"I told Lizzie that Lady Wrayburn knew about her condition." Miss Ashton bit her lip in dismay and lowered her head. "I apologized for my wretched tongue. I had never meant for the news to come out that way."

The girl looked up to Freddie for reassurance and received it at once. "One cannot, after all, hide the fact for very long," Freddie pointed out.

"That is what Lizzie said, Your Royal Highness. When we got to Lady Wrayburn's chamber, I tried to remain in the room to protect Lizzie, but her ladyship ordered me out. I stayed outside the door, though, because . . . well, sometimes Lady Wrayburn . . ."

Again, Miss Ashton lowered her head. "Every once in a while, Lady Wrayburn has been known to strike the servants."

The sentence ended in a whisper as if even now Miss Ashton feared reprisal for speaking against her mistress. I gritted my teeth but said nothing.

"Contemptible," Freddie stated flatly.

Miss Ashton continued. "Lady Wrayburn said ugly things to Lizzie. Lizzie began crying hysterically. I suppose the enormity of what was happening dawned on her. And Lizzie is a good girl. Truly. She was crying so hard, I feared for her and the baby. Unable to bear it any longer, I rushed into the room just in time to catch Lizzie ready to faint from upset. Lady Wrayburn was standing over her, her face red with rage. I put my arms around Lizzie and, I am ashamed to say, I tricked her ladyship into letting the poor girl alone for the rest of the evening."

"Tricked her?" I inquired softly.

Miss Ashton nodded. "Yes, I made as though I feared

for *Lady Wrayburn's* health—a tactic always sure to please—and told her I would take Lizzie away and bring her ladyship her evening milk so she might calm her nerves."

"Trickery or not, it was an excellent way to handle the matter. Did it work?" Freddie asked.

"Yes. I managed to get Lizzie upstairs, tucked away in her room. Then, feeling overwrought with worry and guilt, I went to my own chamber for a few minutes to compose myself."

I put my teacup down and leaned forward. "Naturally you were upset. What person of any sensibility would not be? You were frightened for Lizzie and the baby and yourself. Where would you go if Lady Wrayburn made good on her threat to have you removed from the house?"

Miss Ashton took a shaky breath. "I could not think about it at that moment. My head was in a whirl. I concentrated on simply getting through the rest of the evening. A few minutes went by—"

"How long?" I interrupted.

"Perhaps fifteen, even twenty minutes. Then I went down to the kitchen to get the milk."

"Try to remember exactly what happened then," I pressed her. "Who was in the kitchen?"

"George!" Freddie protested at my probing questions, but Miss Ashton raised a hand indicating it was all right.

"No one was about. The kitchen had been cleared of the servants' meals, and everyone was gone. That is the way it is almost every night by the time I go down for the milk."

"What time is that?"

"Just before nine. Lady Wrayburn takes her milk each evening promptly at nine o' clock. A milkmaid brings it fresh, by Lady Wrayburn's strict orders, daily around seven-thirty in the evening. Lady Wrayburn is . . . was . . . most particular about her milk. The milkmaid has special glass containers marked with Lady Wrayburn's initials that she picks up in the morning, and she returns them filled at night. It is my duty to bring the milk upstairs—on a special monogrammed silver tray—add three drops of laudanum, and give it to her ladyship."

"Laudanum?" I asked. "Every night?"

"Oh, yes. Lady Wrayburn cannot sleep without it. It serves to relax her," Miss Ashton explained. Then her brow creased in anxiety. "That is what I thought I had done wrong. Added too much laudanum to the milk in my distress. I was so upset, and it could have been four drops, or—"

She broke off, overcome with the very thought of having caused the old lady's death. Freddie rose and crossed to Miss Ashton's side. She bent and put a comforting arm around her. "But that is not what happened, is it, 'Becca?"

"No," Miss Ashton replied on a sob. She brought herself under control and looked at me, her cheeks damp with tears. "The doctor assured me that because of the condition of the body, he knew it was a strong poison, not simply a drop or two of extra laudanum, which caused Lady Wrayburn's death."

"Which doctor is that?" I asked in a mild tone, but I still received a glare from Freddie.

"Doctor Profitt."

"Ah, yes, a good fellow. Known him for donkey's years. He mixes some potent cures." I stood and addressed Miss Ashton. "I believe it might be beneficial for me to inspect Lady Wrayburn's chambers."

Freddie gasped. "George, it would be most improper for you to go upstairs to the countess's bedchamber."

"While she was still alive, certainly you would be right. But the woman is dead, and we are trying to find out by whose hand she was poisoned. There may be something in her room of importance to our inquiry."

"Mr. Brummell has a point, Your Royal Highness," Miss Ashton said. "I think we can trust Riddell to escort him."

Good girl, I thought silently. My esteem for Miss Ashton grew, as did my instinct that she was not the killer.

"Very well," Freddie conceded. "Do hurry, George, before we cause comment by the family."

Miss Ashton summoned the butler. In hushed tones, she explained the situation. He glanced at me once, then nodded and motioned for me to follow him.

We did not encounter anyone on our way up the stairs. Riddell stopped in front of a door at the end of the corridor. "Shall you require my assistance, sir? Or will you go in alone?"

"Thank you, Riddell, I shall be fine on my own. You may return to the ladies."

"I believe I'll wait for you outside the door, sir," the butler replied with a stubborn line to his old lips.

Loyal to the end, or should I say, *beyond* the end? "Tell me, Riddell, did her ladyship have friends in London?"

A shuffling of his feet preceded his answer. "No, she

never had callers and didn't go about much. The countess had many years in her dish. At her age, many of her contemporaries had already gone on to greater rewards."

"Of course," I agreed, though I reflected that nastiness, rather than death, had caused Lady Wrayburn to be friendless. "I shall not be above a few minutes in her ladyship's chambers."

Riddell's face remained gloomy.

I entered the room and closed the door quietly. Turning around, my first thought was that there had been some mistake. This spartan chamber, furnished with the minimum of necessities, could not have belonged to a woman of the countess's wealth and position.

But then my eyes adjusted to the dim light, and I saw that though the furniture was dark and depressing, and the pieces few in number, they were of the best quality.

The purple draperies hung in folds of heavy silk, closed tight against the outside. From the musty smell in the room, I felt they had rarely been opened.

Although the chamber was clean, without a particle of dust, an entire apothecary's worth of bottles stood cluttering the bedside table. I strolled over to examine them, harboring the feeble hope that perhaps Lady Wrayburn had given herself a deadly combination by accident. Reading the labels, however, I had to discard the thought. The bottles contained harmless preparations an old lady might turn to for the relief of minor pains, as well as some cream guaranteed to "ease the swelling of joints."

I turned toward the Sheraton desk. Conscious of Riddell just outside the door, I opened the drawers with stealthy care. They were almost empty, with only sheets of Lady

Wrayburn's personal stationery, a few pencils, and a quill pen stored in their depths.

On the polished top of the desk, more stationery rested under the countess's seal along with a partially used stick of sealing wax. Hmmm. Now that was interesting. Lady Wrayburn was writing to someone.

I shuffled through the pieces of parchment until I came upon one with writing on it. I almost yelped a cry of glee, but remembered Riddell just in time.

The letter had been tucked underneath the other papers, in the manner one might employ to keep others from reading their correspondence. I quickly scanned the few lines and realized that what I held was the second page of a letter. All it said was, ". . . he spends his money as if his very life depended upon his getting it out of his pockets as fast as possible. None of it goes to anything commendable either. Excessive amounts are wasted on gambling, and, I am ashamed to say, his clothes! Mark my words, he is the most ramshackle of fellows and will come to no . . ."

I raised an eyebrow at this. Obviously, the countess was interrupted here before she could complete her condemnation.

But of whom?

And for whom was the letter intended?

And where was the first sheet?

I turned toward the fireplace and strode to view the contents of the ashes. Nothing that looked like a burned letter, discarded by someone—perhaps the murderer hoping to conceal its contents—could be found.

The sound of Riddell clearing his throat in the hallway

caused me to hasten through the remainder of my search. All I discovered was that if one's bedchamber could be seen as a window to one's character, Lady Wrayburn was a stark, unforgiving landscape.

Much to Riddell's relief, I exited the room and shortly rejoined the ladies.

Miss Ashton looked at me expectantly.

"Well, George, what did you find?" Freddie asked.

"Nothing of apparent import," I replied, noting the crestfallen expression on Miss Ashton's face. "You are not to worry excessively, Miss Ashton. I shall come back tomorrow, and perhaps then I can meet the family. I want to get to know them better. Who is in residence?"

The strain on Miss Ashton's face seemed to lessen at the news that I would be returning on the morrow. "There is Mr. Timothy Hensley, who is Lady Wrayburn's younger son, and his wife, Cordelia. Then we have Mr. Sylvester Fairingdale. He is Lady Wrayburn's nephew."

"I know I have seen him around town," I remarked in a dry tone. Indeed one could hardly miss Mr. Fairingdale's salmon-colored coats, yellow breeches, and shirt points which reached his ears.

Fairingdale! *But of course*, I suddenly thought. Sylvester Fairingdale was a fop of the first degree. He could very well have been the subject of Lady Wrayburn's letter. At the least, he would bear further investigation.

Miss Ashton rose, and we all moved toward the chamber door.

Freddie spoke soothingly to her friend, while I stood deep in thought. Freddie's last directive called me to attention.

"And, 'Becca, in addition to writing to me, you have only to send word to George if you need anything."

Miss Ashton looked at me uncertainly, and I smiled at her. "Yes, please do, Miss Ashton. But as I said, I shall return tomorrow to see how you go on."

"Thank you, Mr. Brummell," Miss Ashton said, and I was touched by the sincerity in her voice.

Freddie and I took our leave and paused for a moment on the front steps. I shook off the melancholy that the murky atmosphere of the house had pressed on me. My mind raced with questions. Uppermost was: who had access to the milk while it was still in the kitchen waiting to be retrieved by Miss Ashton? The answer had to be anyone in the house. Including Sylvester Fairingdale. And including Lizzie, the pregnant lady's maid with so much to lose if Lady Wrayburn was allowed to carry out her threat.

Freddie's lips curved as she looked at me. "I can see from your expression that the affair has caught your interest."

I could not resist smiling in return. "You wretched woman, you knew it would."

Freddie laughed, but the amusement quickly died from her lips. For down on the street a carriage had slowed. Through the window, a gentleman could be seen. He raised his quizzing glass and peered at us curiously. I recognized the man at once. He was the Duke of Cumberland, Freddie's brother-in-law. Her face paled. I grasped her arm gently, but firmly, and escorted her to her carriage, all the while mentally cursing the Duke of Cumberland and the Duke of York.

I know Freddie refrains from coming to London for the

sole purpose of avoiding her husband . . . and the mistress he goes about with openly. To be seen in town by the Duke of Cumberland would most certainly mean that the Duke of York would be apprised of his wife's whereabouts. Her presence in London would give him an opportunity to amuse himself at her expense, flaunting his mistress in her face. Without a doubt, I knew Freddie would want to leave for the peace of Oatlands immediately.

Ignoring the outstretched hand of her coachman, Freddie accepted my assistance into her carriage. She seated herself, staring straight ahead.

I remained standing in the doorway of the vehicle. "My princess," I murmured, and she turned slightly toward me. "You can go back to Oatlands with a quiet mind. I promise to look after Miss Ashton. But perhaps I should escort you home?"

Some of the tension drained from her lovely features. "Thank you for offering, dear. I shall be quite safe with my coachman and two outriders. As for Miss Ashton, I knew you would agree she is innocent."

I neglected to remind Freddie that I had reached no final conclusion in the matter. Instead, I smiled at her and gave her gloved hand an affectionate squeeze.

She tried to return the smile, but failed. Then she spoke in a low voice. "I fear, George, that my mind will not be quiet until I leave the turmoil of London and reach the comfort of home. Besides, I must see to Minney and the pups, you know."

I drew a deep, dispirited breath. Out of the corner of my eye, I caught sight of a mongrel dog making his way down the opposite side of the street. Even though his shabby brown coat was matted and caked with dirt, a young girl accompanied by her governess stopped to pet him.

About to close Freddie's carriage door I said, "And you do take such good care of your dogs, Freddie. Why, I almost envy them. But I fear I should make a very poor canine myself. Only think of my frustration over not being able to change my coat."

She succeeded in smiling then. To me, it was a beautiful sight. I felt a burst of an emotion best left unsaid, considering Freddie is a married woman, and I am an honorable gentleman.

I bowed, closed the door, then stepped back from the curb. The carriage rolled away, and I watched it until it could be seen no more.

Across the street, the mongrel seemed to have found a new home with the young girl.

Dogs are devilishly lucky creatures.

❦ 6 ❦

As I had anticipated, by the time I had visited with Freddie and she had departed, the hour was such that the auction at Talbot's Art Gallery would have been well underway. I pushed aside thoughts of hurrying over to Pall Mall at the last moment. Such a late arrival would be viewed as rude.

No, I had made my decision to sacrifice the painting, and that would be the end of it. Or so I thought.

For the remainder of the day, I retired to my bookroom. I often sit there when I have something weighty to contemplate. I like to think that the wisdom of the sages who line the numerous shelves will somehow be imparted to me simply by my proximity to them. I needed their intelligence if I was to help Freddie and Miss Ashton by solving the mystery of Lady Wrayburn's demise.

Perhaps you might not think aged brandy can possibly

help this process. As it turns out, you would be accurate in your assessment. While I lounged in my snug chair by the fire, the level in the decanter growing ever lower, my thoughts centered more on Freddie than the mystery I should have been contemplating.

Sweet, dear, Freddie who had come to England from Prussia fourteen years ago with hopes, if not expectations, of a comfortable marriage. Shakespeare's question of "to be or not to be" could hardly have been uttered regarding the union, before clearly the answer was "not to be."

While most of Society, including me, thinks the Duke of York a figure of distinction, as he is, after all, the Commander in Chief of England's land forces, I cannot help but believe he falls short of being a true gentleman. A gentleman, in my view, does not bring dishonor to his wife by his behavior. A gentleman honors his marriage vows.

I poured myself another brandy. Next to me, at arm's length, stood a smallish mahogany revolving bookcase with a gilt Greek key apron. I absently twirled the circular book-holder round and round while thinking of Freddie and her husband.

The Duke of York had married Frederica Charlotte Ulrica Catherine in two ceremonies. The first time was in Berlin with her family, the second shortly thereafter in London. 'Twas a shame neither ceremony had affected the Duke of York, who currently kept Mrs. Clark as his mistress. How His Royal Highness could choose such an uncouth woman over Freddie was the mystery I did ponder over two more glasses of brandy. In my view, Mrs. Clark, a faithless creature if there ever was one, was bound to bring calamity onto the Duke's head someday.

Meanwhile, Freddie chose to stay at Oatlands with more loyal companions, even if they were animals rather than people.

Such pointless, depressing musings carried me through the evening with my only conclusion being the one I have known all along: sometimes being the leader of Society and the arbiter of fashion does not bestow one with the rewards one wishes for most.

The candles burned low when Robinson came downstairs clucking like a mother hen and ushered me up to my bedchamber.

I slept the next morning away like most members of the *Beau Monde*, only rising when the sounds of peddlers calling their wares on the street below penetrated my muddled brain.

Robinson pulled back the curtains of my bed and handed me my morning chocolate. Unlike some fellows, a night of drinking rarely puts me off my breakfast. Robinson's news that André was bustling about the kitchen preparing his special toast almost made me hurry through The Dressing Hour. Almost. My stomach does not take priority over faultless grooming.

Once properly dressed in a simple costume of buff-colored pantaloons, white waistcoat, Spanish blue coat and Hessian boots polished to a shine that could lead ships ashore, I made my way to the dining room and thoroughly enjoyed my repast.

André has a way of making a French-style of toast. Cut slices of bread are dipped in a mixture of cream, sugar, and nutmeg. This concoction is then fried in butter and served with a wine sauce that is delicious. Back in my school days, I was considered top of the class in Cheese Toasting, so I tip my hat to anyone skilled in the realm of the toasting arts.

I felt invigorated after two cups of coffee and settled in with the *Morning Post* to consume my third. Unlike the *Times*, which restrains itself from reporting rumors, the *Morning Post* feels no need to restrict itself to facts. The following was listed under the "Deceased" section.

Hester Billings, the Countess of Wrayburn, has been consigned to her tomb under the most shocking of circumstances. According to confidential information obtained from the Bow Street Police Office, and other most reliable sources, her ladyship was transported to the hereafter following the consumption of a glass of poisoned milk given to her by a member of her very own household staff. The *Morning Post* has learned the evil staff member in question—a young woman—was recommended to Lady Wrayburn as trustworthy by the reclusive F———, a lady of the Blood Royal. An arrest is said to be forthcoming in this scandalous crime.

I threw the newspaper to the floor in a fit of fury. *How dare they?* My every feeling revolted at this luridly scandalous account of the crime. Evil staff member? Reclusive lady of the Blood Royal? That they had presumed to make reference to Freddie was the outside of enough. Burning down the *Morning Post*'s building would not be too severe a punishment in my view. That way they could not put out any more of their filthy papers.

I reached for my coffee and took a swallow, my heart pounding in my chest. In an effort to calm down, I told myself that burning the building to the ground would most likely result in soot and ash ruining my clothes. The publishers were not worth it.

No, I decided, feeling my heart rate return to normal, the answer was to prove Miss Ashton's accusers wrong, and that I was determined to do. I wondered if she had seen the article.

This afternoon, I would fulfill my promise to call on her. The girl was having a wretched time of it and for no reason. Assuming, of course, that as Freddie said and I was inclined to believe, Miss Ashton was innocent.

Thoughts of Freddie reminded me that even though she was in the country at Oatlands, she still received the newspapers. I needed to write her a letter, assuring her I was her humble servant and would help in any way I could. I knew her utmost concern was for Miss Ashton, but I wanted to let her know I would not allow her own name to be bandied about by blabber-lipped newsmongers eager to sell their tainted papers.

I exited the dining room, once more in control, and returned to my bedchamber.

In addition to my desk in the bookroom, I keep a rosewood and mahogany portable writing desk in my bedchamber. It is especially useful when traveling, but many times I use it to write letters late at night when I do not wish to traverse the stairs to the bookroom. It has a collapsible nest of drawers, a writing surface, and a secret drawer. No, I do not wish to disclose what is in the latter. That is why it is called "secret."

My pen moved across the paper steadily for a time before Robinson entered as I was folding the missive.

"Sir, Mr. Griffin has called. He and your new sedan chair await you downstairs in the hall."

These glad tidings served as a temporary diversion from Lady Wrayburn's murder and, in fact, catapulted me from my chair. Excitement at finally obtaining my new mode of transport and a strong need to shout "What the devil took so long?" warred within me.

But as I descended the stairs at a decorous pace and entered the hall, another emotion took hold when I observed the sedan chair. I found myself calling on every ounce of my famous control not to wrap my hands around the diminutive merchant's throat and throttle him.

W. Griffin, dressed in a coat of an inferior black material topped by a spotted neckcloth, nervously cleared the very throat he was unaware was in danger. "Mr. Brummell, I apologize for the delay in the making of your sedan chair. As much as I tried, sir, I could not construct the conveyance to the exact specifications you gave me."

I raised an eyebrow. "That is apparent to anyone with the slightest degree of intelligence."

Robinson coughed.

Mr. Griffin swallowed painfully. He raised his hand and motioned to the sedan chair with a sweeping gesture. "Sir, I could not in good conscience use the wood you requested. Sandalwood, while a very handsome wood and one that possesses a pleasing fragrance, I fully agree, is not strong enough for the purpose and is likely to break.

"Not," he rushed on at my frown, "that I am in any way saying that your trim figure, sir, could be a hazard to the construction. It is more a question of sandalwood holding up under the weather and the test of time."

"Is that so?" I had remained standing at the bottom of the stairs during this exchange, but now moved slowly forward to examine the sedan chair. Two of Mr. Griffin's lackeys held it a few inches off the ground by a pair of removable wooden poles attached to the sedan-chair's sides. These poles extended about three feet in front and to the back of the equipage. The men positioned themselves between the poles, one fore and one aft.

In such a vehicle, I could be carried about town without ever setting foot in London's muddy streets. The sedan chair could be brought into the hall of my house, convey me to White's Club, or Almack's Assembly Rooms, or any other destination, and ferry me to the front door without the risk of marring my boots or evening pumps. As a further benefit, I would not be subjected to the rain that so often lingers in London, nor to windy days which have the cruel effect of ruffling my cravat. What could be worse, I ask you, than the hand of nature wrecking what human hands have worked so hard to achieve?

A sedan chair was perfect for my needs for yet another reason. It did not require horses. I prefer not to keep horses. They are a drain on one's pocketbook when one could better put one's funds to use buying Sèvres porcelain, fine wines, or new clothing.

Furthermore, there is a tavern nearby called The Porter & Pole which I hear can be depended upon to provide me with men to carry the sedan chair at my summons. The sobriety of the men might be in question, but then oftentimes so was mine.

I stood by the vehicle and ran my hand along the wood Mr. Griffin had used.

"This is a rather unknown wood called calamander, Mr. Brummell. I had it specially sent from India."

"Hmmm. It seems strong."

Mr. Griffin nodded his agreement. "Yes, sir. A heart wood, it is both dense and heavy."

The wood was dark and subtly striped. It had been varnished to a high gloss. Admittedly, the craftsmanship was superb.

"Sir," Mr. Griffin said, "calamander was well known to the Greeks and Romans. Today, it is . . . ahem, costly to be sure. I thought it might be in keeping with your fine taste."

Robinson had been standing mute while I examined the wood, but now gave voice to his opinion. "If calamander wood is as rare as Mr. Griffin explains, sir, perhaps you will set a new fashion."

Now there was a pleasing idea.

My face must have reflected my interest as Mr. Griffin seized on the comment. "That's true, Mr. Brummell. Everyone follows your lead."

He swung open the door of the sedan chair's box-like structure, showing off the construction of the portal. "I consider myself an artist, if I may be so bold to say so, and I am proud of this chair. I have long wanted to work with calamander wood. Will you not view the inside?"

I remained stubbornly doubtful, but complied with his request to inspect the interior of the vehicle. Ah, here I must report that everything was what I had hoped for. The perfection moved me to cry out, "Robinson! Come and see the white satin lining. Is it not everything I envisioned?"

Robinson came to stand beside me. "Yes, indeed, sir." He reached inside and touched the seat. "Down-filled?"

I nodded. "And feel this rug. White sheepskin can only be the height of elegance in sedan chair floor coverings."

Mr. Griffin entered an enthusiastic voice to the praise of the interior of the chair.

The three of us were so absorbed that a knock on the front door barely registered a response. Out of the corner of my eye, I saw that one of Mr. Griffin's lackeys took it upon himself to open the door to a servant delivering some sort of parcel.

But I did not give the matter my immediate attention. Instead, I straightened from my examination of the inside of the chair. "Mr. Griffin, as pleased as I am with the interior, I cannot help but feel dubious about the wood used to construct the frame."

"I see, sir," the merchant acknowledged. "But perhaps you might live with it for a week and delay a final judgment? It is my hope that the calamander wood will reveal to you its silent strength, its regal beauty, and its practical worth. Will you not agree to keep the chair for a week with my compliments?"

With his compliments? Well, I could hardly be rude enough to say no to this, could I?

As if in answer, an eardrum-piercing, angry shriek rent the air. Startled, everyone looked to see the source.

" 'Tis the very devil!" Mr. Griffin's lackey shouted, jumping back from the parcel he held, allowing it to drop to the floor.

No one moved.

Then, out of the parcel, which I now saw to be a lidded wicker basket, an animal emerged. The creature sprang to the black and white tiled floor with the agility of one of Freddie's monkeys.

However it was not a monkey. It was the most singular feline I had ever seen in my life.

The cat's face, ears, paws, and tail gleamed a rich, dark brown. The rest of his body was a pale fawn color which was slightly more deeply shaded on his back. He was smaller and more compactly built than the felines of my experience, with exceptionally elegant long legs. His body appeared lean and muscular.

But his large eyes were his most startling feature. A brilliant blue, they brimmed with intelligence. He stood proudly, lashing his whip-like tail and looking down his white whiskers at the company in haughty disdain.

"Reeoow!" he pronounced in a loud, commanding tone.

Robinson fainted.

7

Chaos reigned in the hall. Mr. Griffin stood in front of the sedan chair, arms spread wide as if to protect his creation from an onslaught of Napoleon's army.

His lackey swooped down in an attempt to capture the cat. In a lightning-fast move, and with seemingly little effort, the feline avoided his grasp. Instead the cat reached out a paw and drew a red line across the man's hand.

The servant howled, clutching the back of his hand. "The thing ain't natural, I tell you! 'Tis some demon from hell!"

Fangs bared, the cat hissed at him. I would too if someone called me a demon from hell.

Not wishing to look anything less than in full command of my household, I said, "Mr. Griffin, have your men carry Robinson into the bookroom. There is a sofa in there upon which you can rest him. I am certain he will recover presently. He has fainted before on occasion." Once, when I had a sky-blue coat and matching sky-blue breeches made, Robinson had swooned at the sight.

At a nod from Mr. Griffin, the two men gave the cat a wide berth and lifted the unconscious valet. I led the way into the bookroom. I spared a backward glance for the feline, who was calmly licking the paw he had used to scratch the servant, as if the act of touching such an ill-bred fellow disgusted him.

Inside the bookroom, Robinson moaned when placed on the long sofa across from the desk. I walked to a side table and poured him a glass of brandy.

Once the valet was sufficiently revived and could hold the glass and partake of the contents, I turned to Mr. Griffin, who stood anxiously in the doorway. "I have the situation under control. You may leave the sedan chair with me. I shall let you know my decision regarding it in a week's time."

"Thank you, Mr. Brummell. Are you certain I cannot assist you where the, er, animal is concerned?"

"No, thank you. I can handle him. One of my friends' idea of a joke, no doubt."

They departed, being careful to walk far around the cat, who had now progressed to cleaning his face with a well-licked paw.

I stood over Robinson. His supine form rested on my carved and gilt-wood sofa. It is adorned with lion's head uprights and lion's paw feet, and is cushioned with a handsome gold brocade. At almost seven feet, the sofa more than accommodated Robinson, whom I could see was revitalized by the brandy. "Are you all right?" I inquired.

His pale countenance told me he was shaken. "Sir, a—a feline in your house! We must be rid of it at once," he gasped.

I glanced speculatively out into the hall. The cat held his tail between two paws and washed the length of it. "Why? You know I favor animals. This cat is different from any other I have seen. He intrigues me."

Robinson struggled to sit up, his expression indignant. His voice regained its strength. "Only think of the cat hairs on our clothing!"

I patted his arm. "Oh, I have more faith in you than that, my good man. You would never permit such a thing."

Robinson rose slowly to his feet and faced me. "Sir, we have no idea where the cat came from. He may carry disease. And cats can be destructive. His claws will shred your furniture. He will knock over your Sèvres porcelain, sending it crashing to the floor!"

I raised an eyebrow at these ominous prognostications. "You are correct in that we do not know where he came from. Let me see that basket he arrived in."

Robinson's lips pursed. He stood his ground, refusing to go back into the hall where the invader was. I sighed and braved the front lines. The cat barely spared me a glance as I walked past him to retrieve the wicker basket. It appeared the feline had decided his entire body needed a wash and was concentrating on the task. I approved of his fastidiousness.

Back in the bookroom, I sat behind my desk and opened the basket. "Ah, success is at hand. Here is a note."

Robinson stood, arms folded across his chest, while I read the letter aloud.

Dear Mr. Brummell,

I am pleased that you so wisely decided not to bid against me for the Perronneau painting. You must have realized that such a prize belongs to a king. As a reward for your good judgment, I send you this gift.

In my country, we have been breeding special felines, fit for royalty. My connections with the palace in Bangkok enabled me to bring a female cat with me to England for companionship while away from home. I did not know when I left Siam that the cat was already pregnant. She gave birth to five kittens ten months ago, not long after my arrival in England.

I shall return to Siam with only four of her litter, and my ruler will not know the difference. I do this out of gratitude to you for your respect for my country. Because these cats are distinctive and unique to Siam, I have taken measures to see that this one is unable to breed. You will be the only person in England to own a Siamese cat.

The cat I have chosen for you, Mr. Brummell, I chose because his personality reminds me of yours in a great many ways. Over time, perhaps you will see this for yourself.

His name is Chakkri, after one of our great generals.

The letter was signed by Mr. Kiang.

"Good God," I muttered. "First an imported wood, now

an imported cat. I thought the purpose of the English Channel was to keep unwanted foreign objects away."

"Precisely, sir. You must find Mr. Kiang and return his 'gift' at once."

I sat back in my chair and considered this. Through the open door to the bookroom, I saw Chakkri moving cautiously and with stealth through the hall toward us. His dark nose sniffed close to the floor. When he reached the doorway to the room, he stopped.

After stretching his neck and peering into the room, he did an odd thing. Instead of simply walking across the threshold into the room, he crouched down, then leaped across the threshold. He then resumed his slow, suspicious inspection of the premises. Suddenly, he froze in front of the sofa, rose up on his hind legs, and stared into the eyes of the gilt lion's head. A moment passed. Chakkri touched his nose to the lion's nose. He pulled away swiftly, shook his rear leg in disdain, and continued his exploration.

Robinson watched the process with a curled lip. "As I said, the feline must return to Mr. Kiang."

My indecision must have shown on my face, prompting Robinson to say in a lofty tone, "Lord Petersham has oftentimes indicated that a place for me in his household would always be open. His lordship is a *viscount*, you know, and has a strong sense of fashion. He confided in me recently that he is designing a new style of greatcoat."

Our eyes met.

This is the one challenge Robinson can throw out that I invariably back down from, a truth that irritates me, make no mistake. But that does not change the stratagem's effectiveness.

As you have no doubt learned by now, I am rather careful of my reputation as the arbiter of fashion. While under no circumstances do I give *complete* credit to Robinson for the genius of my clothes and grooming—far from it, I am my own man—I do value our *partnership* in obtaining the ultimate result.

So I relented. "Very well. I shall return the cat to Mr. Kiang. Send round to The Porter & Pole for two men to carry me in my new sedan chair. I do not know Mr. Kiang's direction, but expect I could find out at White's Club."

"Yes, sir. Very good, sir," Robinson said and hurried to obey the order before I could change my mind.

In truth, I felt sorrowful about returning the cat. As fond as I am of animals, for some reason I had never considered obtaining one for myself. Now that Chakkri was here, I thought it might be pleasant to have a feline for a companion. And the idea that these cats were bred for royalty and were not yet in England held appeal. What would the Prince of Wales think of my having the animal?

On second thought, perhaps it would be best not to tell Prinny. We were already at war with France. We need not add Siam to the list of our enemies.

I rose from my seat at the desk and located Chakkri. He was sitting tall in the manner of a ruling monarch on the side table. The one that contained two crystal glasses and the crystal decanter of brandy I had served Robinson from earlier.

I held my breath. Would the cat knock the decanter to the floor, shattering the expensive crystal?

With a movement so delicate and intricate I could not

help but be impressed, Chakkri moved sinuously past the crystal. He hopped lightly onto the large bookshelf against the wall. There, he investigated the spines of several books before moving down the bookcase toward a Sèvres plate I had recently acquired and displayed. The plate, I noted, sat dangerously close to the edge of the shelf.

My heart almost stopped in my chest. True, the plate is not one of my very best. As you know, I keep those in my bedchamber. Still, it is Sèvres and lovely. It is a portrait plate I admired because the lady painted in the center has brown hair the exact shade as Freddie's.

I could not decide whether to make a grab for the cat before he could send the plate crashing to the floor as Robinson had foretold, or if such a sudden motion on my part would startle Chakkri and create an even more likely catastrophe.

Standing motionless, I watched as he sniffed discreetly at the plate. In the absolute silence of the room, I suddenly heard a sound.

Chakkri was purring.

I felt my shoulders ease and my jaw relax.

Then, a thought flickered across my mind. Was it possible the cat actually appreciated the exquisite artistry of the plate?

No! That was nonsense. His purring had to have been a coincidence.

After a few more moments of delicate sniffing, the cat apparently wearied of his explorations. Moving past the plate with the grace of a dancer, he executed another flying leap and jumped onto my chair by the fire. He turned around once, curled into a perfect circle, and closed his eyes.

I admit I stood there watching him sleep. The rise and fall of his beautiful fawn-colored fur mesmerized me. Occasionally, his whiskers would twitch, or his ears would quiver. I wondered if he was dreaming. More likely, I was.

A short while later, Robinson returned to inform me the men from The Porter & Pole had arrived to carry my sedan chair. Warily, I picked up the wicker basket and moved toward the sleeping animal. I slid my hand under him, half expecting him to hiss as he had done at Mr. Griffin's servant, and perhaps even take a slice from my hand.

Chakkri defied prediction though. He opened his incredible blue eyes and gazed at me. I looked back, feeling a strong reluctance to put him into the basket. Rather, I wanted to stroke his fur and hear him purr again. I felt I should speak, but it seemed ludicrous to talk to him. What would I say? Chakkri, old fellow, would you kindly enter this conveyance so I may return you to your sender like a rejected pair of breeches?

Robinson cleared his throat.

I eased Chakkri into the basket. He went without complaint. Before I closed the lid, he was once again asleep.

I accepted my hat, gloves, and greatcoat from Robinson, forgoing my stick. "After I have returned the cat to Mr. Kiang, I shall be calling at Wrayburn House. Also, there is a letter for the Duchess of York in my bedchamber. See that it is sent to her at once."

"Yes, sir. Will you be dining at home this evening?"

"I shall. Ascertain if André can be persuaded to prepare his luscious matelote shrimp."

"Very good, sir."

I left my rooms with the basket in tow. The ride over to White's was heavenly. I felt majestic being carried in my new sedan chair. The seat was most comfortable, and a square pane of glass allowed me to see outside.

During the ride, the occupant of the wicker basket next to me remained silent. Upon my arrival at White's, I alighted and instructed one of the polemen to be certain to keep the door to the vehicle firmly closed until my return. I did not want Chakkri to awaken and exit into the London street.

I shuddered thinking what might happen to him alone. His future, I feared, would not be the same as the mongrel dog I witnessed being adopted yesterday. Why, his small, lean frame could easily be crushed under the wheels of a passing carriage as he tried to dart to safety. Or, if he survived that fate, he might be picked up by an unsavory character who would sell him to Astley's Royal Amphitheatre to be shown as an oddity. Chakkri's royal connections would go unknown. He would live pent up in a cage!

I hurried into White's.

As I walked into the hall, Delbert greeted me. "Good afternoon, Mr. Brummell."

"A bit chilly today, Delbert."

" 'Believe me, 'tis very cold; the wind is northerly,' " was the reply.

I handed over my greatcoat, my expression bland, but my brain working quickly. Suddenly, it came to me. "*Hamlet*."

Delbert let out a guffaw. "Haven't been able to gammon you yet, have I, Mr. Brummell?"

"Not yet, but we are both still young, Delbert. I know it is too early for Lord Petersham to be here, but what of my musically inclined friend Lord Perry?"

"In the morning room playing cards with Mr. Skeffington and Mr. Davies."

I found the three just ending a game of hazard. I could smell Skiffy before I could see him. He loves perfume. Despite my advice for a light hand with scent, a strong air of jasmine surrounded him.

Skiffy's dark hair flowed to his shoulders in the romantic ringlets favored in the last century. Paint made his face white, and two rosy spots of color adorned his cheeks, giving him the appearance of some sort of French toy. "Brummell, my friend, 'tis been too long since we have seen you at the theater. You must view the new play I have penned, *The Diligent Daughter*. I wager it will amuse you."

"You may count on me, Skiffy," I replied.

"The famous Beau!" Scrope Davies called. "Come join us! I warn you, though, I've just won a hundred pounds from Skiffy. If my good fortune holds, I'm off to Newmarket to try my luck."

I executed a mock bow. "I am tempted, gentlemen, truly I am. Scrope, I wish you all good fortune at the racecourse. But today, I must forgo the pleasure of your company and speak with Perry here. It is a tender matter involving an affair of the harp."

Perry chuckled at this, and we ascended the stairs. Upstairs, we settled in matching chairs in front of the fire. He said, "Did you read the article in the *Morning Post* about Lady Wrayburn, Brummell?"

I nodded. "Yes, and I think it to be a disgraceful piece of fuel for the scandalmongers. I did not realize the *Morning Post* had sunk so low."

Perry looked at me steadily. I wondered if he was thinking about Freddie's connection to the matter. My close association with the Royal Duchess is known among my friends, but never discussed in anything more than a cursory manner. "Gossip about Lady Wrayburn's murder is all over town. The general consensus is that pretty companion of hers is responsible."

"Do you believe that, Perry?"

He stopped to consider a moment before answering. "I am not certain what to think. From the way Lady Wrayburn treated the girl one could almost believe it. Still, Miss Ashton, I believe her name is, seemed a well-bred girl. My friend Mr. Dawlish says her father was Lord Kirgo. A bit of a romance there, you know, between Mr. Dawlish and Miss Ashton. He turned down an offer from me to view Lord Boden's new harpsichord this morning to be at her side. Actually, Brummell," Perry went on, warming to his favorite topic, "the harpsichord is not new. It is a rare find. Appears to be made in Naples and has a date on it of 1643."

I casually adjusted the sleeve of my coat and remarked, "Interesting. Getting back to Lady Wrayburn's demise, we do not know much of the rest of the Wrayburn household, excepting that fop, Sylvester Fairingdale, who is a nephew, I believe."

Perry snorted. "Fairingdale! His tight neckcloths might have cut off the blood supply to his brain and caused him to commit a beef-witted act like poisoning his aunt, thinking he could get away with it."

"Perhaps." I sat back in my chair. "Lady Wrayburn's older son is abroad, but the younger is in residence."

Perry nodded. "Yes, Timothy and his wife, Cordelia Hensley. Mrs. Hensley would not lower herself to live anywhere that was not fashionable. She exists solely to be in Society, and of course, Wrayburn House is a good address."

"She rules the roost, eh?"

"Completely. Hensley is totally under the cat's paw."

This comment reminded me of the question I had for Perry. Not that I did not relish gleaning what information that I could about the Wrayburn household, mind you. It was just that I had a more pressing need. "Perry, do you know Mr. Kiang's direction? I need to speak to him."

"Certainly, I know where he was staying, but it will do you no good. He left after the auction yesterday for Dover. He was due to sail home to Siam this morning."

I groaned aloud.

"What is it, Brummell? I confess I was rather surprised you did not attend the auction. Mr. Kiang did get the Perronneau painting you wanted, but I was able to obtain my lute. Petersham almost fell into strong convulsions when Mr. Kiang outbid him on a snuff box. And after he ventured out of doors early to bid, too."

I shook my head sadly, imagining Petersham's chagrin over losing the snuff box. I hoped he would not go into a decline. To answer Perry's question, I said, "It was not convenient for me to attend the auction, after all."

I avoided telling him the whole story. It was not that I do not trust him, because I do. It is simply that I have no inclination to discuss Freddie's visit or her request of me to investigate Lady Wrayburn's murder. A gentleman does not gossip about a lady for whom he cares.

"What did you want to see Kiang about, Brummell?"

"Mr. Kiang left me a gift, and I wish to return it."

Perry's face registered astonishment. "He left you a gift?"

"Yes, and a devil of a gift. A cat."

"What?" Perry exclaimed, leaning forward in his chair. "Why would he do that?"

I outlined Mr. Kiang's note and ended by saying, "The cat is a beautiful creature, but sure to turn my household on end."

"Robinson threatening to present himself at Petersham's doorstep again?" At my nod, Perry said, "Really, Brummell, he is forever saying he will leave but never does. Seems his way of winning an argument."

"Dash it all if you do not have the right of it," I said, wondering why I had not realized Robinson was bluffing and why I still did not think I could bring myself to call the bluff.

"About the cat, something to consider is that in quite a few of these foreign countries to refuse a gift is a high insult. And if, as you say, the animal is rare, news of your giving it away might eventually reach Mr. Kiang's ears even in Siam."

Perry had a good point. I thanked him, and after a few minutes, I made my way out of the club, slipping some coins into Delbert's hand after he handed me my belongings.

Outside, all appeared quiet in my sedan chair. I gave

the order for home, determined to consider my next move on the way. On the seat next to me, there was a stirring in the wicker basket. Slowly, the lid rose and a wedge-shaped brown face appeared. Chakkri sniffed the air and looked toward the window. He yawned at the sight of the London streets. Then he gracefully hopped out of the basket onto the satin seat.

I braced myself for what I was sure would come next. It has been my observation that most cats like to exercise their claws after sleeping. I pictured taking the sedan chair back to Mr. Griffin, the satin seats in shreds.

But it was not to be. The instant Chakkri's paws made contact with the satin, he lowered his nose and began his sniffing routine. Then he promptly dropped to his side and began rolling and twisting on his back, showing every evidence of ecstasy at the feel of the smooth satin. Not once did his claws so much as nick the fabric.

I sat stunned. Here was an animal who seemed to appreciate the finer things in life. You think me mad? Only remember the care he took with the crystal and the Sèvres plate. Why, he actually purred after sniffing the Sèvres!

He slipped off the satin seat and landed on the white fur rug at my feet. Immediately, he repeated his joyous writhing on the soft fur.

This was no ordinary feline, I tell you. And the little fellow was immaculate—no disease-ridden varmint as Robinson had theorized. I judged his fur was softer than the rug on the floor. I remember thinking it was the softest fur I had ever beheld when I picked him up earlier.

Suddenly, I remembered what Mr. Kiang had said in

his letter. How he chose Chakkri for me because his disposition reminded him of me. Was Chakkri's appreciation for beauty and quality the trait Mr. Kiang meant?

No, that was silly. I disregarded Mr. Kiang's remark and gazed down at the animal on the rug. He lay on his back in a position which begged me to rub his stomach. You know a dog or cat does not offer an exposed belly to pet to just anyone. I reached down tentatively and stroked his soft fur. He began to purr.

Really, when I thought it over, Chakkri would pose no problem to my establishment. He would be content with inexpensive fishheads from the local market to eat. A small box of sand would take care of his most personal needs. And it would be a novelty to own such a unique animal. I would be the only person in England to own a Siamese cat.

Besides which, it was my duty to my country not to strain relations between England and Siam by giving the little fellow away. Who knows, Mr. Kiang might one day return to England and demand a progress report on Chakkri's life.

My mind was made up. I prepared to face Robinson and determined I would not argue further with him on the subject. I would call his bluff on taking employment with Petersham if I needed to. Then, I would see Chakkri settled and pay an afternoon call on Wrayburn House. I did not want to postpone interviewing the family members any longer.

The vehicle halted in Bruton Street. I placed Chakkri in his basket. "Welcome to the Brummell household,

Chakkri. Continue on your best behavior, and I daresay we shall rub along together well enough."

I thought I caught a smug expression on his face.

I probably imagined it.

After his initial shock at seeing me return home with Chakkri in tow, Robinson grudgingly agreed to my arguments that the cat remain with us. Added to my persuasion, a lavish increase in his wages, one which would enable him to indulge his passion for collecting Derby china, helped my valet reach this positive decision. Still, I knew he viewed the cat as trouble.

I left Robinson searching for a box he could fill with sand to meet the cat's private needs; a task he took great exception to until reminded of his newly acquired funds.

Downstairs, the men from The Porter & Pole were waiting for me to give the signal to depart. As I entered the sedan chair, the thought crossed my mind that it would grow devilishly inconvenient for me to have to send round for two men every time I wished to venture beyond my own four walls. In addition, the men sent were strong enough, but hardly clean.

The solution would be for me to employ my own servants, but I shuddered at the expense, which I felt could be better spent on wine, Sèvres, clothing, or wagered at White's. Although I must say I have been sadly unlucky at gaming recently.

A short time later, when I arrived at Wrayburn House, I noticed a burly man lingering by the front door. Inside, the morose Riddell silently led me to the same dreary drawing room I had been in on my previous visit.

There, Miss Ashton and the Reverend Mr. Dawlish sat together on the brown settee. The rector had seated himself close to the young woman and appeared to be speaking to her with great passion.

". . . protection of my name," were the only words I caught before Miss Ashton saw me and their conversation ceased.

"Mr. Brummell," she cried, rising to greet me, the skirts of her black bombazine gown rustling. Her expression led me to believe she perceived my arrival with some measure of relief. "How good of you to come. I must speak with you. Oh! Where are my manners? May I introduce Mr. Dawlish?"

I bowed to her, observing the lines of worry creasing her ivory brow. "Here I am as promised, Miss Ashton. And I have already met the rector at Lord Perry's musical evening. Good afternoon, Mr. Dawlish."

Like Miss Ashton, the rector was dressed in black, making me feel a bluebird in a nest of crows. He had risen from the settee with obvious reluctance. Perhaps he did not appreciate his privacy with Miss Ashton being interrupted.

"Mr. Brummell," the rector said. "I fear I'll not be able to enjoy music—nay, *any* of the delights God has given us here on earth—until this dreadful business unjustly involving Miss Ashton has been put behind us."

I raised a brow at this speech. Miss Ashton colored a bit, the pink serving to emphasize her pallor. Dark smudges under her eyes implied she had slept poorly the night before.

She did not appear to appreciate Mr. Dawlish's cloying attention either. Remembering Perry's comment that there was a romance between the rector and Miss Ashton, I reflected that it might be one-sided. Freddie had told me Miss Ashton shunned the married state. Like the proverbial leopard, the independent Miss Ashton did not appear likely to change her spots.

"I was not aware you were acquainted with Mr. Brummell," the rector said to her. His manner implied he resented her keeping this deep, dark secret from him.

"The Duchess of York introduced us," Miss Ashton gave the rector a quelling look before answering. "Shall we all sit down? I confess I am awfully glad you are here, Mr. Brummell."

She and Mr. Dawlish resumed their places on the settee. After declining her hasty offer of tea, I took a place in an armchair across from them. "Miss Ashton, tell me what has happened. Has there been a further development in the investigation?"

To my exasperation, Mr. Dawlish seemed determined to control the conversation.

"You will forgive us if we are not very entertaining company, Mr. Brummell. I fear we have serious matters to contemplate this afternoon," the rector said in his best pious tone.

Although he had spoken to me politely enough, disapproval at my association with Miss Ashton radiated from him. I could not think what I had done in our brief meeting at Perry's house to earn his censure, so I gathered it must be my reputation which had put him off. Remember, I am known to be a foolish dandy. I reflected that a man of the cloth could not be expected to hold a man of clothing in high regard.

If Mr. Dawlish was intent on keeping me out of Miss Ashton's troubles, I would have to let him know I was bent on assisting her. There was my promise to Freddie to be considered, and even if I were to be released from it, I found that I genuinely wished to do whatever I could to help the girl. Heightening my resolve was that cursed article in the newspaper. By their deplorable lack of decency, the *Morning Post* had cast doubt upon Freddie's reputation. And that I could not have.

I settled my gaze on Miss Ashton. "I hope you know I did not come here to be entertained," I told her candidly. "What has upset you? Have you had another visit from the Bow Street investigator?"

"Not a visit, at least not yet. I have had a distressing note from Mr. Lavender. In it, he says he will be calling on me later today to discuss some new evidence that has come to light regarding Lady Wrayburn's murder." Miss

Ashton struggled to maintain her composure. "He said I was not to leave Wrayburn House! He has actually positioned a guard outside."

I remembered the loutish fellow I had seen outside upon my arrival.

Mr. Dawlish patted Miss Ashton's hand and turned a dark look on me. "Mr. Brummell, I cannot help but feel this is an inappropriate time for an afternoon call. You can see Miss Ashton is not in any fit state to receive admirers."

What one could see was that Mr. Dawlish had an overly loving relationship with the pomade jar. Truly, you could view your reflection in his hair.

"I agree with you completely, Mr. Dawlish. I am the only *Beau* she needs to see, since I am the one wishing to help her by discovering who really poisoned Lady Wrayburn's glass of milk," I told him pleasantly enough.

Mr. Dawlish folded his arms across his chest.

I smiled at Miss Ashton and attempted a bit of levity. "You must use the excuse of not being able to leave the house to commission your friends to execute your errands. What may I bring you? A pastry from Gunter's? A book from Hatchard's?"

Miss Ashton's expression eased a bit. "Mr. Brummell, you are kind. There is nothing I need, though, except perhaps a new journal."

"A journal?"

"Yes, you will think me the veriest peagoose, but I have misplaced my journal. I am afraid I am one of those creatures who likes to record her daily activities no matter how mundane."

"I see nothing wrong with keeping a journal, Miss Ashton. I have been known to keep one myself. Life is fleeting after all, and it can be comforting to record its trials and tribulations as well as its joys," I said.

"Exactly," Miss Ashton concurred. "I always leave my journal in the desk drawer in my room, but now I find it has disappeared. In the confusion of the past few days I must have put it down somewhere else, although I cannot remember where."

A disturbing thought occurred to me. "In his note, did Mr. Lavender mention what this new evidence he has might be?"

"Why, no. He merely said some new evidence had come to light." Miss Ashton pressed her fingers to her temples. "I cannot think what it might be."

Mr. Dawlish had sat by quietly long enough. "Miss Ashton, why do you not go upstairs and lie down for a while. I am persuaded you have a headache coming on and would be the better for some rest."

"Perhaps I shall, later."

I hesitated, not liking to upset her further, but I saw no choice. "Miss Ashton, you say you like to record your daily activities in your journal."

"Well, yes," she answered, puzzled that we were back to the topic of her journal.

"It would only be natural to also include your feelings about places you have been, people you know. Did you do so in your journal?"

"Yes, I did. Sometimes, writing about my feelings helped me sort them out."

"That is understandable. You must have written often about Lady Wrayburn."

Miss Ashton suddenly sat very still. Her eyes met mine, and I hope the sympathy I felt for her showed.

"See here," Mr. Dawlish said. "This conversation grows tiresome."

"On the contrary," I said. "Now, Miss Ashton, you must not feel ashamed about anything you wrote in your journal. Lady Wrayburn was a . . . difficult employer, I have no doubt. Concentrate on the members of this household. Who here would like to see you charged with the murder of the countess enough to turn your journal over to the Bow Street investigators?"

Mr. Dawlish looked at me in surprise. "Are you saying someone *stole* Miss Ashton's journal?"

I tilted my head to one side. "What do you think? Miss Ashton writes out her feelings each night before she retires. She may have expressed some completely understandable frustration about Lady Wrayburn in that journal. She kept the journal in the same place at all times. Now, it is suddenly missing."

"Oh, Mr. Brummell," Miss Ashton said weakly, "I did indeed air some angry feelings about the countess in that journal. How astute of you to know. But, upon my honor I did not truly mean any of the ugly things I said."

"Of course not, my dear," the rector proclaimed roundly. "No one in their right mind would think you did."

"True," I said. "However, someone who wished to cast blame on Miss Ashton might have done a casual search through her room and stumbled across the journal. It would have been simple enough to wrap it up and send it to Bow Street anonymously."

"But there is no one here who would wish me harm!" Miss Ashton cried.

"It may not be so much a matter of wishing you harm as much as protecting himself or herself from a charge of murder," I pointed out. "Think it over, Miss Ashton. And if you find the journal in the meantime, do send me word."

"I shall."

"How is the maid Lizzie?" I inquired.

Miss Ashton opened her mouth to speak, but Mr. Dawlish was ahead of her. "God will provide for Lizzie. As it says in Psalms, 'In times of disaster, they will not wither.' "

"No doubt you are correct," I agreed amiably. "However, I cannot help but feel *He* appreciates it when we mere mortals do our part to help *Him* out. With Lady Wrayburn's son, Lord Wrayburn abroad, I imagine Mr. Hensley will make all the decisions now. Are you aware of his feelings on the matter of Lizzie's continued employment, Miss Ashton?"

"Yes, thank goodness. He told us in a most discreet and kind manner that there would be no staff changes for the time being. I believe he must be waiting for the will to be read tomorrow—"

The rector interrupted her, staring at me with a shrewd expression. "Perhaps he has been *too* anxious for the will to be read."

"Indeed?" I encouraged this all too obvious hint.

"Mr. Dawlish!" Miss Ashton exclaimed. "You cannot mean to cast doubt upon Mr. Hensley's character. I shall not have it."

"And why is that?" the rector peered at her through his

spectacles. "You told me yourself that you saw Mr. Hensley dressed for the outdoors the night of the murder. Mayhaps he poisoned the milk before he left the house."

"When did Mr. Hensley leave?" I queried.

Miss Ashton shot the rector an exasperated look. "I saw him when I came downstairs from Lizzie's room in the attics. But it signifies nothing, as Mr. Hensley remarked to me that he was going out for a walk—"

Mr. Dawlish spoke heatedly. "*Someone* murdered Lady Wrayburn, and the investigator from Bow Street thinks you did it. Your friend Mr. Brummell here asked you to think if there is anyone in the household who might wish to cast suspicion on you. I know you are innocent, as I know that there are those in this world who cannot wait to get what they consider to be rightfully theirs. Some, like the prodigal son, wish to hasten their inheritance."

Miss Ashton rose to her feet. I immediately followed suit, the rector more slowly.

She gave voice to her frustration, her tone terse, her cheeks flushed. "Mr. Hensley is no prodigal son. He does not squander his wealth. It is too much on top of everything else to hear you, Mr. Dawlish, whom I have considered to be my closest friend, cast aspersions on Mr. Hensley's character. Doing so is just as dreadful as Mr. Lavender assuming I am guilty."

Mr. Dawlish appeared remorseful, but before he could move to make amends, we were interrupted.

"Did I hear you say you are *guilty*, Miss Ashton?" a female voice asked in a dry tone. "Was that a confession?"

We all turned to see the new arrivals. A lady and gentleman—whom I could only assume were Mr. and Mrs.

Hensley—stood framed in the doorway. The woman was attired in a strikingly elegant bronze silk gown. However, the pleasure afforded me by its resplendence was somewhat marred by the wearer.

Although Mrs. Hensley must have been a beauty during her come-out into Society, two decades of marriage had etched lines of dissatisfaction around her mouth. Frown lines creased her brow above a nose which could not escape being called sharp.

Her husband was a clear contrast. His face was smooth, almost boyish. Where one felt an air of strength and determination about Mrs. Hensley, Mr. Hensley did not seem to have an ounce of fight left in him.

Miss Ashton made a quick recovery at Mrs. Hensley's barb and stepped forward. "Good afternoon, Mrs. Hensley, Mr. Hensley," she said calmly. Then her eyes widened. "Oh, goodness! Mrs. Hensley, is that Lady Wrayburn's topaz broach you are wearing?"

Cordelia Hensley eyed the younger woman coldly. "Yes, it is. With Lord Wrayburn unwed, the countess's jewels would remain in some musty box. I saw no reason why I should not have them. Not that it is any of your business."

"No, ma'am. It is only that Lizzie, as part of her duties, took inventory of Lady Wrayburn's jewels and noticed that several pieces were missing."

Mrs. Hensley raised her nose. "There is no sense in making a fuss. I am entitled to take whatever I want now that the spiteful old woman is gone."

My right eyebrow shot up at this callous speech, but I said nothing.

Mr. Hensley gave Miss Ashton a twisted smile and stood with his hands thrust into his pockets.

Mrs. Hensley led the way inside the room, her steps taking her to the decanter on a nearby side table. Before she could reach it, she discerned my presence and her direction abruptly changed. Her demeanor also changed, and the difference was almost comical. She went from sullen superiority to gushing graciousness in an instant.

"Mr. Brummell! How remiss of Miss Ashton not to let me know you were here. Why, I confess myself charmed that you would visit Wrayburn House."

I bowed. "Good afternoon."

Mrs. Hensley and I had never been formally introduced, but a woman like her would never let a little nicety like that get in her way. Mentally, I heaved a tired sigh. I run across women of Mrs. Hensley's sort oftentimes. I know enough to tread carefully, maintaining a polite reserve. Because if I did not give her my unfailing acceptance and approval—which I never would, considering her capable of the very heights of presumption—she would join the legions who spoke disparagingly behind my back. Why give her any ammunition?

Her smile faded when she turned toward her husband. "Timothy, what can you be thinking? Fetch Mr. Brummell a glass of Madeira at once, and you may bring me one as well."

I stretched out my hand to a man I could tell led a dog's life. And I am not speaking of one of Freddie's pampered pets. "Hensley."

"Brummell, good to see you." He clasped my hand with a weak grasp and then scurried to do his wife's bidding. I would wager he had been scurrying his entire married life. His thick, dark blond hair fell in heavy waves, and he frequently pushed it back in a nervous gesture. I had seen him at entertainments, but rarely, if ever, could I recall seeing him at White's. He probably was not allowed to leave his wife's side for very long in case she needed him to "fetch" something for her.

I accepted the glass of Madeira more for his benefit than for mine. Mrs. Hensley was sure to find fault with him if I rejected it.

"I have a sermon to write," Mr. Dawlish informed us. "I promise to return on the morrow, Miss Ashton."

The rector took his leave; then Mrs. Hensley seated herself in an armchair. I sat next to Miss Ashton on the uncomfortable settee.

Mr. Hensley joined us with the drinks. I accepted mine and took a sip. Excellent stuff, Madeira. Noting Mrs. Hensley's zealous gaze on me, I took a bigger swallow.

"Mr. Hensley, you have suffered a terrible loss," I began, although the fellow did not strike me as grieving for his dear mama. More like harassed. I felt a rush of pity for a man caught between a tyrant of a mother and a domineering wife. "May I offer you my condolences on the death of your mother?"

"Ah . . . yes, kind of you and all that," he replied in a vague way. He swallowed the contents of his glass and crossed the room for another.

Mrs. Hensley, her faded blonde hair swept up in a severe style, could not sit by and let someone else be the center of attention. "What you *could* offer, dear Mr. Brum-

mell, is your advice on a problem I mean to correct here
at Wrayburn House."

"A problem?" I asked, thinking of Miss Ashton and
Lizzie's fate.

"Many problems," Mrs. Hensley assured me fervently.
"How I have longed to take the reins of this household
and change this depressing old barn into the stylish house
it should be. Why, my friends have twitted me on the subject time out of number. Now, at last, I am in command."

It is a testimony to my ability to keep a cool countenance and a civil tongue that I did not simply rise from
my seat, state that I would not waste my time trying to
discuss elegance with a woman who had already sunk to
the very depths of vulgar behavior, and make a swift exit.
Instead, I remembered my mission to draw the Hensleys
out on the subject of the late Lady Wrayburn. "Was Lady
Wrayburn reluctant to make changes in the decor of Wrayburn House?"

Mrs. Hensley completely ignored mention of the dead
woman. "What think you of the new Egyptian style of
furnishings, Mr. Brummell? Will they be fashionable? I
saw a delightful sofa with crocodile legs I do so adore.
But I wouldn't dream of purchasing it without your rec-
ommendation."

"Mrs. Hensley," I said in a low voice, leaning forward
in the manner of a conspirator. "A sofa depicting croco-
diles would be perfect for you."

Miss Ashton made a choking sound, Mrs. Hensley
preened, and I rose, my patience tried. I would get nothing
out of them this afternoon. Perhaps later, if I contrived to
encounter each individually, I would meet with success.

Mr. Hensley, for one, would never speak of personal matters in front of his wife. "Ah, Riddell, after you have taken that tea tray away, would you alert my men that I am ready to leave."

The butler shuffled out of the room.

"Oh, but you mustn't go," Mrs. Hensley protested. "I haven't asked you about my draperies."

Running my gaze down Mrs. Hensley's ample form, I replied, "I imagine something voluminous is needed."

"Precisely my thought," Mrs. Hensley crooned.

"I rather think not," I muttered. Miss Ashton's eyes glowed with perception of my subtle insult of Mrs. Hensley's figure. I bowed over the younger woman's hand and whispered, "I shall return tomorrow."

Mr. Hensley shook my hand again. "Good of you to come. Must see to something in my library." He hastened out of the room.

"Good day, Mrs. Hensley," I said and walked out into the hall where the polemen had brought my sedan chair.

"Oh! Look at that sedan chair!" Mrs. Hensley had followed me into the hall. "It's most unusual, Mr. Brummell. Why, I've never laid eyes on a wood such as that. It's different, isn't it?" she asked with disapproval.

The fate of Mr. Griffin's creation was decided in that instant. "Yes, Mrs. Hensley, how clever of you to notice. It is indeed *different*. This is calamander wood, a rare wood formerly only used for royalty. I imagine there will be quite a crush of customers vying for it in the future."

Mrs. Hensley stood with her mouth open. One could almost see her brain working, trying to devise a way to

obtain the wood for herself before her friends caught wind
of the new discovery.

I took the opportunity to enter my chair. Riddell opened
the front door, and I was mercifully away.

As the polemen carried me toward Bruton Street, I reflected on my visit to Wrayburn House. Without doubt,
there were more questions now than ever. And with the
new development of Mr. Lavender's posting a guard to see
that Miss Ashton remained in the house, coupled with the
ominous news that he possessed additional evidence, I felt
an urgent need to narrow what seemed to be an ever-
widening list of suspects.

Mrs. Hensley was currently uppermost in my thoughts.
A domineering sort, she obviously resented having to bow
to another woman's wishes. Was she capable of murdering
Lady Wrayburn in order to run Wrayburn House the way
she wanted? Her casual dismissal of the mere mentioning
of Lady Wrayburn indicated the coldness required of a
murderess.

I felt sorry for Timothy Hensley, ruled by his mother
and his wife. Was he frustrated enough to dispose of one
of them? Divorcing Mrs. Hensley would have been out of
the question. Divorce is a long and scandalous process. I
could not see the weak Mr. Hensley putting himself
through it. But a few drops of poison in his mother's evening glass of milk might be an act he could carry through.
I definitely had not perceived any familial devotion there.

And why had Mr. Hensley kept Miss Ashton and Lizzie
on? Neither one would have any duties, unless he decided
they could serve his wife. Somehow, I think Miss Ashton

would have relayed such an insufferable change in circumstances to me.

As for Miss Ashton, although I could not logically rule her out as a suspect, my instinct still told me she was innocent. She really was an independent girl. I could see her leaving Wrayburn House with Lizzie in tow, determined to eke out a living, before I could see her murdering the countess.

Very well, perhaps it was her beautiful eyes which blinded me to the thought of her committing any wrongdoing.

And who had taken her journal? I was convinced that it had been stolen, not misplaced.

Just as troubling were the two missing suspects. I had yet to interview Lizzie, the pregnant maid. Tomorrow, I planned to return to Wrayburn House around the time of the reading of the will. I would try to interview her then.

As for the other member of the household, Sylvester Fairingdale, I thought I could find him at a *Beau Monde* entertainment tonight. When I returned home, I would ask Robinson to enlist the aid of his league of fellow gossipy servants to find out what gathering Mr. Fairingdale planned to attend.

That is, if Robinson was still in my employ after spending the last hour with Chakkri.

9

"*Eleven, sir,*" *Robinson* stated.

I had just come in my front door from Wrayburn House and handed the valet my hat, greatcoat, and gloves. We headed for the stairs. "Eleven what?"

"Cat hairs on your bed. I picked them off, but the feline has taken possession of your bedchamber, and even though I tried my best, I cannot remove the hairs as fast as they rub off the creature and onto the coverlet."

I hid a smile. "Surely you know I do not expect you to remove every cat hair from the furnishings, Robinson."

"But, sir," Robinson protested, his voice urgent, "it is not so much the furniture as it is your clothing I am distressed about. If you sit on a chair with cat hairs on it, some are bound to attach themselves to you. I cannot have you leave my care with animal hairs clinging to your person! My reputation as a valet is at stake."

"Hmmm, quite right. Well, I suppose the thing to do is brush any hairs off my clothes before I leave the house."

Robinson gave me a sour look before opening the door to my bedchamber.

I entered cautiously, uncertain of the reception I would receive from Chakkri. Even though he had shown every evidence of being a feline who appreciated the finer things in life, I experienced a moment of concern for my Sèvres and my ivory silk bed hangings.

I need not have worried. There he was, reclining like a head of state in the exact center of my bed. Chakkri yawned, rose on his long legs, stretched, and hopped down. He walked over to meet me, but stopped at a distance of about three feet from my Hessian boots, requiring me to meet him halfway.

He let out a faint, "Reow." I bent, and he allowed me to stroke his incredibly soft fur before strolling over to the blazing fireplace to warm himself.

Robinson watched this scene with pursed lips. I transferred my attention to him, and The Dressing Hour began.

When I finished bathing, Robinson imparted some happy news. "André has prepared his matelote shrimp as you requested."

"André is no end of a good fellow. Was he able to obtain fishheads from the market for Chakkri?"

Another pursing of the lips preceded Robinson's reply. He handed me a pair of black breeches. "As to that, sir, I am afraid the feline has earned André's wrath. The cook had the boy from the market deliver the animal's dinner, but the cat refused to eat the fishhead provided."

I darted a glance at Chakkri while buttoning my white

waistcoat. He had turned around and was now warming the other side of his body. His air of nonchalance was remarkable. I pushed aside thoughts of concern over his lack of appetite. Perhaps the cat had simply not felt hungry the first day in his new home.

"André was angry, was he?"

"Yes, sir," Robinson reported triumphantly, eager for an ally in his war against Chakkri.

"I shall speak to him after dinner. By the way, I desire to know someone's destination this evening. A Mr. Sylvester Fairingdale."

"He lives at Wrayburn House, does he not, sir?" Robinson paused in the act of drawing a Turkish-blue coat out of the wardrobe. His curious expression told me I had best tread carefully if I wished to keep my investigation of the inhabitants of Wrayburn House secret.

I assumed a perplexed look and adjusted my watch chain. "Does he? I believe you have the right of it. At any rate, I had planned to spend the evening playing hazard at White's, but with my luck devilishly low of late, I thought I would amuse myself by beholding Mr. Fairingdale's latest idea of a coat."

Robinson relaxed. "Fancies himself a fashion plate, doesn't he? But in truth he is more a figure of fun. His valet's taste runs to extremes too. I daresay he encourages Mr. Fairingdale. Now that Lady Wrayburn has died, I expect Mr. Fairingdale will have more money available to spend on garish clothes."

"No doubt," I agreed. Robinson helped me into my perfectly fitted coat, and I slipped on a pair of glossy black evening shoes.

Once faultlessly attired, I crossed into the dining room and seated myself at the table. Robinson poured me a glass of claret before leaving to alert André I was ready for my meal.

I sat enjoying my wine and admiring a pair of Sèvres vases which reposed on the sideboard. They are green with flowers and fruit depicted on their smooth surfaces. They have gold trim, and a matching cup and cover sit next to them. Ah, the comforts of home. Is there anything to equal it?

I frowned suddenly. Was the vase on the left slightly farther away from the cup centered between them than the one on the right? I rose from my chair, repositioned the wayward vase, and sat down once more, pleased.

Robinson returned carrying a heavy tray. He placed a plate in front of me, and I breathed in the aroma appreciatively. Plump shrimp, accompanied by onions, mushrooms, and oysters, nestled lovingly in a white wine sauce. Delectable!

"Enjoy your meal, sir. You have only to ring if you require anything," Robinson assured me, indicating a small silver bell next to my plate. "I'll just go downstairs and see about finding out Mr. Fairingdale's plans for the evening. I've sent round to The Porter & Pole for two men to carry your sedan chair wherever you go."

I nodded in silent agreement to all these plans, a forkful of shrimp already on its way to my mouth.

A few minutes later, the sound of raised voices coming from below interrupted my culinary bliss. I tried to ignore the intrusion as I had barely begun to savor my meal, but my curiosity got the better of me, and I rose from the table, napkin in hand.

I strode to the landing and looked down upon an amazing scene. Robinson stood militantly in the hall confronted by a pair of tall, ruddy-cheeked, muscular young men.

"You are not the usual two Mr. Conte sends. Also you are not clean enough to serve Mr. Brummell. Now off with you!" Robinson held the door open.

"Wait just a minute here," one of the boys said, twisting a worn hat around in his hands. I noted it was the sort of wide-brimmed, round black hats favored by farmers. "Ned and me are good country lads, fit enough to serve his lordship. And that there smell you mentioned is only what makes crops grow. We come from Dorchester by boat up the Thames."

I could bear to be a silent witness no more. For while there was nothing amazing about The Porter & Pole having employed two boys fresh from the country, what was amazing was their appearance.

They looked to be identical twins.

What, I ask you, could be more aesthetically pleasing than *matching* polemen to carry my sedan chair?

"You are mistaken," I said, coming down the stairs. "I am not a lord."

"Sir—" Robinson began, but I held up a forestalling hand. Gaining close proximity to the twins, whom I judged to be about nineteen years old, I thought of holding my napkin to my nose. They did, indeed, reek of fertilizer. They were dressed alike in collarless smock-frocks that sported puffy sleeves and came down to their knees. Their breeches were of a coarse fabric in a brownish color and they wore short boots, caked in mud. At least, I hoped it was mud.

But I envisioned them in matching livery, perhaps blue and a gold that would not clash with their blond hair. Oh, joyous rapture! The scene they would present carrying me about in my sedan chair! Prinny would be prostrate with envy!

"I am George Brummell. Did I hear you say you came up from the country this morning?"

"Yes, sir," one twin said respectfully. "Me and Ned heard we could earn a good livin' in Lunnon."

Ned, whom I thought might be incapable of speech, proved me wrong. Very wrong.

"I says to Mum that we could earn her money for her calves foot jelly—she swears by that stuff—now that she's got the arthur-itis real bad after she got caught out in that snow storm last winter tryin' to round up the pigs. Mum's got a taste for bacon like nothin' you've ever seen, and for a woman with only four teeth she does real good. You know, Mum lost most of her teeth defendin' us ten years back when the Widow Freyne accused her o' sleepin' with the devil to get two boys that look the same and—" Ned broke off abruptly and looked to Ted. "What was I sayin'?"

Robinson turned a horrified look on me.

"Er, your mother did not come to London with you, did she?" I asked warily, ignoring Robinson.

"Oh, no, your lordship—I mean, sir," Ted replied. "Nobody could convince Mum to leave her pigs."

"Naturally not," I said. "It so happens I have been considering hiring two men to carry me in my sedan chair. I grow weary of forever having to send round for men from The Porter & Pole. Did you sign any agreement with them to remain in their employ?"

Ted scratched his head. "Me and Ned don't know 'ow to write."

Ned nodded his agreement. "That's right, though once there was a lady who tried to teach us. A purtier thing than her you never did see, she had the shiniest hair, shinier than them shoes you're wearin'. I always wanted to run my hands through it, but Mum made me promise not to. And her skin—well, all I can say is have you ever seen the underside of a pig's belly?—it was silky like that, but she run off one day kinda like Mum's pigs and—" Again, he looked to his brother for help. "What was I saying, Ted?"

"Then there is no impediment to your coming to work for me," I interrupted.

Robinson whimpered.

Ted's ruddy face creased in a wide grin. "No, sir, there isn't. I mean, I don't know what that word—impediment—means, but we'd be happy to work for you."

"Good. For tonight, I will use someone else to carry my sedan chair. I must insist you both bathe before you begin your employment and that you continue to bathe regularly thereafter."

The two looked at each other, clearly baffled by this request. However, they shrugged good-naturedly and assured me they would.

"Robinson, I think there is enough room in the attics to set up two small rooms for Ned and Ted."

"But, sir," Robinson said through gritted teeth, "the attic

has our cast-offs from our Chesterfield Street address."

"Quite right. Good of you to remind me, Robinson. Those things can be taken away to a charity house. We should have done so before now."

Robinson drew a deep breath, preparatory to delivering me a blistering set-down, I was sure, but I held sway. "I am persuaded having Ned and Ted here will take some of the burdens off your shoulders."

"That's the truth," Ted chimed in without malice. "A puny fellow like you couldn't possibly do all the things we strong men can."

"Nor would I want to," Robinson said coldly.

"Then it is settled, and I can return to my dinner," I said.

"Thank you," Ned and Ted chorused. They slapped each other on the back, obviously thrilled to have money to send back to "Mum."

Robinson snorted.

I climbed the stairs, merry thoughts of the *Beau Monde*'s reaction to the twins dancing in my head. For everyone strove to obtain footman of identical heights; it was the thing to do. I, now, had taken this notion a step further. My polemen would be *completely* identical. My place as leader in all things fashionable was that much more secure.

And wait until Freddie saw them!

I sighed happily as I entered the dining room.

Then I froze.

Sitting in my place at the table was Chakkri. He licked his paw and then used it to clean around his whisker pad. The plate in front of him, which had previously contained my dinner, was bereft of a single shrimp. He had carefully eaten around all the mushrooms, onions, and oysters. They had been pushed to the side of the plate, no doubt with his efficient pink tongue. The wine sauce, I noted with astonishment, had also been consumed.

Chakkri stopped his cleaning process long enough to look at me with approving blue eyes, as if to say, "Now that was a meal! You can keep your fishheads!"

Then, I give you my word, he emitted a delicate burp, hopped down from my chair, and retired to my bedchamber.

10

As I climbed the stairs of Lord and Lady Crecy's town house, I heard the orchestra playing a lively reel. A wigged footman dressed in gold and white livery threw open the doors to the ballroom when I approached.

Inside, elegantly dressed couples danced to the music. The ladies were in flowing gowns of colorful silks, velvets, and satins; the gentlemen were in the style I had brought about—immaculate dark coats and light-colored breeches.

People mingled among their friends, chatting and drinking champagne. Young ladies not fortunate enough to obtain a partner for the dance sat with their chaperons in a row of gilt chairs placed against the wall.

The chamber was decorated in the Chinese style. Silk wallpaper depicted a river landscape in great detail, with water flowing, birds flying, and trees swaying. The room had been cleared of most of its furnishings, but a few pieces of Chinese porcelain were placed about on pedestals. The delicate objects stood in each seemingly protected corner of the room, shrouded behind tall potted palms. Yet I still feared an over-zealous dancer might threaten their safety.

"Mr. Brummell! Oh, I am so glad you changed your mind and decided to attend our little party." My hostess, Lady Crecy, was a short, plump woman with too-tight curls ringing her head. They bounced with her excitement over my unexpected presence.

I bowed.

Lady Crecy struck a gloved hand to her chest. "Upon my honor, Mr. Brummell, you have the most exquisite way of bowing I have ever seen in my life."

"Thank you, my lady. As to my attendance here this evening, I assure you I put my valet on a diet of bread and water as a punishment for failing to send my card of acceptance."

She tittered. "Never mind that. What is important is that you are here. I hope you will not find us dull. London is thin of company at the moment, but I felt I should do something to amuse my dear daughter, Penelope, before she perishes from boredom."

Dash it all, I had forgotten Lady Crecy had a girl she was desperate to marry off. The poor thing had been through two social seasons thus far without a single suitor. She suffered from some sort of nasal difficulty and could not stop sniffing, an unfortunate mannerism that even her enticing dowry could not overcome.

By the sheer force of her will and a penetrating stare, Lady Crecy brought her daughter to our side from where she had been seated across the room. "There you are, Penelope. Here is Mr. Brummell come to our party."

Penelope's grey eyes opened wide. She dropped me a curtsy and sniffed loudly.

I bowed and studied her, knowing Lady Crecy had maneuvered me into this position so that I might dance with the girl and thus create interest in her. Usually, I am an expert at gracefully extricating myself from circumstances exactly like the one I was faced with at the moment.

However, as I gazed upon Lady Penelope's rather plain countenance, I saw a hopeless look in her eyes which prompted me to say, "Lady Penelope, I know I have arrived frightfully late on the scene, but would you do me the honor of standing up with me for the next contredanse?"

Grey eyes blinked in surprise. Lady Penelope nodded shyly and dabbed at her nose with a crumpled handkerchief, while her fond mama looked on with satisfaction.

Now, I was free until the contredanse to find Sylvester Fairingdale. I had been surprised to learn from Robinson that Mr. Fairingdale would be attending an entertainment that included dancing. The customs of mourning for a loved one restrict the bereaved's activities to more sedate forms of amusement such as card parties, a friend's musical evening, or venturing to the opera or theater. Dancing is considered bad form.

The reel ended, and flushed dancers waved fans to cool their heated cheeks. Footmen circled with more glasses of champagne. Procuring a glass for myself, I nodded to acquaintances, keeping an eye out for Fairingdale.

I did not see him, and made my way to where Petersham and his friend Lord Munro stood conversing. Petersham's winning smile was not in evidence tonight. At his side, Lord Munro looked sullen.

"Et tu, Brummell?" Petersham accused at my approach.

The snuff box! I had not obtained his snuff box from the auction, sacrificing it along with the painting. I recalled Perry had told me Mr. Kiang won it and that Petersham had been cast into the dismals.

"There is no need for Shakespearean references, Petersham. I hear enough of the Bard every time I go to White's and Delbert is on duty. I do beg your pardon, though, for not being able to obtain the box."

"And beg you shall!" Petersham retorted. "What the devil happened? When I woke around two in the afternoon, I expected to have word from you saying you'd ridden out to Sidwell's and struck a bargain."

"I know, I—"

"And when I hadn't received anything by three, I had my valet, Diggie, you know, run over to your rooms only to be told by Robinson that you were not at home. I suffered a great deal of inconvenience, I can tell you. I had to shave all by myself because Diggie was out."

"Tricky business with those side whiskers," I threw in.

Petersham narrowed his eyes at me. "Then, I had to *hurry* while dressing and attend the auction myself. You *know* I do not leave my house until after six."

"It's bad for his asthma," Lord Munro put in.

"I give you my humblest apology, Petersham—"

"Only to arrive at the curst auction and have that garishly clad Mr. Kiang fellow have the riches of Midas at his disposal. His outrageous bids left me in the dust. My precious snuff box, gone to that foreigner! It's too much for a man to shoulder."

Lord Munro tsked sympathetically, all the while glaring at me over Petersham's bowed head.

"Look here, Petersham, I have given you my apology. I did intend to ride out to Sidwell's, but an urgent matter required my attention. I lost the Perronneau painting too, you know."

"I can't imagine any matter being more urgent than a snuff box promised to a friend," Lord Munro chided.

Can it be he dislikes me?

Petersham lifted his head. "What 'urgent matter'?"

I signaled a footman and exchanged my empty glass for a fresh one. Munro handed a glass to Petersham and secured one for himself.

The distraction gave me the opportunity to avoid Petersham's question. He and Munro could hardly be counted upon to remain silent if I shared with them the details of Freddie's call and my subsequent investigation into Lady Wrayburn's murder.

"Allow me to make it up to you," I finally said. "I shall draw a design of the snuff box and commission Rundell and Bridges to make you one. The jeweler created Sidwell's; he ought to be able to replicate one for us."

Petersham brightened. "You are no end of a good fellow, Brummell. Even if you are damned secretive," he added, letting me know he realized I had not answered his question.

Lord Munro could not allow the issue to be resolved so easily. "But, Charles, are you sure you want a snuff box exactly like one that someone else has? Even if that Siamese man is across the world, won't it bother you that your box is not an original?"

Petersham turned a stricken expression on me.

I restrained myself from shaking Lord Munro until his teeth rattled. Instead, I raised my hand in a forestalling gesture. "You and I can collaborate and make up a *similar* design, one even superior to the box we lost."

Petersham favored me with his brilliant smile, and all was well with our friendship, much to Lord Munro's disappointment.

"Egad!" Petersham cried abruptly. "Look at that waist-coat!"

He and Lord Munro raised their quizzing glasses in unison.

Sylvester Fairingdale emerged from an anteroom where Lady Crecy had set up card tables. He entered with a mincing step, walking on the balls of his feet.

Mr. Fairingdale had a forward jutting chin, an infirmity which was not helped by the fact that he had wound his cravat around his neck to dizzying heights. The results were an unnaturally elongated neck, and a man who looked far down his nose at the world.

Robinson's notion that Mr. Fairingdale would have more money now to indulge his foppish taste in clothing seemed to be alarmingly accurate. Taking in the glory of his costume, I had to forcibly stop my hand from grabbing my own quizzing glass and raising it to my eye.

The waistcoat Petersham referred to was of a rhubarb color and had embroidered pears stitched about the material at random. A spinach-green coat topped it. Breeches in a shade of dull olive green hung loosely about his skinny legs.

The man was a walking salad.

Lord Munro summed up my feelings. "I'm feeling bilious."

"Is he trying to outdo Henry Cope?" Petersham asked, referring to the eccentric Green Man of Brighton. Mr. Cope habitually dresses in green from head to foot. Everything in his house is said to be green, and the fellow eats nothing but greens, fruits, and vegetables.

"Perhaps Fairingdale is *green* with envy," Munro quipped.

He and Petersham chortled with glee.

"I'm certain Fairingdale feels superior to anything Cope does. Always has been an insufferable snob," Lord Munro pronounced when he could speak again.

The snob in question perceived our interest and pranced his way to our side. I trust my expression did not reveal the extent of my disapproval of his manner of dress and deportment. In truth I felt ill from the sheer horridness of such a combination of colors.

My ability to keep a bland countenance must have failed me under the weight of Mr. Fairingdale's folly.

"As well you might look, Brummell, for I know you have never seen anything to equal my costume. I daresay Lady Crecy is quite happy to have me here this evening to display it."

"Indeed. Any hostess would be pleased to have you at her table. Perhaps before the soup course," I added thoughtfully.

Petersham sniggered.

The barb sailed over Fairingdale's head.

A few people started to gather near us, unobtrusively, mind you. But I knew they wanted to hear what my reaction to Fairingdale's clothing might be.

"It must be difficult for you to bear that I have outdone you, Brummell, but I have long known my taste to be superior to yours," he said, raising a hand to adjust the huge asparagus-colored peridot pinned among the folds of his cravat. I was surprised he could lift his hand, his fingers were so laden down with garish rings.

He went on, "I daresay by tomorrow everyone across the streets of London will be talking about your downfall as the arbiter of taste, and how I surpassed you in dress."

"How sad that would be, if true," I said in my best sincere voice. "For I have always felt the severest mortification a gentleman could incur is to attract observation in the street by his outward appearance."

Mr. Fairingdale looked confused for an instant before regaining his air of supremacy.

"May I offer you my condolences on the loss of your aunt, Mr. Fairingdale?" I said, neatly turning the topic. "It is good to see you enjoying the comfort of your friends at a time like this."

"Pshaw! I don't care two straws about the countess," Mr. Fairingdale declared with a careless wave of his hand. "The real loss will be that of Rebecca Ashton. A fine looking woman. Too fine to hang at Newgate. In time, I might even have considered bestowing my attentions on her, overlooking her position as a paid companion. But, although her beauty might have enticed me to set her up as my mistress, it is not enough to convince me to disregard the fact that she murdered my aunt."

I felt myself tense at this public pronouncement by a family member, no less, of Miss Ashton's guilt. And public it was. For while Mr. Fairingdale did not exactly shout his words from a rooftop, his voice had grown louder throughout his speech. The music had ceased, and much of the gathering were listening to us while trying to appear as if they were not.

I called upon every ounce of my ability to remain outwardly tranquil, though inside I seethed with anger at the fop's impudence in purposefully degrading a young lady's character. "I have met Miss Ashton. She is, as you say, a beauty. She is also Lord Kirgo's daughter and not one to dirty her gloves in *any* manner."

This time, the barb hit its target, and this time Mr. Fairingdale did bellow.

"What the devil do you mean by that, Brummell? The chit would have gladly laid on her back for me, had I asked. But I didn't. And then, after some argument with Lady Wrayburn, when she and that scheming lady's maid were about to be tossed onto the street, she murdered the old harridan."

We had everyone's attention now. Not a soul pretended they were not listening. Petersham touched my sleeve and whispered for me to come away and ignore the jingle-brained idiot. But I could not. Miss Ashton must have a champion lest her name be irretrievably blackened.

"Miss Ashton would not be taken in by the dubious rewards of low behavior. She is a lady of gentle birth," I stated firmly.

Mr. Fairingdale sneered. "Perhaps you only say so because a certain 'lady of the Blood Royal' everyone knows you admire recommended the chit to my aunt."

Sharply indrawn breaths met this comment. Out of the corner of my eye I saw Lord and Lady Perry had arrived and had come to stand behind me. Lady Salisbury joined them.

But I could not appreciate their support just now. Fury almost choked me at the foolish Mr. Fairingdale's reference to my dear Freddie.

"Of your galaxy of stupidities, Fairingdale, that statement must be a shining star. *Everyone*," I said in a deceptively light tone, motioning to the gathering, "knows I am my own man and form my own judgments. Unlike others—" here I nonchalantly raised my quizzing glass and stared through it at Mr. Fairingdale's costume with a mocking eye—"I seek neither the attention nor the approval of anyone."

Mr. Fairingdale began to look uncomfortable. He must have realized the enormity of what he was doing by challenging me in public. His social credit did not extend this far, and he knew it. But pride forced him to take a parting shot.

"You say Miss Ashton is innocent of Lady Wrayburn's murder, Brummell. Well, I say Society will see just how valuable your opinions *really* are when Bow Street leads the chit off to Newgate."

At that moment, a loud crash resounded throughout the room. One of the pieces of Chinese porcelain lay shattered on the floor, a fragile victim of a reckless move.

⚜ 11 ⚜

Having successfully thrown down the gauntlet, Mr. Fairingdale stalked away looking like celery on legs.

Lady Crecy, in high alt because now her ball was sure to be talked about all over London, signaled to the orchestra to resume the music.

"Fairingdale's an impudent dog, Brummell. Pay him no heed," Lord Perry said.

I raised an eyebrow. "You malign the species."

"The man's clothes are uncivilized," Petersham pronounced. "How can you take him seriously? Look here, Munro and I are going to White's. Care to join us, Brummell?"

"No, thank you. I have promised a lady a dance."

The two wandered away, and Lady Perry turned to me.

She smiled and placed a gloved hand on my arm. "It has often been my observation that a gentleman who is a model of masculine perfection is frequently subjected to unconscionable behavior by those who feel inferior. Anthony is correct. Pay Mr. Fairingdale no mind."

I grasped her hand and raised it to my lips.

Perry looked at his wife in mock outrage. "So, you think Brummell, and not your own husband, is the 'model of masculine perfection,' do you? I shall just have to whisk you off to the dance floor and twirl you around until you change your mind."

Laughing softly, Lady Perry allowed herself to be whisked.

Perry winked at me over her shoulder.

A gruff female voice said, "I've been standing here virtually ignored for long enough, Brummell. James is in the card room, and no one has claimed me for this dance. You may have it," Lady Salisbury declared.

"It is my honor, my lady."

"Hmpf," was the reply.

The dance was an old-fashioned minuet; one of my favorites. I led the marchioness out to the dance floor. "Lady Salisbury, may I say you are looking exceedingly fine this evening? Not many women can wear Tyrian purple, but you do so with élan."

"You can compliment me until all the cows in Green Park jump into the Thames, but that is not what is uppermost in your mind."

Performing the steps of the dance, I managed a slight bow. "True. But I would not have a beautiful lady plagued by problems."

She lowered her voice. "The whole of London will have heard of Fairingdale's effrontery by morning. I hope you know with a certainty that Miss Ashton didn't add that poison to Lady Wrayburn's glass of milk, because, depend upon it, your very reputation is at stake after this evening's altercation."

"Yes, it is," I said simply. "But an innocent young woman's character was called into question. What else could I do?"

Lady Salisbury gave a little shake of her head. "I suppose I should be glad you did not challenge that fop Fairingdale to a duel."

"Oh, that would not be sportsmanlike. I believe I would have the advantage of a clear shot, while Mr. Fairingdale would be forced to look down the barrel of his gun through the added length of his nose."

"Be careful nonetheless," the marchioness cautioned. "By the way, I need an escort to the opera Wednesday night. James can't abide all the 'screeching' as he calls it. I know he'd take me if I pressed him, but I'd rather not. Besides, it'll do me good to be seen on the arm of a handsome Beau like you."

"I beg to disagree, my lady. It can only bolster *my* reputation to be seen on *your* arm."

"Just so," the clever marchioness concurred.

The dance ended, and we parted on the best of terms. The strains of the contredanse began, and I located Lady Penelope. The shy miss gave me her hand and amidst much whispering behind fans, I escorted her to the dance floor. It seemed I could do nothing without becoming the subject of conjecture.

Lady Penelope danced gracefully, I thought, and though rather plain in countenance, she had expressive eyes. I was soon distracted from them, however, by her recurrent sniffing.

After a few moments of pleasantries, punctuated by her sniffing, I came to a decision. "Lady Penelope, allow me to offer you my handkerchief."

She blushed at that, but accepted the initialed square of linen. I gazed at her kindly, and in the manner of one waiting an explanation.

"I—I, well, you see, in the spring and autumn I find there is something in the air which causes me to . . . oh, I am so embarrassed," she confessed, her head down.

"You must look up, Lady Penelope, or you will miss your steps," I warned. "And as to your difficulty, it is a common enough complaint. May I suggest you have your Mama ask Dr. Profitt to visit you? I am speaking to you now as a brother might, so you must not take offense."

"Oh, no, Mr. Brummell! I shan't be offended," she said, meeting my gaze. "I have spoken to Mama about the problem, but she says it is of no consequence. I disagree, but have not been able to talk to anyone else about it. You have made it easy for me to speak."

"Good! For your nose is delightfully formed and does not show to advantage when pink. Why, come to think of it, I cannot imagine anyone's who does," I teased.

Lady Penelope's eyes shone. "You are the best of men, sir. I shall insist Mama send for Dr. Profitt. If she refuses, I shall tell her *you* said I was to do so. She can hardly argue with that."

We danced in silence for a moment or two, then Lady Penelope boldly said, "And if I were you, Mr. Brummell,

I would not let Mr. Fairingdale's words bother me one whit."

I raised an inquiring brow.

"He is an odious man," Lady Penelope whispered with passion. "I should not be the least surprised to learn that he is the one who poisoned Lady Wrayburn. Mama says he and the countess quarreled frequently."

"One wonders about what." I let the words drop expectantly and was not disappointed.

"I suspect money," Lady Penelope said in a confiding manner. "Lady Wrayburn did not approve of the money Mr. Fairingdale spends on his clothing. Mama said the countess often remarked that her nephew was no better than a tailor's dummy. I think she wanted him to leave Wrayburn House."

"Hmmm," I murmured noncommittally, remembering the letter on Lady Wrayburn's desk. I wanted to know more, but Lady Penelope showed alarming signs of a growing hero worship toward me, and I did not wish to encourage her.

I was in a thoughtful mood when I returned her to her smiling mama. Because I had danced with her, Lady Penelope was shortly surrounded by beaux eager to take a turn around the room with her. Pleased, I finally took my leave of the party.

Fog covered the London streets in a thick, yellowish haze. The polemen carried my sedan chair through it to Bruton Street at a slower pace than usual.

Once I arrived home, I stripped off my gloves in the candlelit hallway. The polemen stored my chair in a large storage closet beneath the stairs and then left. Where was

Robinson? He normally greeted me upon my return home in the evenings.

I heard a noise from his room at the back of the hall, and shortly thereafter the man himself walked toward me. Was his gait a trifle unsteady?

"Did you have a good evening, thur?"

Thur? "Have you been drinking, Robinson?"

"Only enough to rid my throat of all the barnyard dust," he declared loftily.

"Barnyard? Dust? Have you run mad?"

"No, thur. Have you not noticed that our elegant home hath turned into a common barnyard overrun with animals and country bumpkins?"

He swayed a bit. I fixed him with an impatient look. "I hardly think one cat and two farm boys qualify as 'over-run.' Did Ned and Ted get settled?"

Robinson curled his lip. "They are upstairs in the attic, exhausted after their baths. I had to th-thtop them from bathing out back in the mews for all to see. The one who rambles on like a Bedlamite—Ned, I think—told me a story about the last time they bathed. Apparently, it was the first warm day last summer and they just splashed themselves clean at the pump out in the back of their house."

"Good God!"

" 'Zactly! I made them wait until André had left for the evening before allowing them to bathe in the kitchen. The chef would have given notice, without a doubt, if he knew his spotless kitchen was being used to wash pig manure off two yokels fresh from the farm cart." Robinson ended this speech with a loud hiccup.

"Is that when you started drinking?"

"No, thur. I had a few glasses of your brandy after I finished ridding the chair in your bedchamber of cat hairs. Fourteen of them. Shall we go upstairs so I can help you prepare for bed?" he inquired with the sort of dignity common to those who have imbibed heavily.

Taking note of how the valet teetered, I said, "That is not necessary. I shall put myself to bed tonight."

"Very good, thur," Robinson said. "Oh, and His Royal Highness, The Prince of Fur was reclining on your bed the last time I looked. Have a care not to disturb him," he advised mockingly.

I watched Robinson weave his way down the hall, and waited until his door closed before blowing out the flames of the branch of candles on the hall table and picking up a single taper to light my way to my room.

I climbed the stairs and entered my bedchamber. The room was dark, and I lit the candle by my bedside, the one on my washstand, and another on the crescent-shaped side table near the window. That is when I noticed a black lacquered screen had been set up in a corner.

"Reow," Chakkri said conversationally from where he lay sprawled across my bed. He stood up and stretched, his right front paw reaching out toward me.

"Hello, Chakkri. What is this screen doing here, I wonder?" I walked behind it and found the answer. A porcelain serving tray about two feet long, one and half feet wide and three inches deep was filled with sand for Chakkri's use and set discreetly on the floor.

As I stood there, the cat came over and demonstrated how the object worked. When his dainty paws scratched the sand to cover a damp spot, my eyes widened.

At first I had not recognized the porcelain tray, but now I remembered. It had been given to me during the last Season by a member of the merchant class. He hoped to gain my approval of his daughter and heighten the chances of her making an aristocratic match.

He had had the tray specially made. It was a cream color, with gold trim around the sides. Not so very unusual. But, in the exact center, where Chakkri had done his scratching, the artist had painted a detailed likeness of yours truly complete with tall beaver hat, perfectly tied cravat, and raised quizzing glass.

I chuckled mirthlessly at Robinson's sense of humor. Or was it his sense of retaliation?

Chakkri finished his task, and we walked around the screen.

"A fine night's work this has been, old boy," I said, pulling my nightclothes from the wardrobe and laying them across the high-back upholstered chair by the hearth. The linen garments were scented with Floris's bergamot soap, a small luxury Robinson sees to. I inspected them for flaws.

Chakkri jumped up onto the chair, twitching his long brown tail and watching me with his blue eyes. I pulled off my coat by the warmth of the fire. "I have managed to entangle myself in a bumblebroth, my feline friend. After tonight's doings, everyone knows I believe Miss Ashton innocent of Lady Wrayburn's murder. I should have done better for my investigation to remain silent. Devil take it, I still have not ruled her out completely. I refuse to rule *anyone* out as a suspect. Yet, I stood up like a booberkin and defended her publicly, putting my reputation at stake."

"Reow," Chakkri murmured.

Once clad in my nightclothes, I was chilly. I wrapped my old dressing gown around me, poured myself a brandy, and went to sit in the chair by the fire.

It was already occupied.

"Look here, old boy, this is one of my favorite chairs. You will have to get down. Curl up in front of the fire."

Chakkri slipped down from the chair. I settled myself, the brandy in easy reach on a small table next to me.

Without warning, the cat jumped in my lap, lay down, and started to purr.

What could I do, I ask you? I reached out tentatively and stroked his incredibly soft fur.

"My reputation is what enables me to live, Chakkri. Yes, my father left me a goodly sum, but not enough for my tastes. He was secretary to Lord North, you know, the gentleman whose portrait hangs downstairs in the bookroom."

Chakkri purred harder.

"Growing up, I met influential people, ultimately the Prince of Wales, and developed a taste for fine things. My father had lofty ambitions for me. Despite everything, I never quite believed I lived up to his expectations. Sometimes, I feel that he speaks by way of a little voice inside my head telling me I can do better, strive harder, achieve more."

A moment of silence passed.

"Do not forget, that should I fall from favor, my credit with the merchants will be cut off without delay. No more

Sèvres porcelain, no more coats from Weston, no more matelote shrimp," I ended, eyeing the cat sternly.

Chakkri placed a sympathetic paw on my hand and gazed up at me in concern.

"The only thing for it is to prove Miss Ashton did not commit the crime. Heaven knows, we have plenty of other candidates for the title of Murderess . . . or Murderer. Even that fop, Fairingdale, had plenty of motive. I must find out more about him. Has he been totally dependent on Lady Wrayburn for his financial needs? Was he home the night of the murder and therefore able to nip downstairs and poison the milk while Miss Ashton was in her room? If he has been a resident of Wrayburn House for any length of time at all, he must have known the nightly routine. Although the same could be said for anyone in that house, and it seems to me they all had reason to see the old lady dead. Dash it all! Who did it?"

"Reow!" Chakkri said. He abruptly leaped from my lap and crossed to the crescent-shaped side table by the window. He rose to the surface where the candle burned and where my prized Sèvres tortoise-shell plate rested. I tensed.

The cat walked carefully around the candle and sat in a compact bundle in front of the plate. His dark brown nose sniffed hungrily at the parrot painted in the center. Then he centered his attention on the wide bands of tortoise-shell ringing the plate. A slender paw tapped on the tortoise-shell surface, and the cat turned to stare at me.

"What are you doing? What is it that interests you about that plate? Get down from there before your tail knocks the candle down and we all burn to death!"

Chakkri glared at me but obeyed the command.

I finished my brandy, blew out the candles, and opened the door to the bedchamber. "Come along. It is time for me to go to bed. Go downstairs to the kitchen and sleep."

The cat did not move. Grumbling, I picked him up, deposited him in the hall, and closed the door.

Then it hit me. Good God, had I really been sitting there conversing with a cat? What would the *Beau Monde* think if they knew that?

I walked over to the bed and pulled back the coverlet. A furious banging came from the door. Ignoring it, I removed my dressing gown, climbed between lavender-scented sheets, and laid my head upon a down-filled pillow.

"Reeeooowww!!!" Chakkri shrieked.

I sat up in bed my heart pounding in my chest. Muttering curses, and hoping the cat had not roused Robinson or the twins, I threw back the bedclothes and shuffled to the door. "What do you want?" I demanded.

Repeating his earlier performance of hopping over the threshold of the doorway rather than merely walking across it, Chakkri moved sinuously past me and leaped onto the bed. He curled into a perfect circle and fell into a guiltless sleep.

I heaved a weary sigh and slid in next to him. And to think, prior to a few days ago, my only problem was staving off boredom.

❧ 12 ❧

Through no fault of my own, I awoke much earlier than is my custom the next morning. In fact, it was all Chakkri's idea.

A tickling of whiskers on my face was the opening volley. This was followed by the weight of a cat walking across my back. Finally, a loud "Reow!" brought me reluctantly to consciousness.

Chakkri was hungry.

"Go back to sleep, old boy," I mumbled.

"Reeooow!"

The clock on the mantle, a Louis XVI white marble and bronze timepiece, said it was barely nine. An insupportable hour to be awake, but there was nothing for it, so I rang for Robinson. It was some minutes before he appeared.

He seemed a trifle worse for the alcohol he had consumed the evening before. His eyes were shot with red, and yes, when shaving he had missed a line of stubble on his right jaw. "Good morning, sir. Are we awake this early for a specific reason?"

"The cat wants his breakfast."

Robinson glanced over to where Chakkri stood at the end of the bed twitching his tail. He glared at the animal. The cat glared back.

"I shall see if André has any scraps."

A short time later, Robinson returned with a tray containing a pot of chocolate for me and a plate of scrambled eggs with a light cheese sauce for Chakkri.

The cat paced back and forth at the end of the bed, his gaze fixed on the tray.

Robinson held the tray a bit higher. "André had nothing he felt suitable for the feline, so he prepared these eggs."

"Reow!" Chakkri exclaimed impatiently.

"Are the eggs hot?" I asked, thinking I would not like the cat to burn his tongue.

Robinson pursed his lips, leveled me with a martyred look, and plunged a finger into the eggs. "They seem a moderate temperature, sir."

"Very good, then. Place the plate on the floor and then you may prepare my bath."

While Robinson filled the copper tub as well as a Chinese bowl with water for shaving, I sipped my chocolate and watched as Chakkri devoured the eggs, then meticulously groomed himself.

After about an hour, I was also meticulously groomed, complete with a trim of my light brown hair. Robinson pulled a pair of pantaloons from the wardrobe, along with a buff-colored waistcoat and a long-tailed, blue coat. We fumbled through three cravats over the next thirty minutes before perfecting one, but that was to be expected given the early hour.

Once dressed, I left Chakkri sleeping contentedly across the unmade bed. Devil take him! He got to rest while I had things to do.

Since it was far too early to go out, I sat in the dining room partaking of a hearty breakfast of cold meat, eggs, and toasted bread and butter. Working through a pot of coffee, I managed to complete some sketches of livery I wanted made for Ned and Ted, as well as to dash off a quick note to Freddie. I pictured her traipsing about Oatlands, worrying herself to flinders over Miss Ashton. I wanted to assure her she could rely upon me to help the girl.

Around noon, I donned my black velvet greatcoat, selected a silver-topped walking stick from my collection, placed a tall beaver hat on my head, and drew on my gloves.

Because I did not wish Ned and Ted to make their debut as my chairmen until after they were properly outfitted, I once again had two men from the Porter & Pole carry my sedan chair.

Our first stop was in Jermyn Street where the owner of Floris's greeted me with pleasure.

"Mr. Brummell! How delightful to see you in my shop," Juan Floris declared. "I hoped you would come in, as I have put aside a tortoise-shell comb for your inspection."

"Oh?" I said with interest.

Mr. Floris brought out a beautifully carved comb, which he unwrapped from a piece of silk in his leisurely way. "I have just begun working in tortoise-shell and wanted you to be the first to see the results of my efforts."

"Splendid, Mr. Floris, this is a work of art," I said, examining the fine workmanship of the comb. "I should like two of them."

"I only have the one right now, and you are welcome to it," Mr. Floris beamed with pride. "Rest assured, I shall make more now that I have your approval."

Juan Floris was nothing if not an intelligent business-man. He knew if I favored the new comb, word would spread across Mayfair, and he would be besieged with orders.

Mr. Floris was adding up my purchases—a small tooth-brush, essence of lavender for my bedsheets, a container of starch, and a bottle of my favorite citrus fragrance—when my gaze fell on a pretty, ivory-handled, lady's hair brush.

"Er, one moment, Mr. Floris. I should like to add this brush to my bill, please," I said, thinking Chakkri might enjoy a good brushing. The delicate bristles of a lady's brush would be best suited to his soft fur. Freddie has told me she has a servant whose sole duties are bathing and brushing her dogs regularly, a task which must be taxing.

Mr. Floris wrapped the brush in paper. "You are for-tunate. This is the last ivory-handled one I have. Mr. Tim-othy Hensley purchased the other earlier today."

The offhand remark caused me to raise an eyebrow. It seemed odd indeed that Mr. Hensley would be purchasing a lady's brush. His marriage to Cordelia Hensley did not strike me as the sort where one party remembered the other with an unexpected gift. But, then, if not Mrs. Hensley, who was the recipient of the brush?

"A gift for his wife, no doubt," I ventured.

"As to that, I could not say, sir," Mr. Floris replied courteously, but firmly.

Perhaps Mrs. Hensley had commissioned her husband to obtain the brush for her. Something else she had told him to "fetch."

Arriving at White's, I put my speculation aside. Delbert was not on duty at the door, so I did not have to try my brain with Shakespearean quotes. I found I missed the challenge.

Instead, my presence was met with covert glances and a marked cessation of conversation, most likely due to talk of the Crecy's party and my defense of Miss Ashton.

I affected not to notice. I went directly up the stairs to the coffee room where I found Lord Perry sitting alone in a far corner reading the *Times*.

Slipping into a chair nearby, I said, "I am glad to find you here, Perry, as I particularly wished to speak to you. Though I admit I am surprised you could tear yourself away from your bride. Lady Perry looked radiant last evening."

Lord Perry lowered his newspaper. "I cannot spend my time in my wife's pocket, you know."

"No, that would not be fashionable," I agreed, shaking my head at an approaching footman.

"Well, to tell the truth," Perry said, a light coming into his eyes, "Bernadette is refurbishing the nursery, and the noise the workmen are making is abominable."

"Perry! Am I to assume from that—"

"Yes, Brummell. I am to be a papa."

"That is wonderful news," I told him. "We must celebrate. I am escorting Lady Salisbury to the opera tomorrow. Why do not you and Lady Perry come with us? We can make a party of it with a feast at Grillion's, and then the opera."

"It sounds agreeable to me. I shall put the plan to Bernadette and let you know. Now, you wanted to ask me something?"

"Yes. What do you know about Sylvester Fairingdale?"

Perry frowned. "Has this to do with Lady Wrayburn's murder, Brummell? Are you poking about trying to pin the deed on one of the residents of Wrayburn House other than Miss Ashton?"

"It is rude to answer a question with a question."

Perry sat silent.

"Very well, I have perhaps *rued* the day I became involved in this, but I am nosing around. Forgive me for not confiding the specifics to you—"

Perry waved a dismissive hand. "I am only concerned for you, Brummell. Fairingdale has put you in a deuced awkward position. Should Miss Ashton prove to be the murderer after all, well, you shall look a muttonheaded fool. Talk is already spreading across London about last night's scene at Lady Crecy's party. Upon my arrival here at the club, I heard nothing else and finally escaped to this corner."

"I suppose I am not surprised. Perhaps I should present myself at Carlton House and apprise Prinny—"

"You will catch cold at that. He left for Brighton already."

"What? I thought he would be in London the rest of the week."

"Apparently the Prince feels there is a plot against his life, someone who does not want him to become Regent of England. He felt it prudent to retire to his Pavilion at once."

"Good God. What could have put that maggot into his brain? He usually feels supremely confident in the affections of all the English people. I shall have to join him in Brighton, but not until this predicament with Miss Ashton is over. Which brings us back to Mr. Fairingdale."

"Do you suspect him of something more than bad taste?"

"Everyone is a suspect at present, Perry. Do you know the source of Mr. Fairingdale's income?"

Perry considered. "I am not rightly sure, but one would think with him living at Wrayburn House that Lady Wrayburn was providing him with an allowance. I could very well be wrong, though. It is pure conjecture on my part. But I did just hear this morning that, before her death, Lady Wrayburn allegedly told Mr. Fairingdale to leave Wrayburn House. She could not abide his frivolities."

"Is that so?" I mused on this bit of information. If the countess did ask her nephew to leave Wrayburn House, it gave credence to my theory that Mr. Fairingdale was the subject of the incomplete letter I had found in the countess's bedchamber. It would also give the fop even more motive for murder.

I stood. "Thank you, Perry. Let me know about tomorrow night."

"And you have a care, Brummell. This could be a dangerous business."

I left the club and gave the order for home. It was only half past one; too early to pay a call at Wrayburn House. In response to a query I had sent, Miss Ashton had passed along the information that the reading of Lady Wrayburn's will would be held later that afternoon.

The polemen carried my chair to Bruton Street. Once inside, I alighted from the vehicle to find a stranger standing in my hall with Robinson.

"Sir, this is Mr. John Lavender from Bow Street," Robinson informed me, his eyes rounded in concern. "He is an investigator and wishes to speak with you."

"Very well, Robinson."

This, then, was the man who was looking into Lady Wrayburn's death and who had ordered Miss Ashton not to leave Wrayburn House.

Mr. Lavender stood gazing with narrowed eyes at my sedan chair. "Quite a fancy piece of equipage. Ain't seen nothing its equal and thought I'd seen everything. You George Brummell?"

"Yes," I replied faintly, temporarily distracted by the man's appearance. It looked as if his clothes had found him in a wind storm and adhered themselves to his body in a willy-nilly manner.

He was a stockily built man over fifty years of age. His thick, red bristly hair was going to grey. He sported not only bushy side whiskers, also sprinkled with grey, but an enormous mustache.

Most unfashionable.

Worse, he wore a salt-and-pepper game coat with many

pockets over well-worn corduroy breeches tucked into mud-streaked boots. Perhaps he thought a game coat was appropriate for someone who hunted killers.

Looking at the Bow Street man, I fought the familiar urge to seize my quizzing glass and raise it to my eye, judging such an action ill-advised. I told myself it would be better not to have a closer view of Mr. Lavender's clothes. Without the aid of the magnifier, I could see well enough the garments he wore with a lack of concern. Although he did appear clean.

"When you've finished admiring the efforts of my tailor," he said with heavy sarcasm, "I'd like to speak to you in private."

"You may follow me to my bookroom," I said with great dignity.

We left behind a stricken Robinson. No doubt he was in fear of his livelihood lest I be taken away to the roundhouse for some crime; harboring a foreign cat probably came to his mind.

I entered the bookroom and sat behind my desk, motioning the Bow Street man to a chair.

"Look at this," Mr. Lavender said, indicating my small revolving bookcase. "If I had any grandchildren they'd twirl this around enough to drive you mad. But, much to my sorrow, my only child is not married. My daughter prefers to look after other people's children. She runs a shelter for those poor females disgraced and left to fend for themselves by your fellow members of the Nobility— er, pardon me—you're not a lord, are you? Only a plain mister."

"Quite right," I said, unable to decide if the man was

deliberately trying to be annoying. I decided he was. It is a common tactic used to throw off an opponent's self-control. While the man clearly knew not a jot about sartorial elegance, he seemed to be qualified in his work.

"A plain mister, but Mr. Brummell the famous fashion leader no less." He reached into the pocket of his coat and fished around until he found a toothpick, which he placed between his teeth and put to vigorous use.

I did not cringe. As you are aware, I am known for my reserve and my composure.

The movement of his mouth dislodged a crumb of what looked to be oatcake from his mustache. It fell to his knee. He picked it up and popped it in his mouth.

I gritted my teeth.

"Well, that explains it," he said around the toothpick. "You being the leader of fashion, it stands to reason you'd have something like that sedan chair before anyone else. I reckon it won't be long before the London streets are filled with 'em. Perhaps it'll cut down on the number of carriage crashes."

"That was my intention." Two could play at the sarcasm game, and I found I was beginning to enjoy sparring with him.

He nodded. "So the way I see things, meaning no disrespect of course," he said in a way that implied that he did, "you in the best circles of Society have your boredom to struggle with, unlike the rest of us who contend with things like obtaining food, coals for fire, and so forth."

I rose to my feet, which gave me the advantage of looking down on him. It was time I took control of this interview. "The Bow Street police runners rely, for the most part, on private rewards for their efforts. Who has hired you to find Lady Wrayburn's murderer?"

Mr. Lavender remained seated and undisturbed by the question. He surprised me by answering. "Her man of affairs, who is serving as executor of her estate, felt the matter worth looking into. Lady Wrayburn's son, Lord Wrayburn, lives in Italy, but I am told when word reaches him of his mother's death, he will likely return to England."

"Then again, he may not. Distance can sometimes dull interest in family concerns," I remarked.

Mr. Lavender stood and looked me in the eye. "You yourself would be wise to keep your interest in this case, whatever it might be, at a distance."

So that was it. I raised an eyebrow. "Miss Ashton is gently bred and deserves someone to come to her aid against the Runners. I have chosen to be that person."

"And I, Mr. Brummell, am not a Bow Street *Runner*. I am a Bow Street *Investigator* hired to bring her murderer, gently bred or not, to justice. You'll do well to keep your opinions and your efforts concentrated on fashionable fripperies. Do not be interfering in my work."

I had goaded him into a display of emotion. He had definitely burred his r's on the word "interfering," a fact that gave me a small measure of satisfaction and told me he was a native of Scotland.

A heavy silence fell while we took each other's measure. I perceived that Mr. Lavender held the popular belief I think I mentioned before: that I am naught but a foolish dandy.

"I do not see why you would scorn assistance," I said.

"Assistance? From someone who spends his days fig-uring out ways to tie the perfect knot in his cravat?" Mr. Lavender hooted with laughter, then his voice turned grim. "Lady Wrayburn was a countess. A member of the Nobil-ity's murder is a matter of the highest priority in Bow Street. I'm warning you. Stay out of this."

His was to be only the first warning I received that day.

13

After Mr. Lavender took his leave, I sat at my desk thinking about his visit. Overall, it was to my good that the man had seen fit to visit me. I think it is beneficial to know who one's adversary is.

Also, I wondered if his daughter might be of help in finding Lizzie a place, since apparently she ran a shelter for women. Pulling a piece of paper from the desk drawer, I wrote out a quick note asking Miss Lavender if I might call on her to discuss the plight of a young female with child.

I was just sanding the note when Robinson entered the room with the afternoon's post. "Sir, is there anything I can do to help you in your difficulties?" he asked anxiously, passing me a small tray heaped with letters and cards of invitation.

I accepted the stack of correspondence, wondering if

Miss Ashton proved guilty, and I a fool, how many cards of invitation I would receive then.

Glancing up, I looked into Robinson's face and saw the concern there. I would not fob him off with a lie. "Your interest is appreciated, Robinson, as is your loyalty."

Robinson stood a little straighter.

"You have heard about the Countess of Wrayburn's murder, have you not?"

"Yes, sir," he answered, a puzzled expression on his face.

"A young lady is being investigated by Bow Street, and I feel she is innocent, and her name should be cleared. To that end, I have been trying to discover who really killed the countess." There was no need for me to expound on this explanation and involve Freddie.

Robinson seemed intrigued. He said, "While you were out this morning, Rumbelow, the underbutler at Vayne House, came to the kitchen door and told me what transpired last night at Lady Crecy's party. Do you suspect Mr. Fairingdale of the crime? I know you specifically asked me yesterday to find out his plans for the evening."

I raised an eyebrow. "I have underestimated the speed at which gossip travels through all the classes in London. As for Fairingdale, yes, I suspect him as well as just about everyone else at Wrayburn House."

"I see. If you say Miss Ashton is innocent, sir, I know she is. I sent Rumbelow on his way with an admonition not to spread rumors about you. He drinks, you know, and cannot keep his tongue between his teeth."

"Hmmm. I wonder if he knows the footmen at Wrayburn House. Perhaps we could glean some information through him."

Robinson shook his head. "He would not associate with any footmen, sir, considering them beneath his notice. However, he most likely lifts a glass from time to time with Riddell, the butler at Wrayburn House. Allow me to see what I can find out."

"Discreetly, of course."

"Of course."

Our fellowship was broken by the arrival of Chakkri. The cat hopped over the doorway, as was his odd custom, and went to stand by the fire.

Robinson recalled that he was out of charity with me for allowing the feline to remain in the house. He left the room after receiving my instructions to locate the direction of Miss Lavender and see that she received my note.

Flipping through the cards and letters, I found one from Freddie. Quickly breaking the seal, I read:

Dear George,

I am more grateful than I can say for your letter and your kind reassurances. I know I can count upon you, if no one else in this world, to stand by your word and to be my treasured friend. The warmth that this knowledge brings me cannot be overstated. I confess the article in the Morning Post shattered my nerves all to pieces, until your letter arrived to cheer me. You have a way, dear, of taking my troubles away, or at least, of helping me forget them for a while.

My heart is heavy for Rebecca Ashton. I have written her this morning with what comfort I can offer. It is appalling that she has had her freedom to leave Wrayburn House taken away from her in such a manner. One can only feel Bow Street is rushing to judgment and anxious to bring anyone forward as the culprit.

Here at Oatlands, Minney and Legacy's pups grow by the hour. I long for you to visit us, but know you cannot at present. Please keep me apprised of your progress. And never doubt that I am

Yours, ever, and truly,
Freddie

A pleasant glow filled me. I re-read the letter, wishing I could set out for Oatlands at once.

Chakkri jumped up on the desk with a grunt. He sat tall, his long brown tail swishing from side to side endangering the inkstand. I moved it out of jeopardy and perused the rest of the mail.

Casually scanning the invitations to routs, card parties, and soirées, I opened one piece of vellum and my heart jumped in my chest.

It was not a letter, but a drawing. The sketch depicted a gentleman's coat, a most fashionable one, and underneath the coat a cryptic message read: "Stick to perfecting clothes . . . or else!"

I sat thunderstruck. I do not believe I have ever received anything so ugly through the post before now. Not counting my tailor's bill.

Chakkri leaned down, and his inquisitive nose explored the paper. He bared his fangs and hissed at it, the fur standing up on his back and his tail bristling to three times its normal size.

I stared at the drawing and thought it just the sort of cowardly threat Fairingdale might send me. The fop was determined to disgrace me. I could not help but think that perhaps his scheme was meant to cover up his own activities; namely that of poisoning his aunt.

The man's lavish style of dress would land him in debtor's prison at any moment unless he had some sort of unknown income other than from the countess. If he stood to inherit at the countess's death, then he had motive enough for murder. When one added greed to the gossip that Lady Wrayburn was about to turn her nephew out of her home . . .

I tossed the drawing into a drawer and decided it was time to visit Wrayburn House.

The door to Wrayburn House was opened by a young woman I had never seen before. Dressed in a plain cotton black gown, she looked to be one of those voluptuous sorts of girls normally found serving ale in country taverns. Her face was wholesome-pretty, though, and she glanced up at me shyly through her lashes, her head tilted down.

"Yes, sir? Can I help you?" she asked.

"Good afternoon. I am George Brummell, come to call on Miss Ashton." I handed her my card.

The girl opened the door wide. "Please come in, sir. I

am Lizzie. 'Becca—Miss Ashton, that is—told me about you and how you are trying to help her."

I entered the hall and studied the pregnant lady's maid. Her condition was not yet apparent, but the dress she wore fitted loosely.

"I wish to help you as well, Lizzie," I said, entering the hall.

The girl smiled. "There is no need, Mr. Brummell, though I do thank you. The baby's father will provide for us," she said serenely, placing a hand on her stomach.

"Oh?" I expected her to expound on this pronouncement, but was doomed to disappointment.

"Yes, and in the meantime, Mr. Dawlish, the rector, is teaching me my letters so I might better myself. He is ever so generous a man. Always helping those less fortunate. I suppose it's his Bible learning. He's in the drawing room with 'Becca right now."

"And where is Riddell today? Should he not be answering the door?"

Lizzie accepted my hat, walking stick, and greatcoat. Her movements were calm and unhurried. "Mr. Riddell is busy serving the family. They are in the library with the solicitor for the reading of Lady Wrayburn's will."

"Is that so? Well, I shall join Miss Ashton then."

Lizzie bit her lip, perplexed. "I suppose it will be proper for you to do so. Yes, I think it will be good. 'Becca and Mr. Dawlish are not alone. That man from Bow Street is with them, sir."

"No need to show me the way," I told her, suddenly in a hurry to join them and hear what Mr. Lavender had to say. I threw open the double doors to the drawing room and stopped.

Rebecca Ashton, dressed in black, stood in the center of the room. Tears flowed silently down her cheeks. The rector stood beside her, one arm lightly about her waist in a protective manner. Mr. Dawlish glared through his spectacles at Mr. Lavender, who held a book in his hand.

Only Miss Ashton appeared happy to see me.

"Mr. Brummell, how good of you to come, and at this particular moment too," she said, raising a lace handkerchief and swiping at her tears impatiently.

Mr. Dawlish acknowledged my arrival with a curt nod.

Mr. Lavender eyed me with disapproval. "Ah, here he is himself. Come to give advice on fashionable mourning attire, I'm sure, since I know after my warning he would not be here for any other reason."

I inclined my head in his direction. "My limited intelligence prevents me from doing otherwise."

Miss Ashton ignored the exchange. "Mr. Brummell, it is just as you surmised. Someone has taken my journal and sent it to Bow Street! Now Mr. Lavender thinks he has proof that I meant Lady Wrayburn harm. Why does he not see that I did not? And I cannot believe anyone in this house would steal my property, wishing me to be accused, taken away—" She broke into fresh tears.

The rector gave her shoulders a bracing squeeze. "No one believes you killed Lady Wrayburn. I doubt even Mr. Lavender here truly believes it. He is just trying to blame the murder on someone, anyone, in order to prove his worth to his superiors."

"That is a low accusation," Mr. Lavender said frigidly.

Miss Ashton drew a deep breath and regained her control.

"I quite agree with Mr. Dawlish," I said. I shot the Bow Street man a mocking smile. "Mr. Lavender no doubt hopes to gain the reward provided by Parliament for felony convictions, so he might indulge his passion for—" I stopped myself with an exaggerated frown. "Oh, dear me. What is it you hunger for, Mr. Lavender? Surely not clothes," I ended, raising my quizzing glass.

"Justice," the Bow Street man said succinctly. "And I'll have it, I promise you."

He turned to Miss Ashton. "What is your explanation for this?" He read from the journal. " 'Today I could have cheerfully wrung the countess's neck when she made a public spectacle of me at Mr. Talbot's auction.' "

Miss Ashton's chin trembled. "It is not what you think."

"She was merely airing her frustrations, a perfectly human thing to do," Mr. Dawlish cried hotly, defending the woman he obviously cared about. "It is cruel of you to make more of it than that. Indeed, it is heartless to have read Miss Ashton's private thoughts in the first place."

Mr. Lavender looked at the rector as if he was not quite sane. "I am conducting an investigation into the murder of the Countess of Wrayburn. I'll read whatever I please if it means bringing her murderer to justice. Furthermore, I have not heard one solid explanation today which would lead me to believe that I do not have the guilty party already."

"But you also have nothing tangible to take to a magistrate," I said. "Else you would be carting Miss Ashton here off to the roundhouse."

"Don't you be telling me my job, laddie," Mr. Lavender said, pointing his finger at me.

"I would not presume to do so. I am merely stating the obvious. And if you have finished your questioning, I would advise you to leave. Miss Ashton is not looking at all well, and I am certain you would not wish to be responsible for her becoming ill," I said, perceiving Miss Ashton had grown quite pale.

Mr. Dawlish nodded his agreement. "Mr. Brummell is correct," he said, though it seemed to pain him to concur with me. "And do not think to interrogate Lizzie either. In the Bible, Moses warned that men should not create turmoil in the presence of a woman who is with child."

Mr. Lavender popped a toothpick in his mouth. His gaze did not leave Miss Ashton. "There is no need to trouble the pregnant lass. No, I'm off to see Dr. Profitt to question him on the nature of the poison used to kill Lady Wrayburn, and how readily available it was to anyone in this house."

"Do give the good doctor my regards," I said. "Tell him that potion he mixed to cure the stomach disorder I endured after foolishly trying a dish of haggis was most efficacious."

Mr. Lavender bit his toothpick in half. His freckled complexion grew as red as his hair when he heard this slander of Scottish cooking.

Shoving the broken toothpick into his pocket, he delivered a warning that did not bode well for the woman I believed innocent. "Miss Ashton, remember that you are not to leave Wrayburn House. If you attempt to do so, you will be arrested at once."

14

Miss Ashton swayed where she stood.

"Lean on me, my dear," the rector said, guiding her to the settee. "Mr. Lavender is gone now, and you are safe."

"But for how long, Mr. Dawlish?" Miss Ashton murmured weakly. "How long will it be before he returns to arrest me?"

I poured a glass of wine from a decanter on a side table and brought it to her. "Please try to be as calm as you can under the circumstances. It is difficult, but you must try. I am working to discover the killer."

Miss Ashton drank the wine, and a bit of color returned to her pale cheeks. "Mr. Brummell, I heard what happened last night at Lady Crecy's party, that Mr. Fairingdale made public your defense of me. I cannot help feeling mortified that your good name is now at stake in this as well."

Mr. Dawlish curled his lip. "Fairingdale is a useless

popinjay. He cares for nothing but selfish pleasures. Attending a party while in mourning and dancing, as I hear he did, is most improper. Mr. and Mrs. Hensley are no better. They are going to the opera tomorrow night as if nothing untoward has happened."

I took a seat opposite, not missing the fact that the Hensleys would be attending the opera the same night I had agreed to escort Lady Salisbury. That was all for the better, because I would have more of an opportunity to study them.

Though I viewed Sylvester Fairingdale as the probable killer, I wanted to keep an open mind. Besides, I would have to obtain evidence to present to Mr. Lavender if I accused the fop of the deed. I could not just tell the Bow Street man that Mr. Fairingdale was guilty because he dressed badly.

"Mr. Fairingdale's uncouth behavior toward me is of no consequence," I assured Miss Ashton. "What matters is that you and Lizzie are safe, and that we strive to discover who really killed Lady Wrayburn. By the way, I met Lizzie in the hall. She seems most certain that the father of her baby will take care of them."

Miss Ashton dropped her lashes under my intent gaze. I sensed she knew the identity of the baby's father. As the silence grew, it became apparent she would not speak on the subject. Lizzie had most likely told her in confidence, and Miss Ashton was not the sort to betray her.

"As to Miss Ashton's safety," Mr. Dawlish suddenly burst out, his hand placed in a proprietary way on her arm, "I have offered her the protection of my name—"

"Mr. Dawlish!" Miss Ashton gasped, swinging around to face him. "I beg you not to—"

The rector interrupted her with heat. "I am convinced that Mr. Lavender and his cohorts at Bow Street would treat a rector's wife with due respect. And, if you wish it, we could even provide Lizzie with a home. Despite what Lizzie claims, it has been my sad experience in these matters that the cad who fathers the baby rarely lifts a hand to help. Lizzie and the child would flourish in a place where the Bible guides behavior. Indeed, there can be no better atmosphere for a child to grow up in. Why can you not see that this is the best plan? Why have you refused me, when you know how much I care for you?"

"I have told you, what I feel for you is friendship, nothing more." Miss Ashton's cheeks were certainly pink now, and I could not blame her.

Mr. Dawlish's romantic words and promises should have been spoken in private. Apparently, they already had been without success. I could see clearly just what an independent lady Miss Ashton was. Another woman in her circumstances might welcome the sanctuary the rector offered, regardless of whether she loved him.

Clearing my throat, I said, "As to Lizzie, I have learned of a woman who is the directress of a shelter for women. I am inquiring into the suitability of her establishment for Lizzie in case it is needed, and will report back to you shortly."

Miss Ashton sat in a state of embarrassment, and merely nodded her head at this plan. Mr. Dawlish's expression reflected his deep frustration at being refused his heart's desire. A film of perspiration glistened on his forehead.

A shout of laughter, followed by loud voices coming from the direction of the library, served as an interruption. I rose and opened the door to the drawing room.

A man carrying a sheaf of papers hurried past us. The family solicitor, no doubt. Apparently, the reading of the will was over. Lizzie, still on duty in the hall, let him out the front door.

Sylvester Fairingdale and Mr. and Mrs. Hensley strolled out of the library. My gaze immediately fell on a smirking Fairingdale. Yes, I mused, he was exactly the sort who would have sent me the drawing.

Then, I looked at the married couple.

Mr. Hensley appeared relieved.

Mrs. Hensley had a smug smile on her face.

Mr. Fairingdale sauntered toward us. Today, his coat was a vibrant lemon color. "I always knew the old squeeze-purse hated me. Ha! Two shillings and a lecture on my wastrel ways! Oh, that's rich indeed!"

Miss Ashton glared and turned away when Mr. Fairingdale ceased laughing and raised his quizzing glass at the bosom of her gown.

"Be quiet, Sylvester," Mrs. Hensley admonished. "We know you've plenty of money from your Uncle Williams. And all you have to do is spend summers with him in Bath. You're lucky the countess never succeeded in convincing Uncle you are a wastrel."

Shock held me rooted to my place by the doorway. Fairingdale did not need Lady Wrayburn's money. Fairingdale had a wealthy benefactor, the previously unknown recipient of the countess's last letter. Fairingdale had no motive to kill Lady Wrayburn.

"Would anyone care to join me for a drink?" Mr. Hensley asked, wiping his brow with a linen handkerchief and heading for the brandy decanter.

"I would," I responded.

Everyone else trailed after him into the drawing room.

Mr. Fairingdale said, "Pour me one as well." Moving past where I still stood motionless, he paused and spoke in a low voice, "Defending that pretty piece of goods will be your downfall, Brummell. But then, I feel sure under my leadership London will become a more colorful place," he taunted, looking through his quizzing glass at my subdued coat.

"Impossible," I said, forcing my expression not to change. "Despite a marked resemblance to the species, you could not lead a parched peacock to water."

I moved away and accepted a glass of brandy from Mr. Hensley.

"Mr. Brummell!" Mrs. Hensley trilled. "Do come over here. I want you to know that on your advice I purchased the new Egyptian-style crocodile sofa! Now that this tedious will-reading business is over, I shall be able to fill Wrayburn House with all manner of sphinx heads, serpents, and sarcophaguses. I shall be the envy of all my friends!"

"Indeed," I remarked. "Such items will be quite fitting for Wrayburn House."

Out of the corner of my eye, I saw Mr. Hensley toss back another drink. Then, he quietly said, "My mother left you a small bequest, Miss Ashton."

Miss Ashton's hand flew to her throat. "Oh, I did not expect—"

"The countess must not have had a chance to change her will," Mrs. Hensley said archly. "But then, I imagine she did not expect to be murdered."

Mr. Hensley acted as if his wife had not spoken, a tactic I was sure he often employed. "I have already extended an offer for you to remain here as long as you need to, Miss Ashton."

"Timothy!" Mrs. Hensley hissed.

"And that offer is still open," he finished.

Mrs. Hensley's face mottled with rage.

I swallowed the remainder of my brandy in one gulp. I felt disgusted. Disgusted with myself for following the wrong path toward a resolution of the crime and disgusted with Lady Wrayburn's family for their callous treatment of her death. I wanted, no needed, to get away from Wrayburn House and sort out my thoughts.

Ready to take my leave, I crossed to Miss Ashton's side. She was deathly pale once again, no doubt from Mrs. Hensley's obvious belief in her guilt. She, too, needed a respite from the family.

Mr. Dawlish looked about to speak, but I was before him. "Miss Ashton, I have kept you from your rest long enough. I know you wished to retire to your room. Please forgive me." There, that should give her a gracious way to escape.

She managed a weak smile. The rector helped her rise.

"Good day," I said to the company in general and walked from the room.

Reaching the hall, I surprised Lizzie dreamily brushing her short curls in the mirror. She quickly pocketed the brush and retrieved my things. "It was a pleasure to meet you, Mr. Brummell. I know you are trying to help 'Becca."

"Yes, I am," I said, slipping on my greatcoat. "By the way, the night of the murder, Lizzie, did you hear anyone go down to the kitchens?"

The girl frowned, then said, "I was in my room in the attics, sir, and didn't hear a thing. However, I know 'Becca could never do anything so evil as to poison anyone."

"Have you any idea who could?"

The girl's pretty face was a blank. "No."

"Here is my card," I said, extracting a square calling card from a silver case. "If you need anything or if you think of something that might shed light on the murder, come around and tell my man, Robinson, who you are."

Lizzie's face brightened. "Or, since Mr. Dawlish is teaching me my letters, I could write you a note."

Smiling at the triumph on Lizzie's face at her achievements, I left the house.

My smile soon disappeared, as the pleasure I took in Lizzie's pride evaporated. I was in a glum mood when I entered my house.

Robinson took one look at my face and poured me a large measure of claret. "Sir, has something else happened?" he asked, taking my greatcoat and hat.

"Nothing I understand," I bemoaned.

Climbing the stairs with Robinson behind me, I said, "I shall be going out for the evening. It will not do for me to remain at home. I must be seen in my usual good humor by as many people as possible. Otherwise, it may be perceived that I am taking Fairingdale's taunts seriously."

"An excellent plan, sir. While you are gone, I shall step around to The Butler's Tankard and see if Riddell is there." The tavern is a popular gathering place for male servants. "Oh, and perhaps it will cheer you to know André has prepared your favorite lobster patties for dinner."

I sighed. "That is welcome news."

We crossed into my bedchamber, and I stopped. Chakkri was on my bed with my package from Floris's in front of him. The paper was torn and the contents scattered. He held the tortoise-shell comb between his paws.

"Put that down!" I commanded.

His intelligent blue eyes gazed at me unconcerned.

I walked across the room and snatched the comb from his grasp.

"Reow!" he cried in protest.

Examining the comb, I found he had done no damage aside from a faint set of teeth marks on one end. Even so, with the cat's penchant for fine things, I was amazed that he would treat the carefully crafted comb with such disregard.

"That was a bad-cat thing to do, Chakkri," I scolded. "I am sure you were attracted to the string tied around the package—or was it the tortoise-shell of the comb?—but either way it is no excuse for marring one of my possessions."

Chakkri looked at me askance. Then he hopped down to the floor and went behind the screen. Shortly thereafter, a scratching sound could be heard coming from his tray.

I turned to Robinson. "About the container you chose to hold his sand—"

But Robinson stood with an appalled look on his face.

Between two fingers he held the box of starch I had purchased at Floris's. "If you find the stiffening in your cravats inferior, sir, I should be willing to pack my things and leave at once."

"Why, no," I said, perplexed. "The starch we currently use is quite acceptable. I purchased this thinking it would be a convenience."

Robinson regarded me with the look of one dealt a supreme insult. "A convenience? Sir, I spent months experimenting to discover the exact formula for the best starch."

"Is that so? A job well done then. You may throw the one from Floris's away."

Robinson did just that and then hurried to the washstand to fetch water for shaving. His demeanor was a trifle chilly over the starch incident, but life went on. "Would you like a salad with dinner, sir? I could step downstairs and ask André to prepare one."

I sat under Robinson's ministrations during The Dressing Hour, but, for once, my thoughts were only half on dressing for the evening. That should tell you the extent of my chagrin.

Robinson's mention of salad reminded me of Fairingdale's clothing at Lady Crecy's party. Which made me think of the man himself.

I had been so sure Fairingdale was responsible for Lady Wrayburn's death!

He would be the sort to commit murder in a nonviolent way. He would be the sort to send me that drawing, which, in my view, was a cowardly thing to do. He would be the sort to murder for money.

Only there was the rub. It turns out he did not need the money.

Everything had pointed to him. Or had it been just my wanting him to be the murderer that made it seem so?

"Sir?" Robinson said, holding aloft a cravat.

I raised my chin so he could wrap the material around my neck. The thought crossed my mind that I deserved to be choked for allowing personal prejudices to interfere with my investigation. Mr. Lavender was right. I should leave the work to the professionals.

I lowered my chin, creasing the linen material of the cravat in just the right way. The cloth around my neck triggered the mental image of Miss Ashton with a hangman's noose around her pretty neck. I shuddered.

"Cold, sir?"

"No, I am fine." When was the last time a woman had been hanged in London? It did not happen often, but it was certainly possible for someone who committed a heinous crime. Poisoning your employer would fit into that category snugly. Of course, she might only be sentenced to be transported. Australia was the popular place England sent their criminals. Another dreadful fate. No one bathed there.

I must not and would not give up easily. Too much was at risk. Miss Ashton's life. My reputation. Freddie's good name.

Freddie's favorable opinion of me.

I would continue to try my best, although I am no expert like John Lavender. I simply must bring the real murderer to justice.

Slipping into a Saxon-blue coat, I said, "If you do speak

with Riddell, find out what he knows about Mr. Hensley in particular."

"Very good, sir."

"Did you send the designs for Ned and Ted's livery round to Guthrie?"

"Yes, sir. The garments will be ready tomorrow. Mr. Guthrie was honored you chose him."

"Well, Weston would have been a bit much for servants' livery. I am not one to go to extremes, you know."

Robinson's mouth dropped open.

(Yours did too? How singular.)

"Where are Ned and Ted?"

"They have been seeing the sights of London, sir, like the country bumpkins they are," he replied, then pursed his lips.

I put my feet into polished black pumps and walked to the dining room.

"Do you wish me to send for some men to carry your sedan chair, sir?"

"That will not be necessary tonight. I am bound to meet up with friends and will no doubt travel about with them."

Robinson went downstairs to get my dinner. I walked across the hall to the dining room.

"Reow!"

Sitting down, I glanced up and saw a brown face with twitching ears, an overactive nose, and blue eyes perusing the table. Chakkri sat like a person in a chair across from me.

"You rogue! Get down from there!"

At that moment, André himself entered the room carrying a heavy tray. The Frenchman's dark, wavy hair was combed back from his sallow face. The large, white apron he wore over his massive girth was unmarred by a single spot.

The chef spied the cat and grinned. "Ooooh, the little one will not eat the fishheads, sir. He likes only André's cooking! *N'est-ce pas*, my little one?"

"Reow," Chakkri answered and jumped down from his place to rub at André's ankles. The chef chuckled.

André presented me with my plate of lobster patties and my salad. Then, he took an extra plate—of my good china, mind you—and cut one of the patties in small pieces the cat could manage. All the while, Chakkri purred and gazed up at André adoringly. The scamp!

"If it pleases you, sir, I shall place this plate on the floor for the little one."

I waved a careless hand. "As long as he does not eat at the table."

André laughed and set the plate down. "No, that would be indulging him, and we would not want to do that."

He watched the cat eat for a moment, a wide smile on his face, before going back downstairs.

Chakkri and I relished our meal. When I finished, I left him cleaning his face with a well-licked brown paw.

Downstairs, Robinson opened the front door for me. I stood a moment on the threshold pulling on my gloves. "Do not wait up for me," I instructed. "I shall be very late."

"If you say so, sir," Robinson replied. Then, "Er, where will you be going besides your usual clubs—White's, Boodle's, Brooks's . . ."

I raised one eyebrow severely.

Robinson appeared uncomfortable, but pressed on. "It is just that you never tell me your whereabouts on these evenings you stay out all night."

"You are correct. I never tell you." With those words, I walked down the front steps without looking back. I understood Robinson's curiosity, but would not gratify it.

Meeting up with Petersham at White's, the two of us decided to attend Lumley Skeffington's play, the one I had promised him I would view.

After the theater, Skiffy, Scope Davies, and a young friend of Skiffy's, a struggling actor named Edmund Kean who had yet to make an appearance on the London stage, and I all went around from club to club, drinking and gaming and celebrating the play's success. We were a merry party, except perhaps for young Kean, who appeared somber even while growing quite drunk, and who kept trying, without success, to persuade Skiffy to give him a part in the play.

I presented the appearance of one without a care in the world, which was exactly what I desired. Petersham and I worked on a diagram for the snuff box I had promised him. It came out brilliantly, despite our being rather inebriated.

At last, as we were into the wee small hours of the morning, I bade my friends farewell.

And that is all I wish to disclose about that evening. The relaxation I indulged in after I left Petersham is something I prefer to keep private.

But even the distraction of its pleasure did not cease the endless need I felt to uncover Lady Wrayburn's murderer. Nor did it lessen my personal vow not to stop my search until I could hand the criminal over to Mr. Lavender personally.

No matter who he or she might be.

❧ 15 ❧

Because I returned home when the sun was already shining, I did not rise until a rather advanced hour. How advanced? Let us say the muffin bells were ringing outside, and they normally start at about four o'clock.

Chakkri tried to get me to start my day earlier. He shattered my eardrum around ten, with a loud "reow," demanding his breakfast. I stumbled out of bed, opened the door of the chamber, and advised him to go downstairs to the kitchen and give André his order.

A short while later, the cat returned and scratched at my door howling until, awake again and frustrated, I got up and let him back in. Perhaps it would be necessary for me to leave my door ajar so he might come and go as he pleased, I reflected before falling back to sleep.

That afternoon, during The Dressing Hour, I ignored Robinson's Martyr Act from my slight the night before and perused my post. There was a note from Perry saying that Lady Perry was feeling unwell. It was nothing to be alarmed over, merely one of the trials of her condition. They regretted they could not join Lady Salisbury and me at the opera.

I was writing out instructions for having a hamper of sweets made up by Gunter's and sent along to Lady Perry as she was partial to the confectioner's treats, when my attention was caught by another letter.

Rather, it was not a letter, but yet another drawing. It was of the same fashionable coat depicted in the first sketch, but this one was worn by a ghastly human skeleton. Underneath was the command, "Stay out of the murder investigation."

My pulse jumped, and a chill ran through me. Suddenly, I felt vulnerable to the person who drew the sketch, who must be the murderer. Before, when I thought it Sylvester Fairingdale, I felt no fear. Now, I wondered if Robinson checked all the doors and windows at night before we retired.

Then, my anxiety turned to anger. How dare someone threaten me? I would not give in to these cowardly warnings. Weston was in the process of making three coats for me. I would not force Robinson to select one of them for me to wear in my coffin.

I folded the drawing before Robinson could discern its contents. "Did you see Riddell last night at The Butler's Tankard? Oh, and I shall wear the Venice-blue coat."

"Yes, sir, I did," Robinson said, pulling the chosen coat from the wardrobe. "As you directed me, after I felt he had consumed enough ale to be talkative, I inquired about Mr. Hensley."

"And?"

"Well, sir," Robinson said, brightening. He could never remain angry at me for long, especially when he had a choice tidbit of gossip to convey. "It seems that Mr. and Mrs. Hensley are not at all happy in their marriage."

Studying myself in the tall mahogany-framed dressing glass, I said, "That is evident."

"Be that as it may, sir, it seems Mrs. Hensley suspects her husband of infidelity. He has not visited her bed in many months."

"I do not know if I could blame him," I murmured, struggling with the folds of my cravat.

"Here, allow me, sir," Robinson said, lending his aid to the campaign of cravat creation. "The interesting part is that she believes it is Miss Ashton with whom her husband is being unfaithful."

My hands stilled, but my brain galloped along. Now that was interesting. Here might be the person who wished Miss Ashton harm. For if Mrs. Hensley thought her husband was having an affair with the young woman, and wished him to return to her own bed, she would logically take steps to end the affair. Could it be that Mrs. Hensley was the one to remove Miss Ashton's journal from her desk, read it, and after finding its contents damning enough, turn it anonymously over to Bow Street?

Or, could she even be so desperate as to poison the milk herself, knowing it would cast blame upon Miss Ashton?

I suddenly remembered how Miss Ashton had leaped to Mr. Hensley's defense when Mr. Dawlish had accused him of wishing for his inheritance prematurely. Could she have done so out of a finer feeling for Mr. Hensley? Was that also the reason she remained steadfast in her refusal of Mr. Dawlish's proposal of marriage?

And what of Mr. Hensley? Miss Ashton had reluctantly admitted Mr. Hensley had been on the point of leaving Wrayburn House "for a walk" the night his mother was poisoned. I wondered if this was a frequent custom of his. It seemed unlikely when London was rife with pickpockets and footpads whose trade flourished under the cover of darkness.

A knock at the front door prevented me from further ruminations on these fascinating conjectures.

Robinson finished helping me into my coat, then hurried downstairs to answer. He returned a moment later with pursed lips. "Sir, a young female is most insistent she see you."

"A lady?"

"No lady would call at a bachelor's quarters," Robinson scoffed.

I stood very still. My grey eyes probably resembled the North Sea as I glared at him, willing him to remember that Freddie had come to visit.

Robinson caught my meaning. He swallowed, made a slight cough and said, "That is to say, this young woman is unknown to us, and an *unknown* lady would never call at a bachelor's quarters."

I relaxed my posture. "Did she give her name?"

"Yes, sir, Lydia Lavender," Robinson responded, then his eyes grew wide. "Do you think she is a relation of the investigator from Bow Street?"

Ah, yes. I had sent her a letter requesting permission to call upon her. Evidently, she felt no need to conform with the rules of modern society, and had taken it upon herself to call upon me.

"She is his daughter. Escort her to the drawing room, Robinson. Offer her wine and cakes. I shall join her presently."

But that plan did not suit Miss Lavender.

Robinson returned to my chamber, his face pink with indignation. "Sir! Miss Lavender expressed a desire to see the revolving bookcase her father described to her. She insisted on being shown into the bookroom."

I restrained a chuckle. "Very well. I shall meet her there."

I left Robinson muttering about how improper it all was, and went downstairs.

Pausing at the entrance to the bookroom, I saw a slender young woman in a serviceable pale blue gown standing on a stool reaching for one of the volumes on a high shelf. To enable her to stretch higher, she balanced precariously, revealing her blue stockings and neatly turned ankles.

She had dark red hair, not quite auburn, but definitely much darker than her father's, with a plain, high-crowned bonnet covering most of it.

Although I said nothing, she perceived my presence. "Have you actually read this copy of Mary Wollstonecraft's *Vindication of the Rights of Woman*, Mr. Brummell?"

"Yes. I have read all the books in this room."

Grasping the volume in triumph, she stepped down and faced me. Her beauty was startling. The hair I thought to be merely a dark red actually sparkled with gold flecks. Her eyes were brilliant green and her complexion! Ah! What a delight. No freckles, which might have been expected with her Scottish heritage, marred its ivory surface. Instead, here was the smooth, glowing translucence of the finest porcelain. Sèvres could accomplish no better.

She appeared to study me as closely as I regarded her. "Mary Wollstonecraft is a beacon of light in the darkness of ignorance. How do you feel about her ideas?"

Her speech was well-modulated, without a trace of a Scottish accent. I thought a moment before replying. "I concur with the author's feelings that there is a great injustice in the way women are treated presently, and agree that if women should desire learning, that books and tutors should be provided them. However, I cannot go along with her thoughts on women supporting themselves by useful work. Women should, instead, be treasured and valued for their companionship," I ended, my thoughts drifting to Freddie.

"What if they wish to work? What if they desire an occupation, rather than merely to be a companion to some gentleman of means?" she said. "What if, Mr. Brummell, *there is no gentleman of means?*"

Miss Lavender's eyes shot sparks.

I found I did not quite know how to handle such a passionate speech. In Society, ladies avoided overt displays of strong emotion. But then, this woman was not a member of Society. "Please do sit down, Miss Lavender. I see Robinson brought cakes. May I pour you some wine?"

She sat in the chair opposite the desk and accepted the glass I offered. "I perceive you do not wish to debate with me on the topic. I accept that. For now," she said and grinned. "You are a famous man, Mr. Brummell."

"Which, I imagine, is why we skipped the formality of introductions?"

The impudent Miss Lavender ignored this sally. "I admit I was surprised when I received your note asking to meet me. You will forgive me for coming to you rather than sending you a note giving you permission to call? I wished to see what a bachelor's residence looked like, I grant you."

"And now you have done so, and you can add it to the catalogue of your life's experiences."

She chuckled, then turned serious. "Does this have something to do with the murder my father is investigating? For if it does, you are wasting your time appealing to me. My father respects my opinions, but makes his own decisions when it comes to his work. He would like me to spend my time on other pursuits."

I tilted my head and reflected. "Allow me to venture a guess. He would prefer you to be raising his grandchildren?"

Her full-throated laugh filled the room. "Faith! You don't have to be around Father for very long before learning that, do you?"

I took advantage of her good humor to present my case. "I know of a young woman who is with child and may soon need a place to go."

Miss Lavender's expression changed. "Is the child yours?"

"Good God, no!" I expostulated.

"There is no need to take offense. Isn't it common

knowledge that the countryside, the stews of London, and even the ballrooms of London are filled with the Nobility's bastards?"

I drew a deep breath. "I cannot argue with that. The girl in question is a lady's maid named Lizzie."

"So we are indeed speaking of matters pertaining to Lady Wrayburn."

"Yes, but her lady's maid had nothing to do with her murder."

Miss Lavender regarded me thoughtfully. "Perhaps Lizzie herself is not guilty, but her condition might have been what led to the crime."

"If you are speaking of Miss Ashton, and her defense of Lizzie to her now deceased employer—"

Miss Lavender waved an airy hand. "I don't want to know. I have enough in my dish without trying to solve murders. My father must have told you I run an establishment for destitute and downtrodden females."

"Yes, which is why I wrote you. Have you room for Lizzie, should she need it? She says the baby's father will provide for them, but I have my doubts."

"How wise of you, Mr. Brummell," she said with derision. "Members of the Nobility rarely accept responsibility unless forced."

I sat forward, alert. "How do you know the father is of noble birth? Have you been told his identity?"

Miss Lavender took a sip of her wine. "No, I haven't. But it is obvious, isn't it? For if he were a butcher or a shop-keeper he would have stepped forward by now."

She was probably correct.

There was a short silence, then I said, "Will you help her?"

Miss Lavender *leaned back in her chair* and regarded me. Most unladylike, yet it did not appear unseemly when she did it.

"Mayhap we can strike a bargain, Mr. Brummell. I'll help Lizzie, but in turn you must help me."

"I do not know what you mean," I told her frostily, expecting a request to introduce her to some peer of the realm.

"Let us speak without any roundaboutation," she said.

"Have we not been?" I replied with a raised eyebrow.

She nodded, conceding the point. "You travel in the highest of circles, Mr. Brummell."

I braced myself for what I was sure was coming next. She would ask me to introduce her to some lord or another.

"You know all their little secrets, don't you?" she asked, her green gaze pinning me in my seat. "You know who has fathered children out of wedlock, who has abandoned a girl to her fate."

I could think of many such men, unfortunately.

"What I want you to do is gently drop a word or two in those particular *gentlemen's* ears about my shelter and, more specifically, how it is always in need of contributions. My mother left me a small inheritance which I used to set things up, but it has long been depleted."

I admit I was stunned. Was that all she wanted? Money for her shelter? This unselfish need was the one she wished to be fulfilled? I suddenly saw beyond her porcelain-like skin and the appealing figure hinted at beneath her gown, to a beauty not seen often enough in the world.

I cleared my throat. "I feel sure there will be opportunities for me to pass along the name of your shelter and its needs. And I shall be certain to do this when and where it will be likely to kindle a guilty conscience."

Miss Lavender smiled. "Thank you, Mr. Brummell. You amaze me. I had not thought you'd be willing to assist me. My shelter is called Haven of Hope. You may send Lizzie to me at any time."

She held out her hand for me to shake. Surprise held me immobile for an instant. Ladies of my acquaintance may present knuckles to be kissed, but they rarely offer a hand for a gentleman to shake.

I accepted her firm handclasp.

"Reow!"

Miss Lavender turned around to see that Chakkri had entered the room. She squinted, then bent down to examine him more carefully. "What a beautiful cat." He stood calmly under her scrutiny, then purred as she patted his fawn-colored fur.

After a few minutes, I led her to the front door and opened it for her. She passed through the portal, then looked back. "As to Mary Wollstonecraft, I did not mean to imply she was perfect. She suffered for many years of her life from an unrequited love."

With that, she turned and descended the front steps with a sprightly tread.

I closed the door, suddenly thinking of the feelings I held for Freddie.

"She has gone, then, sir?" Robinson said, intruding upon my thoughts. I had not heard him enter the hall.

"Yes," I replied absently.

"Imagine. A *bluestocking* calling on you, of all people." Robinson exclaimed, using the term commonly used to describe a undesirable female with "too much" learning.

"Oh," I said, as I headed up the stairs to my room, "I believe they simply matched her dress."

16

When darkness fell that evening, it could hardly compete with the thick fog hanging over London, winding yellow fingers of haze through the cobblestone streets.

I hired a coach and called for Lady Salisbury at her home at No.20 Arlington Street. Seeing the heavy diamond necklace, earbobs, and three matching bracelets her ladyship wore, I was glad I had chosen to carry my walking stick that concealed a rather deadly sword.

The astute marchioness was a step ahead of me. "Dismiss that vehicle, Brummell. We shall travel in my Town coach."

This was a lumbering old vehicle, done in the first style of old elegance, with two of Lady Salisbury's footmen, armed and riding on the backstrap. Thus, we were provided with not only an impressive appearance, but an added measure of safety.

The marchioness had declined my invitation to dine at Grillion's, saying her digestion was delicate. This was an out and out bouncer, I knew, having seen her put great quantities of food into her tiny frame and never suffer for it. I could only conclude that while the temptations of the opera were enough to take her from her husband for the evening, she would not leave James to take his supper alone.

"I shall be the subject of envy with you on my arm tonight, my lady," I told her once we were on our way and had exchanged *bon mots* about other members of Society.

She rapped me with her fan. "You'll be talked about, but it won't be because of me. What news have you regarding the Countess of Wrayburn's murder?"

I shrugged. "I have my theories."

"Hmpf! You'll need more than theories to keep Miss Ashton from Newgate and your reputation undamaged. Facts, boy, facts. That's what you need," she said, adjusting the folds of her emerald green silk gown. "Facts, and the identity of the real killer would do the trick."

"What do you know of Mr. and Mrs. Timothy Hensley?" I asked, ignoring her good-natured taunt.

The coach rolled to a stop before she could answer. A footman let down the steps and opened the door. The marchioness accepted his hand and alighted from the vehicle. Taking my arm, she said, "I know they have arrived with your favorite crony, Mr. Fairingdale, and are bearing down on us this very moment."

I looked up and saw she was correct. That beastly

woman, Mrs. Hensley, led the way like a general commanding troops.

"Mr. Brummell! Mr. Brummell! How are you this evening? It does so enliven a person's spirits to see one's *friends* when one goes about," she proclaimed in a loud voice, making certain she was heard by other people arriving at the opera house.

Greetings were exchanged all around. Lady Salisbury's manner was cool. She nodded in her grand way at the Hensleys, and gave Mr. Fairingdale's carrot-colored coat a decided look of revulsion.

"I hope you don't plan to come to Almack's dressed like that, Fairingdale. I shall have to tell Mr. Willis to shut the door in your face," the marchioness declared, referring to the fashionable assembly rooms and the gentleman who guarded the entrance.

The fop laughed. "Your sense of humor, my lady, is much to be admired."

"I am not funning!" said the outspoken marchioness.

Mr. Fairingdale's brows drew together, but he quickly recovered.

We had gravitated inside the Opera House where hundreds of candles burned brightly. Tiers of boxes rose up the sides of the theater, filled with haughty members of the *Beau Monde* dressed in their finest in order to best show up their friends.

The Hensley party followed us like sheep.

Mr. Fairingdale, perhaps miffed at Lady Salisbury's acid comment after all and wanting to direct attention away from himself, raised his quizzing glass at me. "I say, Brummell, is that a blonde hair on your coat?"

I glanced down to see one of Chakkri's short, fawn-colored hairs on my sleeve. I raised one of my well-manicured hands and pinched the hair between my fingertips. Holding it up to the light, I allowed myself a smile, then a rapturous sigh. "I never discuss my amours," I declared. Ignoring his sour look, I escorted a chuckling Lady Salisbury to her box.

Society's chief reason for attending the opera was to be seen. Hearing the music was secondary.

Bowing and nodding to numerous acquaintances, Lady Salisbury and I were finally able to take our seats in her private box. Quite a bit of whispering heralded our arrival. The marchioness held her head proudly, and, since the Hensleys were mercifully across the theater, we escaped further chatter.

"You did not answer my question about the Hensleys, my lady," I said, helping her adjust her shawl across her shoulders. "I dislike pressing you, but there are two women whose futures are in peril."

"Well, let me see. You'd have to be blind not to discern that Cordelia Hensley is a pushing sort of woman. She cares for nothing but her place in the world and impressing her circle of friends."

"An accurate assessment."

"As for her husband, he's a mealy-mouthed mawworm who never has a word to say for himself. Although," she went on, her black eyebrows raised, "there's a rumor going about that he has finally got up enough nerve—or something—to stray from his marriage bed."

"Yes, I heard that as well. I am having a difficult time

putting Miss Ashton in the role of mistress. She is too well-bred."

"Ha! Look around you and see all the 'well-bred ladies' who are flirting outrageously. But wait, did I hear you say *two* women were in jeopardy? Who's the other?"

"Lady Wrayburn's personal maid. Lizzie is with child and may not have a place to go."

Lady Salisbury turned sharply and looked at me. "The lady's maid, eh? Hmpf! Wouldn't surprise me if that's where Timothy Hensley has been diddling. Runs in the family, you know. His father, the late Lord Wrayburn, was known in his younger days to have impregnated one of the boys' governesses. Can't remember the girl's name right off, but it will come to me, and I'll pass it along. Lud, but Lady Wrayburn had a fit of hysterics. Tossed the poor girl out on the streets without a reference. At any rate, you know what they say about the apple not falling far from the tree. Mark me, the child is Hensley's."

"Lady Salisbury, you are the best of women!" I cried suddenly, and kissed the marchioness soundly on the cheek.

She giggled like a schoolgirl; people pointed and whispered, but then the singer came on stage, and everyone was diverted.

I sat ignoring the music, my mind racing. Lizzie and Mr. Hensley! Of course. A mental image of Lizzie brushing her hair in the hall of Wrayburn House flashed through my head. She had been using an ivory-handled brush like the one I purchased for Chakkri. The one Mr. Floris said he had sold to Mr. Hensley.

The pieces of the puzzle were falling into place.

Number one: Mr. Hensley, miserable in his marriage, turns for comfort to Lizzie, the docile lady's maid so different from his wife. He genuinely grows to care for her, hence the gift of the hairbrush. A baby will be the result of his affection.

Number two: Lady Wrayburn learns Lizzie is with child when Miss Ashton lets the secret out at Talbot's auction. Mr. Hensley is paralyzed with fear. For he remembers what happened to the pregnant governess many years ago. His mother will surely throw Lizzie out the same way she had that other unfortunate girl. Especially if she finds out her own son is the father. Why, she might even be so incensed that her son is following in his father's footsteps, so to speak, that she might force Mr. and Mrs. Hensley from the house. Such an act would infuriate Mrs. Hensley, who cares so very much for her place in Society. Not to mention what would happen if Mrs. Hensley discovered her husband was sleeping with one of the servants rather than her.

Number three: Mr. Hensley, desperate, slips downstairs and poisons his mother's nightly glass of milk. Then, unable to bear staying in the house while she dies, he goes for a walk. Miss Ashton saw him leave.

This would also explain his generosity in allowing Miss Ashton and Lizzie to remain at Wrayburn House, even over his wife's protests.

Number four: Mrs. Hensley, while knowing her husband is being unfaithful, mistakenly judges Miss Ashton to be his mistress. She subsequently searches the girl's room, hoping to find evidence of the affair with which to confront Mr. Hensley but, instead, finds Miss Ashton's journal.

The journal contains no words of love for Mr. Hensley, but Mrs. Hensley is undaunted. When she reads what can be construed as threats on Lady Wrayburn's life, she promptly turns the journal over to Bow Street, in hopes that Miss Ashton be will accused, removed from the house, and Mrs. Hensley's troubles will be over.

But she had the wrong girl.

17

Excitement produced by my new deductions infused me with energy. After escorting Lady Salisbury home, I made the rounds of my clubs. I hoped against hope that I might run into Mr. Hensley, but I had no luck. Only rarely could he be found at one of the clubs; the leash Mrs. Hensley kept him on was rather short, and most often did not extend beyond the walls of Wrayburn House.

Another missing person was Petersham. He and Munro were frequently among the late-night gamblers, but they, too, were absent this evening.

I did stumble across the jovial Scrope Davies, who invited me to join him and had the decency never to mention Lady Wrayburn's murder. He did want to extol the virtues, or lack thereof depending on your point of view, of his current ladybird and his winnings at the racetrack. During this discourse, we polished off three bottles of White's best claret and participated in a rewarding series of whist games.

Thursday morning, or rather, I should say, afternoon, I woke with a strong sense of expectation. Today, I would wring a confession out of Mr. Hensley. With a somber mien, I would watch him be carried off by John Lavender, who would have a newfound respect for yours truly.

This pleasing prospect moved me to draw a sheet of paper from my portable writing desk and pen a note to Freddie.

My dear Freddie,

Progress has been made in the matter uppermost in both our minds. You will be happy to know an unexpected conclusion to the case is imminent, clearing your young friend's name once and for all.

I should hope to put everything behind me by tomorrow afternoon, in time to travel to Oatlands for your weekend gathering. Need I say how very much I look forward to seeing you? Believe me, I am,

Your most devoted servant,
George Brummell

P.S. If I bring treats for the puppies, will I incur the wrath of the other one hundred dogs?

"Ah, Robinson, there you are. Here is a letter for Oatlands. See that it is delivered at once. What is the day like?"

The valet drew back the curtains. "There is a drizzle, sir."

"Too much to expect otherwise, eh? Is that the post?"

"Yes, sir. And the livery you ordered for the twins arrived from Guthrie. I shall bring it up for your inspection. Will you be wanting breakfast?"

I opened a note from Lady Salisbury and scanned it quickly.

Brummell,

The governess at Wrayburn House who was dismissed all those years ago was named Miss Turtleby. My cursed memory couldn't bring it to mind last night, but I knew it would come to me. Just wait until you get to be my age, and you'll see what I mean.

Mary Amelia

I recalled that Robinson waited for my answer and tossed the missive aside. "Yes, breakfast after I dress. Do bring the garments from Guthrie to me straightaway. I cannot wait to see how the livery turned out."

"You are in fine spirits today, sir. May I hope this means the unpleasantness surrounding Lady Wrayburn's death is over?"

"Not quite over, Robinson, but it should be resolved in time for us to travel to Oatlands this weekend."

I perceived a slight shudder from the valet. The dog hair at Oatlands, you know. Which reminded me. "As much as I hate to say so, I am afraid you were correct about Chakkri."

Robinson's face lit. "You are going to give him away, sir?"

I scowled. "No! It is just that one or two of his hairs have found their way onto my coats. Last night, Mr. Fairingdale remarked on it."

Robinson dropped the Chinese bowl he was getting ready to fill with water for shaving. Fortunately, it landed without breaking on the thick Persian carpet. "Mr. Fairingdale noticed a cat hair on you, sir?" Robinson said feebly. "I-I shall retire to the country then. Perhaps a vicar at some impoverished parish might be persuaded to employ me. Or worse, a huntsman or some other sporting type . . ."

He swayed, and I feared he would faint.

I tossed the post aside and scrambled out of bed in time to ease him into a chair. "Now, now, man, get ahold of yourself! I handled the matter, implying the hair belonged to one of my inamoratas."

This calmed him. The color gradually came back into his face, and he was able to speak with some conviction. "There is nothing else for it. Since you refuse to get rid of the animal, each time before you leave the house, I shall have to brush your coat once more."

"Good man!" I responded bracingly.

Robinson suddenly looked toward the door. His lips pursed.

"Reow."

"Hello, Chakkri," I said, seeing the cat hop across the threshold to the room.

Robinson sprang from his chair and picked up the Chinese bowl from the floor. Without further delay, he went to get the livery and give orders for my breakfast. He glared at the cat as he hastened off.

I climbed back into bed, propping myself up on pillows.

Chakkri joined me, and together we perused the rest of the post.

"Here is a note from Perry," I told the cat.

Last night when I came home, albeit a bit tipsy, I had decided that Chakkri understood every word I said. Besides, I could talk to him about all sorts of things and not have to worry about him repeating them. I had no human I could trust to keep as silent as Chakkri.

"Let us see what Perry has to say."

"Reow." Chakkri nestled in the crook of my arm, his blue eyes fixed on my face. I read aloud.

Dear Brummell,

Bernadette sends her grateful thanks for the hamper from Gunter's, though she fears she will soon grow rotund. Silly girl. At any rate, though the treats were welcome, she is not doing as well as I should like. We may decide to repair to Brighton for a while to get away from the soot of the city.

I have been at Bernadette's side constantly, and as she declares she is ready to throw a chamber pot at my head for hovering, you may find me at White's later today. I wish to hear how matters stand with your "difficulty."

Yours,
Perry

"First Prinny was off to Brighton, now the Perrys, Chakkri. I shall have to visit the seaside town myself. But not until Mr. Hensley has been brought to justice, and I have visited Freddie."

"Reow," he said, placing an agreeable paw on my shoulder.

Thoughts of justice reminded me of Mr. Lavender. "What do you think? Shall I send round a note to the Bow Street man telling him I have solved the case?"

Chakkri bounded from the bed. He walked purposefully over to the crescent-shaped side table and leaped lightly to its polished surface. He went directly to the Sèvres tortoise-shell plate and began rubbing his face against it.

"Get down from there! Are you determined to knock that plate to the floor? I appreciate your interest in Sèvres, but do you have to keep going back to that one plate?"

The cat turned and stared at me. "Reeooow!"

I waved my hand at him. "I do not have time for your foolishness. I have to dress and confront a murderer."

Chakkri muttered something and swooped down from the table. The next sound I heard was a furious scratching of sand coming from behind the screen.

While waiting for my bath to be filled, I decided to delay telling Mr. Lavender of my theory until after I had conducted my interview with Mr. Hensley.

Sipping chocolate, I reclined against my pillows and indulged in a happy vision of Mr. Lavender having to report to his superior that Beau Brummell had solved the case of Lady Wrayburn's murder. Then I frowned. Perhaps it might be best for me to be magnanimous and allow him to take the credit.

Yes, the more I thought of it, the better this latter plan sounded. After all, I would not want Society to know I had to find the real murderer to prove that my opinion of Miss Ashton's innocence was accurate. Better to let the world think I had not troubled myself to give the business a further thought subsequent to my pronouncement at the Crecys' party.

Robinson returned with a load of garments over one arm. Ned and Ted, still wearing their country clothes, followed, carrying the copper bathing tub.

"Hello there, Mr. Brummell, sir. You still in bed?" one of the twins said. "Oof, this tub is heavy even for strong lads like us."

Robinson's lip curled. He handed me a piece of the livery to inspect. It was done in blue and gold, the gold of a shade chosen not to clash with the twins' blond hair, but rather to set it off to advantage.

"Yes, I am certain Robinson appreciates your filling the tub downstairs and bringing it up. It saves him the trouble of carrying pitchers of hot water upstairs," I said.

"Indeed. I hardly remember what my life was like before the arrival of the twins," Robinson declared in a wistful tone.

I glanced at him sharply, but his mockery had gone over the twins' heads.

I ran my hands over the blue velvet material of the livery and noted the cut of the sleeves. Guthrie had followed my detailed instructions to the letter, bless him. "By the way, how the devil do I tell you two apart?"

"I'm Ted. I'm the smart one," he said with a deal of pride.

Robinson snorted. "Between the two of them, they do

not have the intelligence of a turnip," he said for my ear alone.

"Look at that!" the other one, Ned, suddenly exclaimed. He pointed at Chakkri, who had come out from behind the screen and had vaulted to the top of a high-backed chair by the fire. The cat sat proudly, staring down his whiskers at the twins and twitching his tail.

Ned squinted. "I ain't never seen no animal like that there before. It's a cat I reckon, but a funnier lookin' one I never did see. I wonder what his parents were? Reminds me of the time one of Mum's pigs had a litter of the strangest lookin' animals you ever did see. The girl pig had wandered off one day and come back pregnant. The only thing I could figger is that a wild dog had got to her, but Mum said that weren't possible. Still, they had brown spots on 'em, not at all like Mum's Yorkshire pigs that're pure white. You should have seen the set of privates on one of the piglet boys. Zookers!"

Ned fell victim to a sudden fit of hilarity until he comprehended that Chakkri was staring at him without blinking. The country boy abruptly stopped laughing and crossed himself. "Hey Ted, that there cat or whatever it is, is lookin' at me like the devil. What was I sayin' anyway?"

Robinson drew a deep breath and let it out slowly.

"You may retire to your rooms and dress in these clothes," I said to the twins. "Present yourselves to me in two hours' time. I should be bathed and dressed by then."

The twins turned and started to leave the room. As they were crossing into the hall I heard Ned say, "It's gonna take him two hours to get ready to go out? Ted, I've never heard of somebody takin' so long to dress. Even the time

I caught that sickness from the pigs, the one where my joints were all swollen and my skin was . . ."

Thankfully, they were out of earshot and I could hear no more.

"It might be wise to order the twins to remain mute when you use them to carry your sedan chair about Town, sir," Robinson advised. "Oh, and shall I just step downstairs and make certain André is preparing bacon to go along with your breakfast?"

Clad in their rich new livery, Ned and Ted were everything I had imagined. What a sight they made carrying my sedan chair! Two tall, healthy, identical young men dressed in all their blue and gold glory could not help but attract notice. Especially when they were carrying an extraordinary sedan chair occupied, if I may say so myself, by the leader of fashion.

How onlookers gaped as we traversed the streets between my rooms and Wrayburn House. Ladies and gentlemen alike stopped in their tracks to stare. Quizzing glasses were raised, gloved hands pointed, and heads nodded knowingly. Yes, of course that was Mr. Brummell, in his new sedan chair. Yes, that is the most fashionable of woods, calamander. Yes, trust the clever Beau to have everything that matches, down to his chairmen.

I experienced no small measure of contentment as I watched the interplay through the glass. You would feel the same, come now, admit it.

Soon enough, we arrived at Wrayburn House. Riddell was back at his post and did not let any evidence of surprise cross his features when I asked for Mr. Hensley. His rheumy eyes did almost start from his head when he saw Ned and Ted, but, being a well-trained servant, he quickly recovered.

After taking my greatcoat, hat, and gloves, he bid me to wait while he determined if Mr. Hensley could see me. It was not long before he returned and directed me to the library.

Mr. Hensley rose unsteadily from where he sat behind a large desk. "Brummell! Come in, come in. Good of you to visit, to be sure, but I daresay there's been a mistake. Aren't you here to see 'Becca, ah, Miss Ashton, that is?"

I stood politely, as he had not offered me a chair. I fixed an expression of amiability on my face while noticing Lady Wrayburn's younger son had been indulging in a bottle of Jamaican rum. The seal lay on the desk, and the bottle was half empty. His cravat hung loosely knotted, and his hair was in a disarray that was anything but artful. It looked as if he had been raking his hands through it in frustration.

In fact, Mr. Hensley gave every impression of a desperate man.

18

"*I should meet* with Miss Ashton, of course, but things are looking rather bad for the girl just now," I said with a slight shake of my head. "I thought perhaps you might offer me a bit of Dutch courage first."

"Happy to do so. Sit down," Mr. Hensley waved me to a chair and clumsily resumed his own seat. A drawing book lay on the desk, open to a likeness of a country landscape, but before I could get a good look at it, Mr. Hensley snapped the cover shut. "Nothing Dutch here, but I've a good Jamaican rum," he said in a weak attempt at humor.

His hand shook as he poured me a glass.

I sat sipping the rum—not my favorite—and waiting expectantly.

It did not take Mr. Hensley long to become unnerved by my silence. "Pity about Miss Ashton," he bemoaned. "A decent family, you know. Father a viscount."

"I doubt with her background she would be capable of—"

"There's the rub," Mr. Hensley interrupted, pouring himself another glass. " 'Course she couldn't have done Mother in. Not that anyone in this house would give a snap of their fingers if she had." He tried to snap his fingers to illustrate his point, but failed.

"Hmmm. As bad as that?"

Mr. Hensley swallowed his drink. "Good Lord, yes. And Miss Ashton did her best. Tried to please. But it was impossible."

I tilted my head. "What was impossible?"

"Pleasing Mother! Mother had to have everything just her way, you know. Raised hell if anyone took a wrong step. Wrong in *her* view, you see. And so much of what I did fell into that category." He tapped the closed drawing pad. "Hated my fiddling about with pictures."

I experienced a flash of memory of my own father chastising me severely for not being more athletic when I was at school and at Oxford. I ruthlessly pushed the image from my mind, focusing on Mr. Hensley. "It must have been difficult for you and your brother growing up."

Mr. Hensley sat back in his chair. "My brother's moved to another country. May return now that Mother's dead. And as for me," he shrugged. "I don't think of it any more. The whippings on her order, the hours locked in my room, her coldness. It's nothing to me. I've shut myself off from it."

"That would be for the best, I imagine."

"But there's no getting away from her, is there? Here

she is, making life hell for Miss Ashton." Mr. Hensley looked away.

"And Lizzie," I added softly.

"What?" His gaze cut back to me.

"It must be particularly hard for you about Lizzie."

Mr. Hensley sat forward and poured yet another drink, his gaze now on the bottle. "I don't quite know what you mean."

I held out my glass. "May I?"

"Oh, yes, yes." He rushed to pour the rum, spilling a bit on the desk near the drawing book, but he did not notice.

"Thank you," I said. I took a moment and sipped my drink. "What I meant was it must be disheartening for you to watch the girl increase with your child."

Mr. Hensley stared at me. I gave him my best sympathetic expression.

"She told you, eh?"

I remained mute, not wishing to lie. He took my silence as an agreement.

"The women in this house seem to confide in you effortlessly, Brummell."

I managed a chuckle. "One of the perils of being a bachelor, I suppose. They must think that as I have no other females to look after, they can rely upon me."

Mr. Hensley raked his fingers through his hair. A full minute went by. Finally, he spoke in a near-whisper, "The devil of it is that I wish I could acknowledge the child as my own."

"That is natural enough," I assured him quietly. "You

must be terribly dismayed, having no heir to claim your estate."

Anger suddenly gleamed in his eyes. "Damn if you don't have the right of it! And a pretty estate it is," Mr. Hensley said vehemently. He was growing very drunk, I thought. "I'm a rich man in my own right, you know. Didn't need Mother's bequest. Hang it all!"

"Is there any chance that Mrs. Hensley might open her heart to the child?" I ventured, knowing full well Mrs. Hensley would rather appear naked at Almack's Assembly Rooms than raise another woman's bastard.

Her husband's answer surprised me.

"I am determined to see this child grow up. Otherwise, I would have paid Lizzie off and sent her away myself. As for Cordelia, I might find a way to convince her," Mr. Hensley declared boldly.

His daring must be coming from the bottle. I wondered if the bravado would last when he sobered. His next words stunned me.

"If I had something to hold over Cordelia, you know, something she would not want anyone else to know. Ever. If you catch my meaning. Then," he said, nodding, "then she'd let Lizzie stay, mark my words. We could come to some sort of arrangement where I would not go to Bow Street, and Cordelia and Lizzie would go away to the country for a while. When they returned, we would produce the babe and say it was Cordelia's. Lizzie would understand."

I doubted that. But I realized Mr. Hensley was trying to convey to me that he believed his wife had poisoned Lady Wrayburn. Was this a tactic intended to throw me off? Despite the rum, did he comprehend he was sitting across from a man bent on learning the identity of his mother's killer?

Or was it possible I had been wrong about him?

Was he innocent of his mother's murder?

Did he genuinely believe his wife had killed his mother?

"Mrs. Hensley and your mother did not get along," I ventured.

"O-ho! There's an understatement. Cordelia wished Mother at the dower house on my country estate. She wanted to rule supreme at Wrayburn House. Change all the furnishings, entertain as hostess, and queen it over all her friends. Mother stood in the way."

Mr. Hensley began to laugh. He still held his glass, the contents shaking violently. "It's all so damned funny. Cordelia is the same as Mother. Never approves of anything I do. Calls my sketches rubbish. Tells me only females should sketch."

His voice rose. "All these years. No babies. Cordelia blamed *me*. Me, did you hear? When all along, it was *her* fault!"

He suddenly slumped onto the desk, his arms cradling his head, convulsed in drunken laughter which quickly gave way to anguished sobs.

I rose to my feet, put my glass on the desk, and went to find Riddell. He needed to see to his master.

Entering the hall, I saw Ned and Ted sitting on chairs waiting for me. Ned was speaking while pointing to a chair leg shaped like a serpent. "If one of those things was real, I'd shoot it."

Riddell, on duty at the door, was trying not to stare at them.

"Riddell, your master needs you in the library."

"Yes, sir," the butler said and began to tread without sound in the direction of the library.

"Mr. Brummell!" a female voice called.

I looked up and saw Miss Ashton coming down the stairs. "What is happening?" she inquired. "I must know."

Her pale face showed the days of strain she had been under.

I kept my voice low so we would not be overheard. "I have just been questioning Mr. Hensley. Did you know Lizzie's baby is his?"

Miss Ashton looked startled. "Yes, she told me. The poor thing needed someone to confide in."

"Of course."

"Mr. Brummell, I do not know what you think of Mr. Hensley, but he has promised to take care of Lizzie and the baby. I believe him."

"In case he fails, I have spoken with a Miss Lydia Lavender. She runs an establishment for women called Haven of Hope. Lizzie is welcome there at any time. She has only to give my name."

"Oh, Mr. Brummell, that is good news indeed. How very kind you are to have done this," she said, reaching out and giving my arm a grateful squeeze. "But I confess to a certain curiosity. Is the lady who runs the shelter a relation of Mr. John Lavender from Bow Street?"

"Yes, she is his daughter. Do not distress yourself. Miss Lavender strikes me as knowing her own mind. She cares deeply for the plight of women who find themselves in difficulties, indeed for all women. I believe she works hard to put her beliefs into practice."

"Really," Miss Ashton murmured thoughtfully. "If I had my freedom, I would assist her, if she would allow it."

"Is that so?"

"Oh, yes. Pray believe me when I tell you my views most likely parallel those of Miss Lavender. For room and board, I would gladly lend my hands to her cause."

"What of Mr. Dawlish? Has he no chance of winning your affections? I hope you do not think me impertinent for asking, but your future is a concern to me."

Miss Ashton smiled. "You may ask me anything, Mr. Brummell, after all that you are doing to help me. I am sorry to say I do not return Mr. Dawlish's regard. He is a friend, nothing more. He has many fine points, believe me, such as teaching Lizzie her letters. And I know she is not the only girl he teaches. But I fear that Mr. Dawlish's feelings sometimes border on an intensity that I cannot like. His fervent beliefs can, on occasion, be over-whelming."

"I understand."

"It is all a moot point, though," Miss Ashton said rue-fully. "For I may not have a choice to make about my future. Should Mr. Lavender come for me . . ."

"Hold on just a little longer, Miss Ashton. I shall speak to Mr. Lavender and see what he learned from Dr. Profitt about the poison that killed Lady Wrayburn. I want to share a theory I have about the murder as well. No, no, I cannot speak of it yet. Concentrate on what you will do once this is behind you. You know the Duchess of York will allow you to stay at Oatlands for a time, I am sure, if you and Miss Lavender are unable to agree on an arrangement."

Miss Ashton nodded.

"Send word to me if you need me, or if you think of anything at all that might be of help. Otherwise, I shall be in touch with you tomorrow."

I turned to go, but she cleared her throat and said, "Mr. Brummell, I do not like to say this . . ."

"Go on," I said encouragingly.

"I have racked my brain trying to think of who would have taken my journal and given it to Bow Street. Though it pains me to point a finger at anyone, I will say that Mrs. Hensley holds me in dislike. I do not know why, but there it is."

"Thank you, Miss Ashton. I shall bear it in mind."

Bear it in mind I did, as the twins carried me through the darkening London streets to White's Club. Indeed I could think of nothing but the Hensleys.

Mr. Hensley's confession to fathering Lizzie's baby; his feelings about his mother; his none too subtle hints that his wife might have been responsible for his mother's death. These things would all be laid out for Mr. Lavender.

And I had not missed the fact that Mr. Hensley liked to sketch. I wondered if his tastes had recently run to drawing gentlemen's coats and skeletons.

It was too late to expect Mr. Lavender to be at Bow Street now, but I did not want to call on him there in any event. My doing so would surely be common knowledge across London within an hour of the occurrence.

No, it would be best to go directly to the Bow Street man's house. I made a mental note to have Robinson find out his direction so I could go there in the morning. I groaned aloud thinking of the early hour when I would have to awaken to catch the man before he went to his office.

Arriving at White's, I tossed some coins to Ned and Ted. "Go round the corner and have a pint of ale. Come back for me in thirty minutes."

"Yes, sir!" Ted cried.

"We will, but the ale won't be the same. I mean as what's made back in Dorset County. That's where we come from—"

"Step along, Ned," admonished his brother.

"—Have the best malt liquor in all of England, least that's what Mum says . . ." Ned trailed away, giving in to his brother's urging.

I walked up to the door of White's. Delbert sprang from his place to open it for me. "Afternoon, Mr. Brummell. Or should I say evening? Was that *your* sedan chair?"

"Yes," I said, stripping off my greatcoat.

"Very nice, sir. If I may be so bold, I would say, 'I ne'er saw true beauty till this night.' " Delbert accepted my things and waited.

"*Romeo and Juliet*, Delbert. Thank you. Ah! Perry, I was just coming up to see you."

Lord Perry descended the stairs from the coffee room. "I am on my way home. I had about given up on you, Brummell."

We stepped to the back of the hall near the staircase, leaving Delbert to attend to his duties. I said, "My apologies. I have been at Wrayburn House."

"Anything new?"

"Perhaps. Let me ask you something, Perry. With you soon to be a father, perhaps you might have some insight. To what lengths would a gentleman go to to protect his interests in his child? Let us suppose the child will be born on the wrong side of the blanket."

Lord Perry let out a low whistle. "That depends entirely on the gentleman. As you well know, numerous men care nothing for their byblows."

"Correct." I thought of Miss Lavender's work and of the pregnant governess, Miss Turtleby, whom Lady Wrayburn had heartlessly dismissed all those years ago. I wondered what had become of her and her baby.

"But then, other men care for all their children, no matter what. They take whatever steps are necessary to provide for their offspring. I tell you, this thing of becoming a parent is awe-inspiring, Brummell. I have insisted on taking Bernadette to Brighton tomorrow. She enjoys the seaside even at this time of year. And I shall do anything in my power to make her comfortable."

"I know you will, Perry. Thank you for your help. Write me with your direction when you get to Brighton. I may be there myself before much longer. I need to mend my fences with Prinny, since I neglected to call on him before he left Town."

"I shall certainly write," Perry said, moving to accept his greatcoat from Delbert. "Have a care, will you? Oh, and Petersham just arrived and is upstairs looking blue-deviled. Seeing you would undoubtedly gladden his heart."

I found the languid viscount sprawled in his usual chair by the fire looking, as Perry had said, sunk in spirits.

"Where have you been?" I demanded, putting up my quizzing glass to study his pallor.

Petersham gazed at me wearily. "Munro and I had a falling out. I went to bed on Tuesday with a supply of claret and told Diggie not to wake me until Thursday. Today is Thursday, ain't it?"

"Yes. Did you get your snuff box from Rundell and Bridge's?"

Petersham nodded dully and pulled the box from his pocket. "It's even better than the one Sidwell had. See how the Venus is done all in gold?" He raised the lid and took a pinch.

I could not help but remove my own snuff box—a Sèvres—from my pocket, and repeat the performance of taking snuff that had so entranced the Prince.

Petersham seemed equally impressed. "Do that rather well, don't you? Egad, I wish I was good at something."

"Upon my honor, Petersham," I claimed, "no one is better at doing *nothing* than you."

This cheered him. "And when I am doing something, I mix snuff to a nicety, don't I?"

I nodded sagely. "You are in the mopes because of a personal matter, I take it?"

"Devil of a thing, one's finer feelings. Gets one into all sorts of trouble." He looked imploringly at me. "Why can't people always be good to those they say they love?"

I thought of Wrayburn House and its generations of unhappy people, but I could not be maudlin when Petersham needed bolstering up.

"Delbert would quote from Shakespeare. 'Love is

merely a madness, and I tell you, deserves as well a dark house and a whip as madmen do.' "

Petersham looked much struck by the sentiment.

I stood and said, "Come on, then. You can take your dinner with me. André has promised beef croquettes for this evening."

The viscount rose, and we walked downstairs.

"And you have not seen my new sedan chair or my new chairmen. Sad to say, it carries only one person, so we shall have to hail a hackney for the ride. But I do want you to see it. Thank you, Delbert," I said to the footman, accepting my things and dropping coins into his hand. "We need Lord Petersham's hat as well. Have my servants returned?"

"Yes, sir."

We stepped outside. Petersham saw the sedan chair and the twins with their golden hair and muscular physiques.

Finally, I was treated to his famous grin.

❖ 19 ❖

Friday morning at the inhuman hour of seven-thirty, I stepped into a hackney cab and gave instructions to be set down in Fetter Lane. I did not want to call any attention to myself by taking the twins and my sedan chair, which was rapidly becoming well known.

In my estimation, Mr. Lavender would not leave for Bow Street any earlier than eight o'clock. I had plenty of time to see him and present my theories regarding the Wrayburn case.

As I traveled north toward Oxford Street in the chilly air and drizzle, I breathed a sigh of relief at getting away from Robinson. Now that I was out of the house, I hoped he would retire to his rooms and not come out until he had slept off his pique.

After dinner the night before, he had utilized his league of servants and their useful gossip to obtain Mr.

Lavender's direction for me. This task he performed without protest. However, once he learned that I had to be dressed and out of the house at a time when fashionable members of Society were just going home from an evening's entertainment or already fast asleep in their beds, he had become indignant. I had had to suffer through his Martyr Act ever since I had risen.

Granted, I had entertained Petersham until two in the morning. Still, if I could function after three hours of sleep, Robinson could have the common decency to remember to *warm* my shaving water and *sharpen* my razor before attacking my face with it. There is nothing worse for a gentleman's complexion than a dull razor.

Robinson was sufficiently miffed about his lack of rest that he went so far as to point out that even Chakkri was still asleep. Amazing how that creature has accustomed himself to my schedule. Chakkri, not Robinson.

Rattling along the cobblestones, my mind was diverted from Robinson's antics. I was struck by how astounding it was to behold the difference in London once one traveled out of Mayfair.

While that stylish area was quiet with sleep, it was a different story when one passed into Holborn. The streets bustled with lawyers, clerks, merchants, and shopowners on their way to work. Vendors cried their wares. Horse-drawn carts carried goods to markets. Chop houses overflowed with breakfast customers. This world was very much awake.

Mr. Lavender had chosen his lodgings within walking distance of Bow Street. When we reached Fetter Lane, I directed the hackney driver to stop toward the end of the road, near Fleet Street.

After paying him, I made my way around the back of Kint's Chop House, grateful that Mr. Lavender's lodgings, situated above the eating establishment, boasted a private entrance. I did not want to attract any undue notice by going through the chop house and using the inside stairs.

When I reached the door I sought, I raised my ebony stick and knocked. A moment passed, and then I heard footsteps. The door swung open.

I was caught off guard by the sight of Miss Lavender's porcelain-like skin and beautiful dark red hair, radiant in comparison with the grey day.

I cannot say which one of us was more surprised.

She leaned forward and squinted at me. Then she drew back, her eyes wide. "Mr. Brummell! I would never to have thought to see you here."

"I hope the shock might not be too much for your system," I told her gravely. The thought that Miss Lavender might be near-sighted crossed my mind. If so, it was puzzling that a practical girl like her did not wear spectacles, even if they were highly unfashionable.

She opened the door wide, chuckling. Today, she was clad in another serviceable gown, this one in a pretty grass green. "Faith! I'm made of sterner stuff than that. But I must say *you* look burnt almost to the socket."

"Good heavens, I shall have to speak to my valet," I said, removing my hat. "Is your father at home? I hoped to speak with him before he went to Bow Street."

"He is. Please sit down while I let him know you're

here," she said, indicating a small, spartanly furnished room obviously used as a parlor.

I laid my hat and stick on a plain side table on top of the current issue of *Hue & Cry*, the police gazette which details the latest swindles and violent crimes. Then I removed my greatcoat. Placing it across the back of a comfortable-looking armchair, I noticed an assortment of pipes within easy reach of another chair, this one upholstered in a plaid material.

The room contained a not unpleasant odor of pipe smoke. I recognized a hint of cherry in the scent. A few paintings graced the wall, two of which depicted scenes of grouse hunting.

"Well, laddie, I've underestimated your powers of detection. You've managed to find me."

I turned around from where I had been examining a painting of the Scottish moors, to discover Mr. Lavender gazing at me with a forbidding eye. He was dressed much the same as he had been on our first meeting: old game coat with many pockets, worn corduroy breeches, scratched boots. I tried not to stare. After all, I was not here to give the man sartorial advice. Much as he might need it.

"Thank you," I said, ignoring the sarcastic tone of his voice. "I hope I am not intruding?"

"And if you are?" he said.

"I believe you will want to hear what I have to say," I replied with confidence. "It concerns Lady Wrayburn's murder."

The Bow Street man considered this. Then he seemed to recall his daughter standing next to him. "Go on back to whatever you were doing, lass. I'll take care of Mr. Brummell."

Miss Lavender looked from her father to me, reluctant to leave. "Surely you will want coffee?"

Before Mr. Lavender could answer, I said, "Delightful idea!"

She hurried away, but not before throwing a knowing smile over my shoulder. Impudent girl! Maybe that is why I found myself liking her.

Resigned to a few minutes in my company, Mr. Lavender sat in the plaid chair, extracted a toothpick from his pocket, and popped it into his mouth.

Taking the seat opposite him, I forced myself to ignore the thin wooden stick moving back and forth. Instead, I concentrated on telling him of my suspicions about Mr. Hensley, concluding with the conversation we had yesterday in the library at Wrayburn House.

I could see he looked doubtful, but he listened attentively, plying the toothpick. At the mention of Mr. Hensley's admission that Lizzie was carrying his child, the Bow Street man leaned forward in his chair.

He removed the toothpick from his lips and held it. "Did Hensley say his mother knew the child was his? Had they quarreled about it?"

"Well, no," I said slowly. "I do not believe Lady Wrayburn had time to find out her son was responsible before she was killed. But there was a longstanding resentment between mother and son. Mr. Hensley told me as much."

"Is that all? Laddie, if every son or daughter killed a parent they resented for one reason or another, we'd not have anyone in London over the age of twenty."

At that moment, Miss Lavender returned with our coffee. She lingered after pouring out the cups. "Mr. Brummell, did I hear you mention the girl, Lizzie, you were wanting me to take in at my shelter?"

"Yes. Lizzie remains at Wrayburn House for the moment." I had risen at Miss Lavender's entrance and remained standing, waiting for her to be seated. She ignored her father's scowl and sat in the chair next to mine. I resumed my seat and took a sip of my coffee. Mr. Lavender did not partake of the refreshment.

He spoke to his daughter. "Am I to understand from that statement, Lydia, that you are previously acquainted with Mr. Brummell?"

"Yes, Father," she answered. I had to admire the innocent way she put it, as if it were perfectly natural that a girl of her station in life would be known to me.

I smiled at him pleasantly. "Indeed. After you were gracious enough to call on me and mention your daughter's work, I sought her out to ask for advice for Lizzie."

There was no need for me to mention how Miss Lavender had defied the conventions by calling on me at my house upon receipt of my letter. Her father looked peeved enough at our connection.

"I must tell you, Miss Lavender, you were correct when you said the father of the baby was connected to the Nobility."

"I am not surprised."

"What will surprise you is that Mr. Hensley has every intention of looking after mother and baby," I said with a bit of triumph, placing my cup on the table. For some reason, I did not want Miss Lavender to have a poor opinion of *all* members of Society.

Miss Lavender raised a well-shaped eyebrow. "Accepting responsibility is an unusual commitment. Most men turn their backs once a girl becomes pregnant. Lizzie is fortunate in that respect."

Mr. Lavender grew impatient. "Mr. Brummell, I fail to see how Mr. Hensley's relations with a servant, and his supposed fear that his mother would learn of it, would have been motive enough for him to kill his parent. Besides which," he went on, consulting a tattered notebook he produced from his pocket, "Mr. Hensley was out of the house at the hour of the crime."

"Not necessarily," I contradicted. "Miss Ashton said she saw him ready to go out before she went down to the kitchen to get Lady Wrayburn's glass of milk. He would have had time to add the poison to the milk before he left."

"Ah, *Miss Ashton* says so, does she? I'd be thinking of a tale or two to tell if I was about to be arrested for murder myself."

"But what about the baby?" I protested. "Mr. Hensley truly wants to be a father to the child. I think he would take any steps necessary to ensure that he is not denied the opportunity to do so."

"Exactly, laddie," Mr. Lavender said, returning the notebook to his pocket. "If Mr. Hensley is as adamant as you say he is to see the babe reared, then he would not risk committing a hanging offense just to avoid his mother's—or, if it came to it, his wife's—ire."

I sat astonished. Mr. Lavender had poked holes in what

I had thought to be a sound theory. But there was one more suspect to be dealt with. "What about Mrs. Hensley? Have you considered her? Her husband all but came right out and told me yesterday that he suspected her of poisoning his mother."

Mr. Lavender sat back and laced his fingers over his stomach. The toothpick was back in action. "Accusing her of murder would be a convenient way of getting rid of an unwanted wife."

"And men have stooped to worse to disentangle themselves from their wives," Miss Lavender remembered sadly. "You know, I once rescued a lady from a madhouse her husband had her committed to so he could live openly with another woman. He'd bribed a physician to sign the papers."

I knew my expression was grim.

Mr. Lavender shook his head. "No, as I told you, Mr. Brummell, I have the guilty party: Miss Ashton. She's responsible for her employer's death. Above anyone else, she had the motive and, according to Dr. Profitt, the opportunity."

"What did the doctor say?" I asked, angry at myself for neglecting to ask earlier and wishing I knew more about solving a crime.

" 'Twas a common enough poison used, kept in any house in London to eradicate bugs. Miss Ashton would have found it readily at hand when she went into the kitchen to get the old lady's milk."

I looked at him steadily. "Anyone in the house could have done it."

He heaved a sigh. "I'm on my way now to Bow Street to get the papers for Miss Ashton's arrest."

I shot to my feet. "She is innocent! Can you not give me another day or two to prove it?"

Mr. Lavender stood. He pocketed the toothpick. "No, I cannot. I told you before to stay out of this."

I took a step toward him. "You are not the only one who has been telling me to stay out of the investigation. I have received two threatening drawings—"

Miss Lavender gasped.

"What?" Mr. Lavender's voice rose. "What kind of drawings? Why haven't you told me?"

"You would only point out you had warned me. The sketches I received depicted a gentleman's fashionable coat and a message to stay out of the investigation. The drawings were another reason why I suspected Mr. Hensley. He had a drawing book in front of him on his desk."

"I'm telling you, you're wrong about him, drawing book or no."

"Perhaps. But *you* are mistaken about Miss Ashton. Why, when she believes me to be investigating the crime for her benefit, would *she* send me those drawings?"

"I don't know," Mr. Lavender said, his puzzled mind working.

"Mr. Brummell's right, Father," Miss Lavender said.

"Unless she doesn't want you to find out she really did commit the crime," Mr. Lavender said at last. "She knows you to be a man of honor who would turn over any evidence against her despite her aristocratic lineage."

"Well, I thank you for thinking me a man of honor."

Mr. Lavender's eyes narrowed. "Just why are you taking such a personal interest in this case, Mr. Brummell? I thought you dandies cared about nothing but your clothes and fancy parties and card playing."

I waved a careless hand as if my reasons were a mere whim. "I declared my opinion that Miss Ashton is innocent at a public gathering. My judgment, my reputation as a knowledgeable gentleman, has been called into question." There was no need to tell him about Freddie.

"I see," Mr. Lavender said, and I sensed he saw more than I wanted him to.

"As a gentleman of honor, I am asking you to delay making the arrest. Just give me today and tomorrow, at least," I said as close to pleading as I would allow myself. I held his gaze until I saw him weakening.

"Sunday is the Sabbath. We observe the Sabbath in this house. Therefore, I won't be working. You're asking me to give you until Monday," Mr. Lavender grumbled, but I could tell he was going to relent.

"What's the harm in it, Father?" Miss Lavender asked. "You've a man posted outside Wrayburn House, I expect, so there's no danger of Miss Ashton running away."

"Course I have," her father barked. He knew he was outnumbered, and who could resist Miss Lavender's charming appeal? "Very well, Mr. Brummell, I don't see how it will make any difference, but I'll wait to hear from you. Only until Monday, though."

Relief swept through me.

The Bow Street man shook his finger at me. It was a mannerism he had employed before. I had not liked it then, and I did not like it any better now. "You'll advise me immediately if you find any proof whatsoever, no matter whom it implicates."

"Agreed," I promised.

"All right. But be aware, unless you discover anything new, first thing Monday morning, I'll go to Wrayburn House and arrest Miss Ashton for the murder of Lady Wrayburn."

I understood all too well.

"Thank you, Mr. Lavender. You shall hear from me. Miss Lavender," I said, giving her a brief bow, "I hope to meet you again."

"I'm sure you will, Mr. Brummell. At the very least, I'll be hearing from some of your friends," she said coyly, reminding me of my promise to urge guilty gentlemen of my acquaintance to make donations to her shelter.

Her father frowned at her. I would be willing to wager the moment I left he would have a stern talk with her about associating with me. I hoped she would not pay him any heed.

A few minutes later, I walked down Fetter Lane, pausing automatically to admire a display in the window of Allen & Butler, Ivory-Box Makers.

My gaze ran over the intricately carved pieces without really seeing them. Instead, I saw the pieces of the puzzle I thought I had put together fall apart and scatter.

I still did not know who killed Lady Wrayburn. And now I wondered if I was capable of finding out who the murderer was.

Or if I was doomed to failure as Mr. Lavender predicted and Sylvester Fairingdale desired.

❦ 20 ❧

After paying the hackney driver, I let myself into my house in Bruton Street. All was quiet. Robinson must have been sleeping and did not hear me come in.

Weary, I climbed the stairs to my bedchamber and stripped off my clothes. My head reeled from the early hour I had risen and my visit with the Lavenders.

The hour was still too early to do anything about Miss Ashton's plight. Who in Mayfair is abroad at nine in the morning, I ask you?

It seemed only logical for me to get some sleep. Perhaps in the course of my dreams I might be able to decide on the next step I should take to help Miss Ashton. And save my own skin.

Donning nightclothes, I moved a seemingly comatose Chakkri over to the side of the bed and eased my tired body between lavender-scented sheets.

My eyes sprang open. I groaned thinking that from now on the scent of lavender would remind me of the bluff Bow Street man. He had granted me a reprieve, though, I must remember. However, his personal grooming habits and his constant employment of a toothpick grated on my sensibilities.

Perhaps I should focus my thoughts on the lovely Miss Lydia Lavender instead . . .

Some time after one o'clock, I awoke. It required a few minutes to convince myself I really was not staying in a Scottish castle, walking the moors with Miss Lavender, her hair tumbling in a charming way down her back.

I reached over and pulled the bell-rope to alert Robinson of my return to the conscious world. In the meantime, Chakkri opened his blue eyes and stretched. With a soft "reow," he came forward to be petted. He batted at my quizzing glass—yes, of course I sleep with it—and purred his contentment at my attention.

About two hours later, I was freshly shaved and dressed in an Alexandria-blue coat, and had partaken of a hearty meal of cold meat, eggs, coffee, and bread and butter. Some of which I shared with Chakkri. Not much affects my appetite, as I imagine you have noticed by now.

I decided to sit in my bookroom, where I have told you I often go to think out a problem, hoping the wisdom of the sages lining the shelves will inspire me to new intellectual heights. I had just gotten comfortable in the chair behind my desk and had pulled out a sheet a paper to write down possible suspects and motives, when Robinson entered carrying a tray with the day's letters.

"Feeling more the thing, Robinson?"

"Yes, sir. And you? How is your investigation coming along?"

"I should hardly raise my efforts to the level that they be called an 'investigation,' " I replied. "But whatever it is, the word 'impasse' comes to mind. Do recollect that we are traveling to Oatlands this afternoon."

"Very well," Robinson said on a sigh.

"It might be best to order a coach now. You know what a crush there can be on a Friday afternoon."

"Yes, sir."

He left, and Chakkri hopped on my desk to assist my reading in the way cats have of being helpful. A few letters slid to the floor under the impetus of his curious nose, and I had to retrieve them.

I glanced hastily through invitations, a letter from Prinny chastising me for not coming to see him, and a note from Lady Crecy informing me her daughter wished to thank me for my kind assistance. Then my gaze fell on a letter from Wrayburn House pressed under Chakkri's paw.

"Give that to me," I commanded him.

"Reeoow," Chakkri howled stubbornly. I extracted it with some effort.

Hastily breaking the seal, I looked to the bottom of the missive and saw it was from Timothy Hensley.

Dear Brummell,

By the time you read this, Lizzie and I will be on our way to Hensley Cottage. Though it is one of my

*lesser properties, I know we'll be happy there, rais-
ing our child. And I have you to thank.*

*I wouldn't have had the courage to leave Cor-
delia before the talk you and I had, which freed me.
I suppose speaking of matters I had heretofore kept
silent about acted as some sort of release, though I
don't know much about that philosophical stuff. I do
know happiness is more important than keeping up
with Society. To the devil with Society's rules!*

*After you left, and when the rum had worn off, I
went to Cordelia and told her all. At first, I tried to
threaten her by telling her I thought it was she who
had poisoned Mother. But Cordelia laughed and told
me to go ahead and make a fool of myself. Why on
earth, she asked, would she hasten the old lady to
the grave and jeopardize everything she'd worked
for—her position in the world and all her possessions—when she only had to bide her time before
Mother suffered a fatal attack of apoplexy during
one of her tirades? I expect she's right. It was purely
wishful thinking on my part that she was guilty.*

*Regarding my involvement with Lizzie, Cordelia
was incensed until I agreed to buy her a new town
house and give her an unlimited budget for deco-
rating it. What it comes down to is that as long as
she can indulge in her extravagances, I daresay she
won't give Lizzie and me nearly the trouble I'd
thought she would. In fact, Cordelia told me that she
rather liked the idea of being a Tragic Figure, as
she put it, whose husband had obviously run mad.*

She thinks she'll attract sympathetic male attention, something she's sorely missed. Imagine that!

Well, I must dash now. Lizzie is waiting. But I could not go before thanking you for helping me make this fresh start. I tried once before, you know. The night of the murder, I slipped out to a posting house to hire a coach, but my courage failed. Now, I need not concern myself about Cordelia nor, it seems, will she concern herself about me. I care only for Lizzie and the baby. Wish us luck, will you?

Yours,
Timothy Hensley

P.S. About Mother's murderer, it's beyond me who could have done it. Perhaps old Riddell. God knows she badgered him enough.

I threw the letter aside, thoroughly amazed.

Mr. Lavender was correct. It was clear Mr. Hensley did not kill his mother.

I had been so sure Mr. Hensley was a feasible suspect. Going so far as to disclose my views to Mr. Lavender.

I sat disgusted with myself, drumming my fingers on the desk top, barely refraining from drumming my head against the wall. At least Mr. Hensley had taken his chance at a new future. I imagined him sketching in the bucolic countryside, free of Cordelia's nagging.

As for the idea that Riddell had committed the murder, that was absurd. I had questioned the butler the day I searched Lady Wrayburn's bedchamber. He would no more have killed his mistress than Robinson would murder me.

Hmmm, wait a bit. Perhaps that is not a good analogy.

In any event, I would wager my best pair of Sèvres candlesticks Riddell had nothing to do with the countess's death.

I dropped my head in my hands. Obviously, I had failed. I was no closer now to solving the murder than I had been the day Freddie had asked for my help. Foolish girl, placing her faith in me!

Chakkri had been watching me and now walked across the desk to rub his face against my head.

I looked up, petted him, and glanced at the clock. It was after three. I needed to rouse myself from my dejection if I was to leave for Oatlands at the usual time of around five. And I must go. I had sent Freddie that note yesterday apprising her of my imminent visit.

And of my good news.

Now, I would have to face her and tell her I had failed. I contemplated going to the Tower where wild animals are displayed and walking into the lion's cage. It might be preferable to disappointing Freddie.

Miss Ashton would expect to hear from me today as well. I drew out a sheet of paper and quickly wrote her a few reassuring lines. There was no need to alarm her by telling her Mr. Lavender would arrest her on Monday unless I could manage a miracle.

I was about to put the rest of the post aside to read later, when Chakkri began sniffing a square of folded vellum. His tail grew to three times its normal size, and he bared his fangs. He bit down on the paper.

I recognized the now familiar black scrawl written across one side. Lunging across the desk, I seized it from the startled cat. Angry at having his toy taken away, Chakkri sauntered from the room in high dudgeon.

I unfolded the paper. It was another drawing from the killer.

This one had no cryptic message printed at the bottom. But then, it needed none. It depicted the Grim Reaper with a quizzing glass raised to his eye. A small figure I could only assume was myself, from the elegance of its dress, was under the death figure's gaze.

I stared at the sketch. Who could have executed it? I examined it carefully, judging it to be intricate work, from a trained artist's hand. Someone of refinement had conceived of this warning, which took more than a measure of intelligence.

Riddell had told me Lady Wrayburn had no friends. The few she had in her younger days had all died. She received little or no correspondence other than from the uncle in Bath, her husband's brother, I think, she had been writing to.

The murderer had to have been someone in the house in order to get to the milk. I had already discounted Riddell. The cook at Wrayburn House had been with the countess for over thirty years and was reputed to have loved her dearly for all her faults. Riddell said there had been no visitors to Wrayburn House from the time the milk had been delivered earlier that evening.

Unless . . . unless the milk had been tampered with *before* it had been delivered to Wrayburn House.

This new theory made my mind spin. If the milk had

been poisoned before its delivery, then *anyone* could have done it.

My head pounded. I needed to get outside and breathe some fresh air, even if it was full of London's smoke and soot. A walk might help me think. Besides, I wanted to get something for Freddie and her dogs to take with me to Oatlands.

I hurried upstairs and retrieved my greatcoat, hat, gloves, and stick. Outside in the street, I made my way around to the confectioners, all the while thinking.

Someone could definitely have added the poison to the milk before it arrived at Wrayburn House. But that person would have had to have known the countess and her household's routine.

Exiting the confectioners a few minutes later with a lacquered wooden box of chocolates for Freddie, I turned my steps in the direction of the toy shop. The day had grown windy. A few autumn leaves flew about my feet.

My thoughts ran on. Even if the murderer knew about the milk being delivered each evening, how would he obtain access to it? Bribe the milkmaid?

At the toy shop, I purchased a half dozen leather balls for the puppies.

I left there and began walking back home. Turning a corner, I paused out of habit at the window of a print shop. It was my custom to peruse the cartoons and caricatures so artfully drawn by Gillray and other noted satirists displayed in the shop's window. They could also be found around Town for the public's amusement. But mostly people viewed them at the print shop where many were for sale. If a particularly fascinating scandal held Society in its grip, people could be found three and four deep craning to get a look at the latest lampoons.

Today as I walked toward the shop, a throng of people were ahead of me. At my approach, they scurried away. Most odd.

I raised my quizzing glass and viewed the offerings. They included one of Gillray's favorite subjects, King George III, or Farmer George as he was sometimes called, rambling about the grounds of Windsor Castle while making wild proclamations about the country.

A second showed Prinny running down the road toward Brighton, a masked villain chasing him. I frowned at that one. Perry had said the Prince had retired to Brighton because of a threat against him. Again, I thought someone must have done a brilliant job of convincing the Prince this was so. Prinny simply would not believe anyone would wish him harm. I decided to visit Brighton at my earliest opportunity and find out what was going on.

Preparing to view the next print, I was interrupted by an obnoxious male voice behind me.

"Ah! There is the man himself," Sylvester Fairingdale cried with energy. "We were just speculating as to your health. Are you feeling cast down? Or perhaps, cast *aside*?"

I let my quizzing glass fall to my chest and turned around slowly to observe Fairingdale looking at me in high glee. Two of his foppish friends stood by him, grinning. Under my steady gaze, they shuffled their feet and grew nervous.

About to give voice to his taunt, I suddenly noticed Fairingdale's gloves. It is the fashion for gentlemen to wear white gloves when dressed for evening entertainments. Mr. Fairingdale had departed from this custom. His gloves were white, in fact, but small red tulips had been embroidered across the cloth. Ghastly!

"How very kind of you to be concerned. As you can see, I am the pattern card of health." I leveled my quizzing glass at his hands. "And I see you are positively blooming, Fairingdale."

One of the fops snickered. "Fancies himself a real Tulip of Fashion, Sylvester does."

Mr. Fairingdale swung around and silenced his friend with a look. Then he turned back to me, his chin in the air. "Are you admiring your likeness in Gillray's print? Don't let us keep you. That is," he said, pointing at the window, "unless your poor eyesight requires your obtaining assistance to find your way home."

I stood speechless—for once—as the three laughed shrilly and went on their way. My brows drawn together, I scanned the prints trying to discover what that idiot Fairingdale referred to.

Then my gaze fell on the third lampoon, and I understood.

It was a wicked caricature of yours truly with a blindfold on. Standing in front of the cartoon "me" was a woman portrayed as Beauty, obviously Miss Ashton. She held a silver tray with a glass full of some liquid, resting on it. Floating in the liquid was a skull and crossbones. Underneath, the caption read: "Can it be that Prinny's Favorite and the Arbiter of Fashion has been blinded by Beauty?"

I drew in a sharp breath.

The tide had begun to turn against me already.

21

Oatlands Park is situated in Surrey on the southern bank of the Thames River. It is not far from London, which is one of the reasons for its popularity. The other reason is Freddie herself.

She is the most genial of hostesses and cares not if a man talks loudly, drinks excessively, or loses consciousness on her drawing room carpet. An atmosphere of relaxation and good fellowship prevails. The informal company is almost always made up solely of men.

True, one must dislodge a dog if one wishes to sit down. There are between twenty and thirty house dogs at any given time scattered about at Oatlands. They have free reign and command the best chairs by the fire. But this is a minor inconvenience.

I delayed my departure from London until after six that Friday evening so that I might persuade Petersham to come along with me. His estrangement from Munro continued. I felt the viscount needed to be surrounded by friends, and a little distance between him and Munro might improve matters.

In addition, I selfishly wanted someone nearby to keep me from shooting myself after I told Freddie I had not solved the case of Lady Wrayburn's murder.

So it was that our unhappy party of four rode in a hired coach out to the country.

Chakkri was the only contented creature in the vehicle. He entered his basket without complaint and promptly fell asleep. The basket was now on the floor between Petersham and me.

Petersham sat opposite me, brooding, and occasionally taking snuff.

Next to me, Robinson, who is wretched every time we visit Oatlands because of the dog hair, sat clutching my mahogany dressing case and glaring at Mr. Digwood.

Diggie, as he is known, is Petersham's valet. Robinson and Diggie hate one another with a passion. Diggie knows his master would replace him with Robinson if he could. Robinson knows that Diggie feels superior because Lord Petersham is a viscount, not a mere mister. Had there been any way to obtain two vehicles, I most certainly would have done so in order to avoid witnessing the exchange of nasty glares between them.

Just then, I noticed Robinson casting a pointed eye at Petersham's pleated shirt cuff. His gaze lingered long enough for all of us to observe it and Robinson's pursed lips.

I braced myself.

"You know, Mr. Digwood," Robinson said with good will positively dripping from his tongue, "I have often found that pleats that are ironed poorly can indeed be corrected."

Diggie, a portly fellow whose brown eyes tended to bulge, went red.

Petersham extended his arm and looked critically at his cuff.

Robinson blithely continued. "It is true. I have had a special pleating iron made, but you could almost duplicate its splendid effect by ironing the pleats between two layers of muslin dampened with vinegar."

From the look on Diggie's face, I should not hold myself amazed to find Robinson with his throat slit, the smug smile he currently wore wiped forever from his lips.

Petersham dropped his arm and looked appalled.

Robinson was satisfied.

By the time we arrived at Oatlands, darkness shaded the Palladian-style building. Old Dawe—that is the name everyone calls him—opened the door to us, and we could hear laughter coming from the drawing room. The party was already merry.

"Mr. Brummell, sir, it's good to see you again. And Lord Petersham. I hope you are well, my lord," the ancient retainer welcomed us. He is a small man, past sixty at least, with sparse grey hair. Surprisingly strong for his age, he is fiercely loyal to the Royal Duchess.

After settling in and changing into evening clothes, I walked out of my room and down the stairs, anxious to see Freddie. I met her in the hallway just outside the drawing room.

"George!" she cried. She smiled, and my breath caught at the light in her blue eyes.

I bowed low, then took her hand and pressed a warm kiss on her bare knuckles. "Freddie, how can you be more beautiful every time I see you? Animal dander must have a salubrious effect on your person."

"Stuff and nonsense! I see your eyes twinkling," she bantered. "Only I *am* glad you are here. I do so wish you to meet Minney's puppies." She glanced about and then whispered, "And I cannot wait to hear how you untangled the mystery of Lady Wrayburn's death."

I felt a knot form in my stomach.

A great shout of laughter came from the drawing room. The door swung open, and the untroubled face of Scrope Davies appeared in the doorway. I dropped Freddie's hand.

"Brummell! Thought someone said you were here. Come on in and settle a bet between Yarmouth and me. He says Joe Norton beat John O'Donnel in a fight last week. I'm not having it."

"Can Yarmouth think of nothing but contests between pugilists?" I asked, annoyed that my privacy with Freddie had been interrupted.

Scrope shrugged. "I don't know. Never thought about it. Yarmouth fancies himself an amateur pugilist, you know. But, see here, there's money on it, so stop dawdling and join us."

He turned away, but out of the corner of my eye I saw Petersham traipsing toward us. "May I see you alone?" I asked Freddie in a low voice.

She nodded. "If the weather is fine tomorrow afternoon, we can walk together at one."

"Very well," I said, reluctant to leave her. Our eyes met for a brief moment, but then Petersham reached us, and I fell in with him and the others. I saw Freddie throughout dinner and the remainder of the evening, but there was no further opportunity for private conversation.

Happily, the next day turned out to be warmer and the sun shone.

At the appointed hour, I strode outside—steering clear of the monkeys—and meandered around the beautiful grounds—watching where I stepped—until I came to a paddock where Freddie housed a herd of kangaroos and ostriches.

She stood, arm outstretched, feeding one of the kangaroos from her fingertips. Her curly brown hair was held back from her face by a yellow silk bandeau. Clad in a golden-color spencer jacket over a sprigged muslin gown, she appeared young and carefree.

All at once I was struck with a terrible premonition of impending doom. Lady Wrayburn's killer eluded me, and I must tell Freddie. I could not bear the thought of her thinking ill of me.

"Freddie," I called tentatively from a few feet away.

She turned and smiled at me while brushing crumbs from her gloved fingers. Her cheeks were pink from the sunshine. "Are they not glorious creatures, George?"

I glanced at the kangaroos. "Tolerable. But you have not seen my Chakkri. Yes, you may look amazed. I have succumbed to the allure of owning a pet and have acquired a cat."

"A cat! How wonderful. Come, let us take a stroll and you can tell me about him. It is a rare day, and you know

I enjoy being outdoors." She tucked her hand into my arm, and we began walking along a path that ran next to the pine woods.

I told her all about Mr. Kiang and the cat who had come into my life, and promised to bring him to her sitting room so she could see for herself his many charms. She listened enthralled and clapped her hands when I described how Chakkri would only eat the sort of food I ate.

"He sounds so much like you, dear," Freddie said.

"What?"

"Oh, goodness, George, this is making me laugh. Here is Chakkri, only wishing the best food, appreciating your Sèvres collection, cleaning himself meticulously, and—" She broke off laughing.

"Well, I have to say I do not see the comparison," I declared loftily. I could not help but remember Mr. Kiang's assertion that he had chosen the cat because it reminded him of me. For some reason, the assertion chafed.

"That is all right," she assured me, wiping moisture from under her eyes. "Dear, I am thrilled to hear you have allowed an animal into your heart. Having a pet can be rewarding in ways you cannot imagine."

"You would do well to tell Robinson of Chakkri's virtues. He cannot see them himself."

"I shall. But you had best not bring Chakkri to my sitting room. That is where I have Minney and the pups. We will have to make other arrangements. And, by the way, Lord Sidwell is one of our party this weekend. He arrived late last night and retired early, but you will see him today, I expect. Oh, here comes Hero."

A little dog who looked to be a cross between a small terrier and a shaggy poodle bounded toward us at top speed. His hair was mostly black, but his feet, chest, and head were a mixture of tan and cream.

He halted at Freddie's feet and gazed up at her adoringly. She bent and petted him, causing his plumy tail to wag and his black nose to seek her hand.

Freddie looked over her shoulder at me. "Will you not pet him?"

I thought briefly of Robinson's reaction to seeing me covered with dog hair. Oh, devil take it. I reached down and stroked his fur. Hero barked and jumped in doggie delight.

"I am glad you already have a Hero, Freddie, as I am afraid I would make a poor hero myself."

Freddie straightened at my serious tone. The dog lay down and rolled in the grass. "What are you talking about, George?"

I gazed into her eyes and reached for her gloved hand. "It is Miss Ashton." I swallowed and held the precious hand tight. "Freddie, I have failed you. I thought I had uncovered the real killer, but found I was wrong. Miss Ashton's freedom is still at stake, as is your reputation."

I made no mention of the threatening drawings or my altercations with Fairingdale.

She gazed at me steadily for what seemed like hours, so great was my anxiety, but was actually only a moment or two. Then she lifted our clasped hands and patted mine. "Dear George, you must have faith in yourself. I do. You will untangle the muddle."

"Freddie, you do not understand. Mr. Lavender, the

Bow Street investigator, plans to arrest Miss Ashton on Monday. There is nothing I can do to prevent it." I stared at her, waiting for her to absorb the news and for the disillusionment to appear in her eyes.

She stood quietly and considered my words. "Well, if it comes to an arrest, then you will simply keep on working until the puzzle is solved. It shall be dreadful for Miss Ashton to be imprisoned, the poor thing, but you will prevail, George. I know it."

I felt a lump rise in my throat. I let her hand go and brushed a curl away from her eye. My fingers lingered to caress her cheek. "Your faith—"

My voice broke. I stopped and cleared my throat. "Your faith in me gives me strength. I hope it is not misplaced."

"Of course it is not, dear," she said with complete conviction, her face leaning into my hand.

My gaze ran over her features, lingering on her lips. "My princess," I murmured, my heart rate accelerating.

She seemed to come to an awareness and gently moved my hand away. "We must return to the house, George," she said softly.

I looked down at her for a moment. "Yes, of course. You are right," I agreed, disappointed and ashamed of my disappointment.

Being a man of honor is something which a gentleman must constantly work at, you know. When I am with Freddie, I find the work arduous.

We ambled back to the house, and Freddie took me upstairs to her sitting room to see the puppies. They were most appreciative of the leather balls I had brought them. The room quickly turned into a scene of romping canines.

Freddie's maid, Ulga, was in attendance the entire time. Under her watchful eye, Freddie later waited in a small upstairs parlor for me to bring Chakkri to visit. They took to each other immediately. Freddie could not stop exclaiming over Chakkri's beauty and regal air, which pleased the cat no end.

"I hope he is being fed well while he is here, George. Did you ask Robinson to talk to Cook?"

Chakkri purred hoarsely, rubbing his face against Freddie's shoes as she stroked his fur.

"I have not heard any complaints from Chakkri. Believe me when I tell you he makes his needs known."

Later, while Robinson and I were putting the finishing touches to my attire for the evening, a servant brought a tray of food for Chakkri. It contained a miniature portion of everything I assumed we would be dining on, including risolles of fowl and a small saucer of mock turtle soup.

"Her Royal Highness is all that is kind. She thinks of everyone's comfort, even that animal," Robinson remarked.

He had obtained a special cloth which he employed to rid my coat of any lone cat hair before leaving his presence. He used it vigorously on my mazarine blue coat before pronouncing me fit for company.

Meanwhile, Chakkri's nose busily explored the contents of the tray. He sniffed approvingly at each item until he came to the saucer containing the mock turtle soup. Without warning, he bared his fangs and a low growl emitted from his chest, in the same way he had when the drawings arrived from the killer. He then shook his front paw in the manner cats have when something is distasteful to them.

I watched the scene with satisfaction. Here was a contradiction to Freddie's statement that Chakkri was much like myself. For I adore mock turtle soup.

When I noticed that Chakkri was not eating anything, I removed the offending saucer of soup to a side table. I did not want him to go hungry and thought the soup made him reluctant to partake of the rest of the meal.

I was gratified when the cat promptly returned to the meal and ate with gusto.

"Apparently, the animal's preoccupation with tortoise-related items does not extend to turtle soup," Robinson observed.

"I admit Chakkri is unpredictable," I said, watching the cat consume his food. "He taps on my tortoise-shell plate, chews my tortoise-shell comb, but refuses mock turtle soup. His diversity makes him more interesting, do you not agree?"

"No, sir." Robinson stated stubbornly.

Throughout the evening, I presented my usual self to the company, but inside I felt distracted and restless. I could not stop thinking of Lady Wrayburn's murder and trying to come up with suspects. A niggling feeling that some clue to the killer's identity was just out of my reach haunted me.

Despite the comfortable bed, I tossed and turned all night and awoke unrefreshed the next day. I played billiards cheerfully, watched politely while a group of men shot birds out of the sky—although I find the practice repulsive myself—and participated in several lively games of chance with Scrope and Petersham among others.

But it was not until Sunday afternoon when everyone crowded into the drawing room again that I met Lord Sidwell and his friend, Lord Inskip, and received a piece of information which changed everything.

22

Rain drove everyone indoors Sunday afternoon. Some gentlemen decided to head back to London early. Thus, it was a small party that remained at Oatlands.

In the drawing room, tables were set up for cards. Freddie played a game of whist with Petersham, Scrope, and an older man I did not know. A still more elderly gentleman sat nearby, not participating, but watching the game with interest.

I walked over to where Old Dawe stood on duty behind a tray of decanters. A handsome man of about thirty-five years, whom I recognized as Lord Ackerman, berated the servant.

"I asked you for claret. This is Burgundy. It's not the same thing, is it?"

"No, sir. They are similar—" Old Dawe began.

"Whether they are similar or not doesn't concern me,"

Lord Ackerman snapped. "Burgundy isn't what I asked for, and it won't do, will it?"

Old Dawe's hand tightened on the decanter. "No, your lordship."

"That would not happen to be a Chambertin Burgundy, would it, Old Dawe? If it is, I shall I have a glass," I said. "Oh, hello, Ackerman. Care to try the best Burgundy ever to roll past your tongue? Or in your case, I collect I should say slide across the points of your tongue."

Lord Ackerman gave a twisted smile. "I suppose just this once I could."

Old Dawe poured out two measures of the Burgundy. His expression did not change, but I saw the smile in his eyes.

After accepting our glasses, we moved a few feet away, and Lord Ackerman pronounced his wine tolerable.

"Glad you like it," I said, holding my glass up and gazing at the contents. "I hear you like housemaids as well."

Lord Ackerman looked startled at the abrupt change of topic. He let out a snort of laughter. "They're convenient."

"Not so convenient when they become with child, though, are they?" I asked tilting my head in a inquisitive manner.

Lord Ackerman fixed me with a belligerent stare. "They find the door quick enough if they are foolish enough to let that happen."

I felt like punching him, but thought better of it. I would not want to mar the perfection of my hands. "Ever wonder what becomes of the girls?"

"No."

"Really?"

"You know what they say, out of sight, out of mind."

"I have heard that, indeed. But take a girl like Mary, for example," I went on, undaunted. "Or, er, best forget that. I think you already have taken her."

Lord Ackerman leered and swallowed some wine.

"I hear she lives at a place called Haven of Hope. A friend of mine told me her baby should be arriving any day. I daresay the shelter could use a sizeable contribution to help with costs and such, you understand."

I had his grudging attention now.

"Otherwise, Mary might find herself back out on the streets. She could make quite a nuisance of herself, I imagine, what with a squalling baby and a sad story of debauchery. Lady Ackerman strikes me as the type of woman who would object to such a fuss."

Lord Ackerman paled.

I restrained a smile. I had him now. "But it is all conjecture on my part. Pay no attention to me. Enjoy your wine," I said and wandered over to the card tables.

"George! Say you will make a fourth for our next hand," Freddie begged. "Lord Petersham says he is too tired to continue."

Petersham looked petulant.

"Very well," I said, pulling up a chair to the square gaming table and watching the game currently being played.

"I do not think you know Lord Sidwell," Freddie said.

Introductions were made. Lord Sidwell, the gentleman who had been forced to sell off treasured art objects due to gaming debts, was an overwrought man. He was all nervous movement. First, he fidgeted with his cards, arranging and rearranging them in his hand. Then he constantly turned his wine glass round and round. All the while, I could see his right knee jerking up and down in an effort to release his excess energy.

"Good to see you, Brummell," Lord Sidwell said, barely taking his eyes off his cards. "This here is my friend, Lord Inskip. It's his first visit to Oatlands."

"How do you like it, my lord?" I inquired politely. Lord Inskip had to be eighty if he was a day. A ring of white hair surrounded his balding head. Loose flesh hung off his throat and bounced whenever he coughed, which was often.

"The Royal Duchess here is a fine woman," he wheezed. "She runs a comfortable house. Too bad her husband acts like a lout." He placed a card on the table.

Freddie turned pink.

Lord Inskip did not notice her discomfort. "I like dogs, though, so I'm having a fine time. They're better company than some people." The elderly man nodded his head in Lord Ackerman's direction. He was back to badgering Old Dawe. "Watch him, Duchess. He'll get a leg over anything female."

A short silence followed this coarse comment.

"Ackerman's always has an eye for his female servants. Why doesn't he set up a mistress or two like everyone else?" Scrope chimed in. He had just entered the room and stood hovering over the gaming table looking at everyone's hand of cards.

I raised my quizzing glass at him. "There is a lady present, you oaf." His words were especially awkward in light of the fact that the Duke of York was so public with his mistress.

Scrope caught my meaning. He looked ruffled at possibly having embarrassed the Duchess of York and mumbled an apology.

Freddie's features were composed, but I saw she gripped her cards tightly.

Lord Inskip, however, remained oblivious to the implication of his words. "Governesses, companions, lady's maids, and housemaids are always falling victim to the master of the house. They are readily available and cost nothing. Mistresses, on the other hand, are expensive." He ended with a wracking cough.

The cards in Freddie's hand shook.

I felt compelled to change the subject. Anything to spare Freddie humiliation. The first topic that sprang to mind was Lady Wrayburn's murder. Without giving the matter any further thought, I said, "They have yet to make an arrest in Lady Wrayburn's murder, I hear."

"Tight with her money, the countess was," Lord Sidwell bemoaned. His left eye twitched. "Once she held a card party, and I won fourteen pounds from her. She never paid me! When I taxed her on it, she said it was just chicken stakes and I should forget the matter. Imagine that! A gentleman is forced to honor his gaming debts no matter the cost, whereas one is supposed to forgive a lady? Where's the logic in that, I ask you?"

No one answered his passionate query.

"There was something about Lady Wrayburn that gave me a disgust of the woman. Can't remember now . . ." Lord Inskip trailed off.

Petersham said, "She made a terrible scene at a recent auction."

I glanced at him sharply. The auction had been of Lord Sidwell's art objects. Surely, he would be mortified by the reminder of his straitened circumstances. Lord Sidwell, however, was too busy examining his cards with a baleful eye, his leg jumping, to pay any attention to what Lord Inskip or Petersham was saying.

The game ended. Freddie was the winner.

Lord Sidwell groaned.

I was just about to exchange chairs with Petersham when Lord Inskip startled the party by slapping his hand down hard on the table.

"I've been trying to remember what it was about Lady Wrayburn that turned me against her. By God, I have it now!" Lord Inskip drew in a deep, wheezing breath. "She caught Lord Wrayburn with the governess. Sweet girl, she was. The governess, that is."

I listened with half an ear. It was the same story Lady Salisbury had told me. I sat at the table and scooped up the cards.

"Lady Wrayburn threw the girl out when it became known she was going to have a babe. The governess fled up to Yorkshire way, not far from where I live."

The elderly man shook his head. "Damn shame, it was. Her son, for the baby was a boy, grew up angry that his father had abandoned them. But Miss Turtleby never bothered Lord Wrayburn for a shilling. Made her living teaching Bible lessons and taking in sewing." A coughing spell interrupted his story. Lord Sidwell slapped his friend on the back.

My hand suddenly stilled in the process of reaching for my glass. I felt a chill run through my body.

Recovered from his fit, Lord Inskip went on: "Everyone said her name ought to have been Miss Turtle*dove* as she was so devoted to Lord Wrayburn, even though I doubt she ever saw him again. The boy was different, though, more's the pity. Hated his father and the name Wrayburn. He worshipped his mother, even promising her to go into the clergy, which was her fondest wish."

"Whatever happened to him?" I asked. I slowly lowered the cards back to the table and stared at Lord Inskip. Every nerve of my body was on alert.

Lord Inskip squinted beneath his bushy eyebrows. "He changed his name. I don't know what he calls himself now, but the last I heard he was a parson up London way."

I rose to my feet so quickly, my chair banged down on the floor behind me.

The company stared at me.

"Fred—er, that is to say, Your Royal Highness, I must leave at once. Do not worry. I shall send word—"

"What?" Freddie half rose from her place. "What in heaven's name is it, George?" Her blue eyes rounded in concern.

Lord Inskip broke out into a fit of coughing.

I spared a second to right my chair. "Petersham, you ride back to London with Robinson and Diggie. I am going on horseback."

"Now? On horseback? *In your evening clothes?*" Freddie exclaimed.

"What the devil has got into you, Brummell?" Petersham asked, rising.

"I daresay whatever it is, I should not be rushed back to London in such a manner," Scrope declared, "unless it has to do with a horse race. Does it, Brummell?"

I did not answer him. "Old Dawe!" I shouted, heading for the drawing room door. "Send word to the stables to have a horse made ready for me."

"Yes, sir. At once." He hurried away.

I bolted up the stairs to my bedchamber.

Robinson started at my entrance. Chakkri raised his head from where he was sleeping on the bed.

I ignored them and found my Hessian boots. Kicking off my evening pumps, I went to pull them on.

"Sir!" Robinson howled. "What in heaven's name—"

"I do not have time to explain! I need to return to London immediately. I shall be riding. My evening pumps will not serve." I struggled with the boots. My hands were shaking.

"You are *riding* back to Town?" Robinson's lips compressed. Then he grabbed my arm to prevent me from putting on the boots. "Sir, if you are riding, you will ruin those silk breeches."

"I do not care. Let me go at once," I commanded in a strong tone I rarely employ.

Robinson obeyed; his mouth dropped open in shock. He hastily procured a pair of leather breeches from the wardrobe. "At least put these on first please, sir."

Frustrated at the delay, but realizing the wisdom of wearing something sturdier, I stripped off my evening breeches and scrambled into the leather ones. I accepted Robinson's help with the boots. All the while, he flung questions at me about what on earth could be the emergency that could cause me to go running off dressed so *inappropriately*.

I never replied. I was entirely focused on something else. Nor did I pay any attention to Chakkri. The cat remained rooted to his spot on the bed, watching me intently with his intelligent blue eyes.

My mind raced as a clear picture of what had happened fell into place.

All I wanted to do now was get back to London in time to lay a trap for a murderer.

At precisely ten o'clock Monday morning I arrived at Wrayburn House hoping my carefully laid plan would succeed. I ordered Ned and Ted to remain outside, then knocked on the door.

Riddell answered. "Good morning, Mr. Brummell."

I walked into the gloomy hall and handed him my great-coat, hat, and stick. Later, I would regret parting with the stick.

"Good morning, Riddell. May I inquire as to whom is in the house?" I jingled coins in my pocket to encourage him.

"Well, sir," the butler said consideringly, "Mr. Hensley has gone to Hensley Cottage. Mrs. Hensley went to a weekend house party. Mr. Fairingdale has not yet come home from last evening. That leaves Miss Ashton and her visitor, Mr. Dawlish, besides the servants."

"Thank you. Now, Riddell, I have something to ask of you. It is very important and concerns Lady Wrayburn's death."

"Then I shall do whatever you ask."

"Good man." I asked a few questions, then whispered hasty instructions. Certain that Riddell understood what I required, I pressed several coins into the butler's wrinkled hand.

"You may rely upon me, Mr. Brummell," he said, pocketing the money. "Miss Ashton and Mr. Dawlish are in the drawing room. He just arrived. Miss Ashton has not yet rung for tea."

"Excellent. Remain here. I shall announce myself. That way, we will give Miss Ashton no chance to ask you personally to bring refreshments."

I walked toward the drawing room, a wave of apprehension sweeping through me. I felt it appropriate under the circumstances to mutter a silent prayer.

Opening the door, I found a familiar scene. Miss Ashton, clad in her black mourning dress, appeared so pale as to be almost lifeless. Beside her on the settee, the rector sat turned toward her. He held one of her hands. His expression was fervent.

". . . Would just reconsider my proposal. How can I convince you—"

"Good morning," I interrupted. My tone was somber.

Mr. Dawlish eyed my crisp cravat, faultless Bishop's blue coat, tight-fitting breeches, and silk waistcoat—a new one—with obvious disdain. "Hello, Mr. Brummell."

"Mr. Brummell," Miss Ashton said, a small ray of light coming into her eyes. "You are about early this morning.

I know it is on my account." She rose wearily. I could tell her store of hope was almost empty. "How can I ever express my gratitude for everything you have done?"

I moved toward the settee and bowed over her hand. I put the first part of my plan into action. "Perhaps before we discuss recent developments, you might offer me some tea, if you please. I hate to trouble you, but my throat is parched."

"Of course." She reached for the bell rope and gave it a pull. She resumed her place next to the rector. "You must forgive me, Mr. Dawlish, for not ringing for tea when you arrived."

"*I* do not expect you to concern yourself with trivialities when I know you are much distressed. So deep is my anxiety for you that neither food nor drink appeal to me."

"Those are honorable sentiments to be sure, Miss Ashton," I said, then settled into a chair opposite them. "I am afraid, though, I cannot share Mr. Dawlish's finer feelings." I cleared my throat. "Do excuse me. It is just that I am quite thirsty."

Miss Ashton got up again, motioning the rector and me to remain seated. "I do not know why Riddell has not answered the bell. Let me go and see what is keeping him."

"Must you?" Mr. Dawlish protested. "We have matters of import to discuss that surely must come before Mr. Brummell's tea. Can he not refresh himself from the wine decanter?"

"I do beg your pardon." I coughed. "But I never partake of wine this early in the day." I felt my pious tone worthy of the rector.

"Do not give it another thought. I shall order a nice pot

of tea and return in a moment," Miss Ashton said.

The rector and I were alone.

"You will forgive my little machination to send Miss Ashton from the room, Mr. Dawlish." I watched him closely.

"What?" he asked, blinking behind his spectacles.

I leaned forward. "I did want to talk with you privately about a most urgent development."

"Is that why you sent me that letter last night?"

I nodded. "Yes. Thank you for coming here as I asked."

A touch of impatience flickered across his pasty features. "What has happened? Your letter said only that it was imperative for me to be at Wrayburn House this morning at ten. That Miss Ashton would need me more than ever."

"Indeed that is the case. You see, the situation grows grave."

Mr. Dawlish stared at me, his body completely motionless. " 'Becca? Have they found more evid—but, no! There cannot be anything else against her."

So tense was the atmosphere in the room, I thought at any moment one of us would break. Struggling to maintain my calm, I returned the rector's gaze. "It grieves me to tell you an arrest is imminent."

Mr. Dawlish's hands clenched in his lap. "Miss Ashton is to be arrested?"

I nodded sadly. "For a crime she did not commit."

The rector broke the stillness by jumping to his feet.

I stood as well, unwilling to give him any advantage. I watched him closely.

He removed his spectacles. With the fingers of his other

hand, he pressed the bridge of his nose. "I never believed it would come to that." He put the spectacles back on. "Are you certain?"

"Yes, I went to forestall Mr. Lavender, but my efforts were in vain. He let slip that he would be here this morning to take her away."

Mr. Dawlish thrust his hands into his pockets and stared at the floor. "My God! I never once thought it would go this far!"

"Of course not. You care for her."

"Yes," the rector declared vehemently, his head coming up. "I love 'Becca."

My stomach twisted at the idea.

He mistook my silence.

"It can be no secret to you how I feel. And she is innocent of any wrongdoing!"

"We both know that, Mr. Dawlish." My voice was soft. Knowing. Wise.

Our eyes locked for a moment.

He looked away first and began prowling the room. He came to an abrupt halt. "When is this to happen? Perhaps I might still convince Miss Ashton to marry me. We could be away before Mr. Lavender arrives."

I positioned myself near the fireplace.

"Will she go with you?"

The rector moved closer and faced me. "You could help sway her decision, Brummell. She must come away with me. We can go to the Continent. Not France, of course, but perhaps Spain. Now! It must be now!" His voice had risen. A damp sheen of perspiration covered his brow. "How much time do I have?"

I gazed at him steadily. "Mere moments. I wanted you here this morning because Mr. Lavender is coming for her at any minute."

Mr. Dawlish's eyes popped. His breath came in gasps. I had caught him off guard. Exactly as I planned.

"Any minute?" he repeated, his voice barely above a whisper.

"Yes." I reached down to consult my watch. "I expect—"

The rector grabbed the lapels of my coat. I could feel his breath on my face. "You must help me! You must tell 'Becca to come away with me instantly. It is the only thing to do!"

He released me and made as if to leave the drawing room and find her.

I followed and caught up with him halfway across the room, bumping into a side table, causing the decanters to rattle. I grasped his arm in a light hold. "Are you sure? She may not be persuaded. Is it the *only* thing to do?"

He swung around. Uncertainty crept into his expression. He licked his lips but said nothing.

"You know there is another way Miss Ashton can be saved," I said, my gaze boring into his, my voice terse.

"No, I do not!"

"I believe you do, Mr. Dawlish."

"No!" he cried desperately. "I do not know of any other way. Release me!"

I dropped his arm. We were both breathing heavily now. I forced down revulsion and made my expression sympathetic. "Why not tell me precisely what happened the night Lady Wrayburn died. Perhaps I could help."

"I cannot imagine what you are talking about!"

"Yes, you can," I persisted, deadly calm now. "Tell me. Tell me now. I shall try to help you, *Mr. Turtleby*."

The rector sucked in his breath. Fear filled his eyes.

My gaze did not waver.

A chill black silence surrounded us.

Then, like an actor shedding a role, his expression changed to one of resignation. He knew. "How did you find out?"

I struggled to answer lightly. "Oh, Society's secrets rarely stay secret."

The rector turned away and slumped into the armchair next to the little side table we had almost toppled. "He treated her worse than an animal."

"Your father?"

"*Lord Wrayburn*," the rector sneered. "I shall never refer to him as 'Father.' Did he care that Mother's reputation was in ruins? Did he care that she was forced away from London, the only place she had ever known, to live in disgrace in Yorkshire?"

"Apparently not."

"You are damned right he did not care!" the rector shouted. "He never cared for anyone but himself! His selfishness was surpassed only by his wife's, *Lady* Wrayburn." The rector gave a mocking snort of laughter. "*She* was never a *lady*. For what kind of lady throws a pregnant girl of nineteen out on the streets to fend for herself? I grew up hating her! My mother was ten times the lady that Countess Wrayburn was."

Spent, Mr. Turtleby's angry outburst subsided to a tortured muttering. "Oh, dear God, help me," he groaned, over and over.

I leaned down next to his chair. "It must have been horrible for you. Seeing the same thing about to happen to Lizzie. History repeating itself, as it were."

His head shot up at that, his gaze pleading. "You understand then? I could not sit back and do nothing while another girl was caught up in the countess's malevolence, could I?"

I thought of many ways the rector could have helped Lizzie besides murdering the countess, but held my tongue.

He looked off into the distance. "Lizzie is such a guileless girl. As Mother was, before years of fighting to sustain us took its toll on her. I could not bear to see another woman suffer the same fate."

"Or to see her child grow up in the shame that you did?" I asked softly.

The rector produced a handkerchief and wiped his brow. "Mother did her best, but there was always talk. She did not deserve it. And neither did I deserve to be teased unmercifully and called a bastard by the local boys."

"No, of course not. So what did you do to save Lizzie?"

"It was so simple," he said, eager now to share how clever he had been. "Almost like Divine Providence. I teach some of the servants around Mayfair their letters. Lizzie is one of them. Wrayburn House's milkmaid, Belinda, is another. Every evening, Belinda comes to my parish house for lessons."

"Before she delivers the milk?"

"Exactly. Belinda collects the milk for Lady Wrayburn, then on her way to Wrayburn House, she stops by the parish for her lessons. She usually just leaves Lady Wray-burn's container of milk by the door so as not to forget it when she leaves. The countess had to have a special container just for herself, you know." This last was said with a sneer.

"So I have been told."

He nodded. "Such pretension. It was her undoing, though. I keep arsenic powder in the house to get rid of insects. It was the simplest of things to slip some into the milk when Belinda was not looking."

I caught my breath. I could not tear my gaze from his. He made it all sound so reasonable, so logical.

"Belinda and I spent our usual half an hour going over the alphabet, then she went on her way. No one would ever have known except for—"

He broke off, a sudden anger lighting his eyes.

I stood, my knees unsteady from crouching next to him. And, I must say, from something more. For a killer had just confessed to me. It is a decidedly uneasy feeling, let me assure you.

"Everything would have been all right if you had not gone poking into my business," the rector said, rising from his chair. Realization blossomed on his face. A hint of menace entered his voice. "If only you had heeded my warnings."

"The drawings," I whispered, backing away. "You sent me the drawings."

"Mother taught me how to sketch. She was an educated and genteel lady. Dear Mother would have approved of Miss Ashton. 'Becca. I must get to 'Becca and take her away from here."

Mr. Turtleby advanced toward me.

My heart began to pound. Why had I relinquished my cane to Riddell?

The rector's face had changed. He was angry now. Angry that I had figured it out. "I never meant for Miss Ashton to become involved in this. I love her! It is *your* fault that our future happiness is at risk. You will tell that man from Bow Street, and he will see that I hang. I cannot allow that to happen!"

In a split second, Mr. Turtleby seized a decanter from the side table. With a swift motion, he crashed the crystal against the wood. He lunged at me, holding a long, narrow shard of glass.

I feared my perfectly tied cravat was about to be bloodied.

Then a voice with a slight Scottish lilt said, "He won't have to tell me, Rector. I heard every word myself."

John Lavender stood in the doorway, holding a pistol aimed at Mr. Turtleby's heart.

I released my breath in a long sigh. "I say, Lavender, if you fire that thing, I beg you not to miss. This is a new waistcoat."

Mr. Lavender kept the gun leveled at Mr. Turtleby. I could see beyond him, through the doorway. Miss Ashton and Riddell were standing close together, peering into the room. Two burly men, obviously Mr. Lavender's assistants, waited for instructions.

"Take him down to the roundhouse, boys, and lock him up. I'll be there presently." The men marched forward and shackled the rector, who had begun weeping again.

" 'Becca," he sobbed, "I love you."

Miss Ashton's hand went to her throat as the men led the rector away. I hurried to her side.

"I-I cannot believe it," she said softly. "I stayed away, as Riddell told me you had asked. And when Mr. Lavender arrived, I thought he was coming for me. Never in my wildest imagination did I think—"

For the first time during the entire ordeal, I feared she

would faint. "Steady now, Miss Ashton. You have had a shock. Come into the drawing room and lie down for a few minutes." I guided her from the hall to the settee. She lay down without protest.

"I trusted him, Mr. Brummell," she said, gazing up at me. "I trusted him."

I bent down on one knee at her side. "You could not have known to do any differently. He is a sick man. But it is all over. Would you like me to send for Miss Lavender? I am certain she would come. You need another female just now, do you not think so?"

"If . . . if it would not be a bother. I have never wanted to be a burden. Not ever in my entire life."

"You are not a burden," I assured her. "You have all the strength you need. And do you know what strong women—and men—do when they have had a shock?"

She shook her head.

I rose to my feet. "Follow my motto: 'When your spirits are low, get another bottle.' May I bring you a glass of wine?"

She nodded and managed a weak chuckle. I moved toward the remaining decanter and poured her a glass. I paused, then poured myself one, and swallowed the contents in one gulp. It is not every day that my person is endangered, you know.

Returning to Miss Ashton, I said, "This has been a dreadful time for you. You are allowed to ask for the help of friends."

"I suppose you are right."

"Good! I shall send for Miss Lavender."

Giving her hand a squeeze, I left her and stepped into

the hall. Here I found the Bow Street man conversing with Ned and Ted. The twins had come inside at the commotion.

Mr. Lavender eyed me and seemed satisfied I had suffered no harm. "I've been waiting for you, laddie. Everything went according to the plan you outlined in your letter last night. Except for that bit with the rector and the broken glass. Is Miss Ashton all right?"

"She would be better with some company. Do you think your daughter could come to her?"

"Sure, and she would be glad of the opportunity to meet the girl."

I beckoned to Riddell, who lingered in the back of the hall. He took down the direction of Miss Lavender's shelter and walked silently away to send a message to her.

The investigator leaned against the stair rail, plying a toothpick. He indicated the twins. "These are two fine specimens of youth and strength, Mr. Brummell. I'm thinking I could use their help in my work every now and then."

I lifted my right eyebrow and lowered my tone—to about thirty degrees Fahrenheit. "They are in my employ as chairmen."

"But that doesn't take up all of their time, now does it?" Crafty, the man is crafty, I tell you.

Ned's face glowed with excitement. "Ted and me would jump at the chance to help, wouldn't we Ted? Even though we don't rightly have any experience at catchin' criminals. Well, now wait just a minute here whilst I correct myself, because I recollect the time we helped Mum catch a duck thief. I don't know if that counts or not, but we did run the fella down right through the cow pasture. Caught him when he slipped on a pile of—"

"If Mr. Brummell agrees," Ned interrupted his brother, "we would be honored to help you, Mr. Lavender. But our first loyalty is to him."

The Bow Street man looked at me.

I took in the eager faces of the two country boys. "I am willing to discuss it. Another time."

Mr. Lavender whipped out his notebook. "That's good, that's good. Meanwhile, I need to take a statement from you, Mr. Brummell."

I entered the house in Bruton Street worn to the bone.

Robinson met me as I flopped down—quite uncharacteristic of me to flop, mind you—in the chair behind my desk in the bookroom.

"Has everything been resolved to your satisfaction, sir?"

"Yes, it is as I told you last night when you returned from Oatlands. Mr. Dawlish is really Mr. Turtleby. He held a long-standing hatred of Lord and Lady Wrayburn because of what they had done to his mother. When it looked as if another female would fall victim to Lady Wrayburn's wrath, it triggered an irrational, violent response in Mr. Turtleby."

Robinson tsked. "Thank heavens we can put that behind us." He handed me a square of vellum. "Here is a letter from Lord Petersham."

"Oh," I accepted the missive. "Did everything run smoothly on the coach ride home?"

Robinson pursed his lips. "Lord Petersham slept the entire way, leaving me to the company of Mr. Digwood and that cat."

"Chakkri gave you trouble, did he?"

The valet hesitated. "I cannot really say that he did, sir."

"Come now, admit it. The little fellow has gained your affection," I said with a perfectly serious expression.

Robinson narrowed his eyes. "The only time I shall feel the least fondness for that animal is when I see him crated for his return to Siam."

"Pity. For that is not going to happen. Why not take the afternoon off, Robinson? I plan on going to bed after I have written to the Duchess and will not need you again until this evening. You could go down to the Tower and see the lion. Think about how an animal of that size would shed fur. It might make you feel better."

"How tempting," he retorted, his lip curled. "Shall I wait for your letter to the Royal Duchess?"

"Yes. I do want her to get the news about Mr. Turtleby and Miss Ashton without delay."

While Robinson stood by, I wrote out a letter outlining the morning's events. I ended it by begging Freddie's forgiveness for leaving Oatlands so abruptly.

> *. . . For you know I treasure the time I spend with you and would not have departed prematurely without good reason.*
>
> *I might travel to Brighton to see the Prince this week. What are your plans? May I hope you will decide a breath of sea air would be beneficial?*
>
> *Your humble servant,*
> *George Brummell*

I sanded the note and gave it to Robinson. He stalked away without another word.

Petersham's letter lay unopened in front of me. I picked it up and broke the seal.

Brummell,

> *Matters are resolved between Munro and me. He has leased a house in Brighton so we might be fashionable and follow the Prince. I daresay there are a few weeks left of decent weather before the cold truly sets in. Perhaps we shall meet you there.*

> *Petersham*

> *P.S. Munro gave me the most superior snuff box. I cannot wait for you to see it.*

Ah, Petersham had a new snuff box. All was right with the world!

I slept soundly until late afternoon. Cornering a murderer is a tiring activity.

Dressed for the evening in a royal-blue coat, I once again took a hackney cab to Fetter Lane. I wished to learn whether or not Miss Lavender had seen Miss Ashton.

And, I must admit, I owed Mr. Lavender my thanks.

To that end, once I arrived in Fetter Lane, I paid the coach driver and paused to look in the window of Allen & Butler, Ivory-Box Makers. Seeing the very thing I desired, I roused the shopkeeper from his dinner and then made the disturbance worthwhile to him.

Several minutes later, I knocked on Mr. Lavender's door.

The bluff Scotsman answered. "I didn't think to see you again so soon, laddie."

He motioned me inside. We sat down in the small parlor.

Miss Lavender came forward. "Mr. Brummell, I must thank you for sending me to Miss Ashton. But first, would you care for some refreshment?"

I held up a detaining hand. "I am expected at my club, but thank you. The purpose of my visit is twofold. First, I did want to learn Miss Ashton's condition."

"The girl's a brave lass," Mr. Lavender pronounced. "Lydia brought Miss Ashton here, not wanting her to stay at Wrayburn House another night. She's asleep right now. Worn out, I imagine. I'm glad she was not the guilty party."

"Rebecca is coming to work with me at the shelter, Mr. Brummell," Miss Lavender said with a broad smile. "I feel most fortunate. It's extraordinary when one finds another with a like mind. Rebecca will be an invaluable addition to Haven of Hope."

"It pleases me greatly to hear it," I said.

"Indeed, sir, I am in your debt. For our agreement was that I would take Lizzie in, and now it seems she does not need a place to go. Instead, I have Rebecca as a helper, and just today I received a large draft on Lord Ackerman's bank."

I raised my eyebrows in mock surprise. "Is that so?"

She laughed. "Yes. I expect I have you to thank for that, although I confess I do not know how you did it."

"Your debt to me is paid by the pleasure of your acquaintance, Miss Lavender. I have an appreciation for beauty, you see."

We smiled at one another.

Mr. Lavender cast a glare at us that would have withered heather. "If that is all then, you'll be on your way, Mr. Brummell. Unless you care to discuss letting Bow Street have use of the twins?"

I lifted my watch by its chain and checked the time. "Er, I must be off. But, before I go, I did want to give you this, Mr. Lavender." I held out my gloved hand. In my palm lay the purchase I had just made. It was a small ivory box intended to hold toothpicks. In the exact center, a tiny round turquoise stone rested.

Miss Lavender squinted at it, then leaned closer to get a better look. Devil take me if the girl is not near-sighted.

She studied the gift and gasped. "How lovely!"

Her father accepted the slim box. He stared at it, speechless at first. Then, "Don't know if it might not be too fine for a Bow Street investigator."

"Balderdash," I said calmly. "It is a gift from me to thank you for saving my life. Another minute and Mr. Turtleby might very well have accomplished his second murder."

Mr. Lavender looked at me, then said grudgingly, "I suppose I need to thank you, as well. If not for you, I might have arrested the wrong person."

I smiled.

He shook his finger at me. "But don't go thinking you can ever get involved in another murder investigation. Leave such matters to Bow Street."

My smile changed to a wry twist of my lips. "I shall be happy to do so, I assure you. In fact, I am considering a visit to Brighton. Nothing ever happens there."

We walked to the door. I bowed over Miss Lavender's hand, under her father's sharply disapproving eye.

Donning my hat, I put my hand on the door handle and turned to make a final goodbye. Just then I saw something I wish I had not.

Mr. Lavender apparently perceived a minuscule bit of dirt on the top of the ivory toothpick holder. He spat on it, then rubbed it clean on the sleeve of his shirt.

I shuddered.

Lydia Lavender caught my eye and winked.

That night, I made my way through my clubs, ending at my favorite, White's. Talk abounded on the apprehension of Lady Wrayburn's murderer.

Though I knew my story would be relished, I kept silent about my part in the investigation. It was enough that everyone knew I had been correct when I proclaimed Miss Ashton innocent.

At one point during the course of the long evening, I crossed paths with Sylvester Fairingdale. He gave me a most unpleasant look before casting his chin in the air and moving away without speaking.

I noticed his gloves were plain white.

Dawn began to break as I made my way home through the Mayfair streets. I entered the house as quietly as one who had consumed approximately three bottles of wine could. Earlier, I had told Robinson he need not wait up

for me. I imagined he had spent the evening at The Butler's Tankard, perhaps regaling the other valets on my virtues.

Then again, perhaps not.

Slipping into my bedchamber, I saw Chakkri raise his
head from where he was sleeping in his usual place, the
exact center of my bed.

"No need to get up, old boy," I told him somewhat
unsteadily. Robinson had laid out my nightclothes, and I
struggled to get into them. "I shall be there in a flash."

It might have been my imagination, but he seemed to
view my condition with scorn. With a low "reow" he
jumped down off the bed and went to warm himself by
the waning fire.

I blew out all the candles save the one by my bedside
and climbed into bed. "You might greet me with a little
more respect, you know. I am the one who keeps you in
lobster patties."

The cat made no reply. He traversed the room and
leaped onto the crescent-shaped side table.

"Oh, no! Not my tortoise-shell Sèvres!" I yelled.

But for some odd reason, one I shall never fathom, the
cat had no further interest in the tortoise-shell plate. A
fickle fellow, do you not agree? No doubt he would leave
my tortoise-shell comb alone. He might even partake of
turtle soup.

Who could understand it?